WIDE WORLD
IN CELEBRATION
AND SORROW

WIDE WORLD IN CELEBRATION AND SORROW

ACTS OF KAMIKAZE FICTION

LEON ROOKE

EXILE
editions

Library and Archives Canada Cataloguing in Publication

Rooke, Leon
  Wide world in celebration and sorrow : acts of kamikaze fiction / Leon Rooke.

Short stories.
ISBN 978-1-55096-303-8

  I. Title.

PS8585.O64W43 2012   C813'.54   C2012-905879-3

Design and Composition by Hourglass Angels~mc
Typeset in Fairfield and Lucida Bright fonts at the Moons of Jupiter Studios
Printed by Imprimerie Gauvin

Published by Exile Editions Ltd ~ www.ExileEditions.com
144483 Southgate Road 14 – GD, Holstein ON, N0G 2A0
Printed and Bound in Canada; Publication Copyright © Exile Editions, 2012

The publisher would like to acknowledge the financial support of the Canada
Council for the Arts, the Government of Canada through the Canada Book Fund
(CBF), the Ontario Arts Council, and the Ontario Media Development Corpora-
tion, for our publishing activities.

 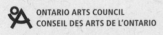 

Canadian Sales: The Canadian Manda Group, 165 Dufferin Street,
Toronto ON M6K 3H6   www.mandagroup.com   416 516 0911

North American and International Distribution, and U.S. Sales:
Independent Publishers Group, 814 North Franklin Street,
Chicago IL 60610   www.ipgbook.com   toll free: 1 800 888 4741

Contents

ADDRESSING THE ASSASSINS

Look at your watch. What time is it? Well, it's too late, much too late. I can't be bothered to go into the matter now. Come back later. Forget it. Go on with what you were doing.

All right, I have six minutes, no more, this will have to be fast. I'll stick to the subject, tell you all I know, all anyone knows. But keep this in mind: I'm getting this *off your chest*, not mine, it serves your interests, I'm not concerned one way or another, the affair has nothing to do with me. It happened I was in the vicinity, that's all.

    Fine, you say, okay, good, why are we talking about it?

Look, I've got my worries too. I'm coming up in the world, I'm going down, no one can keep pace with me. Up, down, up, down, try it sometime. This is what I've learned, this: even if I get nothing, so long as I've *got* it I'm happy, try it sometime. You don't think I mean it? Try looking at me in the eye, you'll see! I'm *alert*, there are people who have looked and never been the same. It doesn't matter to me that I lose, I always lose, I've become accustomed to that, listen, I *like* losing, I recommend it.

1

So what is my information worth, how much would you give?

To put it another way, how much money do you have?

Good, I'll take it all, I'm tired of being poor boy off the farm, I'm fed up with holding up this zoo, I'm after blood now.

How's the family, you ask. Wait, stop the trolley, I'm getting off here. Don't pry. Are we here to talk turkey or are we just killing the breeze?

My family is fine, how's yours?

So it's only conversation you want, well, naturally, I expected as much. Try looking at it from my point of view, have a heart, I'm not the same person I was then.

Yes, yes. I'm familiar with your situation, I know it as well as my own. You hesitate, so do I, you're at sea, so am I, when was this not ever so? Did you think word wouldn't get around? Don't try kidding me, there are no balloons tied to this nose.

Look, the kid wanted a dog and finally got one, that's all there is to it, the dog died, run over by a car while the kid was in a shop buying bread to go with dinner, end of story.

The kid stood out in the street, ruined, the dog in his arms, stopping traffic, stopping pedestrians who were properly horrified: "Little boy, don't you know?... Little boy, you... Little boy, you'll get run over yourself, blood all over your clothes, oh little boy" but why go on, you know the type.

In the meantime, well, it's always in the meantime, every minute you breathe – in the meantime the dog's guts have spilled over the boy's arms, blood flows down his jeans, and the boy – stricken! – what could he do except cry *NO NO NO NO NO you can't take him, this dog is mine*! Sure. Finally someone shows some sense, we are not total morons after all, someone says, "This boy is in a state, can't you see he is, this boys needs looking after!" Others have roughly the same idea, they say, "Little boy, what's your name, where do you live, we must get in touch with your parents!" and so on but of course the boy is dim with grief, he's perplexed, though he still intends to fulfill his purpose here, he's holding the loaf of bread tight, it's mixing with dog to the extent that who can say which is which, musn't disappoint Mom. Well, I was there, I know. Although the dog is dead it takes three people to pry the animal from his arms and three more to hold the boy as he fights to get the dead burden back, so what can be done, that's the question going around and ours is not a total idiocy, we have feelings, finally it occurs to someone to let him have the dead beast back.

You should have heard the kid screaming MY DOG MY DOG MY DOG MY DOG MY DOG MY DOG!

Jesus!

All right, don't get sore, no need to beat your head against the wall, this was a long time ago. Finally the boy's mother is telephoned, she comes running, finds no one, nothing going on, everything quiet, only this puddle of blood on the stones, she goes running back to her own house. She comes running through the door, sees a bunch of people she's never seen before, and hears one of them saying, "Dead, he's dead." He's dead, and naturally she believes it's her own son they are talking about and promptly loses whatever part of her mind she had not lost long before. Rushes forward screaming, beating her breast, shoving everyone aside – and calms down in an instant when she catches sight of the boy in a wing chair with the dead dog dripping in his arms.

Okay, stop the clock, one two three, count to twenty-five, when you're ready I'll go on. I'm not in this business to tug your heartstrings. I've told you frankly and will again: this has nothing to do with me.

She rushes to the boy, shakes him, slaps him, all the time yelling, *"I told you I told you I told you didn't I tell you didn't I mark my words you will never have another dog again I knew this would happen* knew it!" She tears the dog free, she kicks it over the carpet, shoves the boy into the bathroom, rips off his clothes, slaps wet towels all over him.

Okay, to hell with it, you get the idea.

Afterwards, the next day, that very night perhaps, the boy is out in the backyard burying his dog, out there with a flashlight and refusing all help, swinging his shovel at anyone who comes near, going at the earth with grunts, throwing up the dark soil, deep, going down deep, throwing it up hard. *"MY DOG! MY DOG! MY DOG! MY DOG! MY DOG!"*
    Et cetera.

Listen, I'm not concerned, I'm only telling you. Meanwhile, she's at the back door screaming, *"I told you what would happen, told you not to get a dog, warned you, no you had to have a dog, don't blame me!"*

All right, sure thing, that's all there is to it, I'm almost finished, you're not paying me enough to keep me around here, keep your shirt on.

He buries the dog, let another kid try to walk over the grave and he'll get a stick across his head.

So, look, he's a grown man now, you've seen him around. You won't find him owning a dog or any other animal. Hasn't married either. Hates kids. Sure, he loves his mother, no grudges held, what else is new, did I say he didn't? That changes nothing, I look at it this way: he's still guarding holy ground, fending off enemies, rebuilding from that single old violation. Does it make sense, does he know what he's doing? Don't ask me.

Listen, hold my hand, show a little warmth, life goes on.

Listen to me. An attempt has been made on my life. You can dance around it any way you like, but that's the fact of the matter: an attempt has been made on my life. More than once.

Who would want to kill me, you ask. Who indeed. You, them, everyone. I can't be any more specific than that. Proof, I have proof, I have all the proof I need, I was there, it happened to me. What would you have me do, stay at home, lock myself in the cellar, never come out again? Sounds easy, but

I'm not so simple-minded as that, I'm like you, I have needs. I take my chances. I don't expect much.

Oh I have suspects, quite a few, I have names, I'm checking the matter out. It's an emergency, the situation is grave, but it isn't irreconcilable, it isn't irreversible, not by a long shot. I can still negotiate. I know where *I* stand.

And I might get them first, there's always that.

Anyway why worry about it, where's the bad news, I can't say I'm much concerned.

Even so, I'm watching you. Don't think you can put anything over on me. One false move and I'll be at your throat before you can blink, this is *My life My life My life My life*!

BALDUCHI'S WHO'S WHO

1

BEGINNINGS

Pick a spot.

Take the case of Frannie Balduchi, who is forever saying to herself, "Where shall I begin? How do I go on? How might I start over?"

Or consider her father, old Egi Balduchi. Consider *Thamn-al-batn*, Balduchi's stomach price.

Two dark Arabic-type fellows in a café washroom over in the Greek area of the city, on the Danforth, told him one day that that's what they called in their country Balduchi's particular stomach ailment. In Algeria, that was. But then the Arabic-type fellow holding the other's hand explained. "*Thamn-al-batn* is stomach price, yes. Yes, but it mean if someone from another tribe come upon your people and pass the friendly salutation, then that tribe must has to feed the visitor four days. Four days, yes. We can no slice the visitor's throat while he sleep, without is invite the wrath of full tribe. So *Thamn-al-batn*, stomach price, is price you pay for being friendly host."

Balduchi liked the expression, and if his daughter, these days, ever troubled herself to ask how he was, he would say he was A-Okay, except for having to pay the stomach price. "I've got a touch of *Thamn-al-batn* in the gut," he would say. "Otherwise your old papa is fine." Not that Frannie was likely to ask, being too wrapped up in her own troubles to consider another's. A bit loose in the caboose, unstable, unreliable, bookish, sacrilegious, a nutcase, a dreamer, could be. But a good kid all the same.

He wouldn't tell Frannie there seemed to be no cure, any more than he would confess that his brand of *Thamn-al-batn* could take him at any time.

This morning, for instance, waking had been like pushing through a steel door. All those women. All those brooms.

2

SKAZ

Frannie Balduchi, backpack riding high, was jogging west on Queen Street away from the springtime hordes on lower Yonge Street, one sweaty hand clutching a spray of yellow tulips intended for home, when Josephias of Arimathea barred her path. She'd been to the bank. The bank had said no. A sermon was the last thing she wanted. Josephias was as pimply-faced as a boy and sold candles sometimes. He sold straw dolls his mother made, and Frannie had known him all her life. He was sorry and no good but had a good heart, and Frannie liked him. He wore a winter coat grey as spit, which would stand up by itself if ever he took it off. He was swishing that bum's newspaper, *The Outrider*, under her nose. "Ah, de debil wid-yu," Frannie told him. "Ya worthless critter! Ya no-good wastrel! Ya old whisky-breath!"

Josephias came back with, "Save an orphan! Rescue beasts from the storm!"

"Good idea," Frannie said, extracting fifteen cents leper money from a tight jeans pocket.

"Love ya," he said. "The people, yes!"

Frannie went on, sometimes running, her nose sometimes crushing the flowers, eventually turning north into Kensington Market's grungy digs. The whole world had a stake in Kensington Market; goods arrived from the globe's every corner. Frannie had scored her first kiss in Kensington Market. After the long winter the stacked fruits and veggies made her mind fizz. Today she was late for a rendezvous with destiny. She was always late for such meetings. No one liked her. Outside Monsieur's Empire of Cheese she paced up and down, working up the courage to go in and beg samples. She stepped on a tomato. Juices spewed up her leg as though from a lizard's tongue. A wide-shouldered man parking a crumpled van tried to run her over. He looked deeply disappointed at the failure. Ula, dear mama, had worked the counter at Monsieur's. The help had leapfrogged over Baby Frannie, climbed each other's backs, to serve the next customer. Monsieur's had prided itself on quality, quantity, and service. It had run Ula ragged. "Here," someone called. "Use this as a book marker." A wedge of cheese flew through the open door, flopping dead at Frannie's feet. "Midnight at the Purloin," another said. "Wear net stockings." Everyone in Monsieur's had a hearty laugh. Frannie blushed. They knew she was easy and didn't care a tinker's goddamn.

Frannie stepped aside for a Chinese man pushing a cart. In the cart, cushioned by a ratty blanket, a church bell rolled like a bronzed baby. "Where are you going with that?" Frannie asked. She had always been nosy.

"To heaven," the Chinaman said. His name was Ling. Frannie had an arrangement with his son, poor Ling Two, the cripple.

A five-year-old boy riding a painted stick, his face bright as a tray of oranges, took a whack at Frannie's backpack.

"Mother, mother!" the boy cried.

"Quelcazar cazam, kiddo," Frannie said back. Which meant, "Scram, kid, or I shall have to swat you."

A blue-eyed pony-tailed man wearing zigzag cargo pants, good shoes, and a decent shirt, looked on. He slapped a tambourine rhythmically against one leg. He had mean eyes and beautiful lips. Beside him, a heavy woman with braided hair and a red nose softly cried.

"Charlie eats no crow," the man said. "The fuck you lookin' at?"

3

SETTINGS

The Purloined Letter, oasis on a side street in the Market area.

"Hello, everyone. Jump up and live. Win a free seven days, and six great nights, at the Manitoba pig farm of your choice!"

Frannie sang this out upon entering. No one responded. It was afternoon. In the afternoon Purloin regulars were quiet as snakes asleep in a pile. The darkness was shocking. A raven perched on a swing under a sloped ceiling fluttered its wings. Shrieking. Earlier, in the bank, Frannie had done her share of shrieking. She had told the balding, suited man who refused her loan to go stuff himself.

"My books, please."

Because the authors Frannie Balduchi at the moment most adores in the world are Isaac Babel and the French master Giui de Mopassan, Guy and Isaac, Bobel at birth … it is these authors' work now ringing the table where she sits. But it is because she was made uneasy when she did not at all moments comprehend a character's precise geographic location within a tale that Frannie Balduchi, 39, teeth sharp and white, lips black as Black Tuesday, took also the InkSpeak pen from her backpack and wrote on a bar napkin, foregoing in the last second logic to which she was a servant, "Once again I am found in the poverty of my creative labour here in this city of my birth, which shall be nameless that I might protect myself from my creditors, yea, even to the extent that I shall refrain even from identifying my very-most home and native land of true patriots strong and free."

This note she passed about for approval to all of the Purloin regulars who would look at it. Those who did so declared that Frannie's hand was appallingly illegible, and, moreover, they had affairs of remarkable import pinging in their brains.

"Quit mooching our smokes," she was told. "Buy your own."

Whereupon, moping – no one loved her – Frannie composed on the napkin's other side, the two inks bleeding together, this news about herself: "It came to Frannie Balduchi, once upon a time, that Frannie Balduchi was not the person she had been, once upon a time."

"How's my sweet dovecote today?" Gregor the insect bartender said, delivering her poison.

"Go away," she said. She poured the oil of her loathing over his head and away he went.

The sun was shining.

No more muck.

Thank God winter was over.

4

FLASHBACK

"What a ridiculously sunny day," Frannie earlier had observed.

5

A DREDGE OF MAUPASSANT

In the spring of the year 2004, by Odessa's black bay, waters snarling under high winds and Dutch steamers tilting, God met his old combatant, Isaac Babel, uttering threats against the cobblestones as he trudged his wicked way from the station along Pushkin Street up towards Vasatyatava Square.

God was astounded. The dead generally avoided Him.

Next came Maupassant, not exactly behind Babel, nor beside him either. Occasionally scrabbling along on all fours, syphilitic still, the old throat wound clearly visible. As though a door in Dr. Esprit Blanche's madhouse at Passy in Paris had opened and here the wretch was.

Both of them. God's knaves, His villains.

Cursing the dusty startled trees, avoiding lorries, carts, fork-lifters and the like when able.

Two old lyricists paired forever, God thought, rocking on His heels, intent on remaining calm.

Refugees from the storied Hereafter. Arms flailing as they advanced against strong headwinds, their pace now a depraved shuffle-fraught weave of baby steps.

God took refuge behind a decrepit stall selling fish cooked over charcoal fires to housewives of drunken seamen. It would take Him a minute to recover.

Babel, the exact image of a Jew so ravaged, so stunted by time's lashings, that even from a distance God could see through the sockets of His eyes all our tomorrows come and gone.

Yids and shikers.

Dreck.

Babel and Maupassant caught sight of God and their steps quickened.

"Hey, Bigshot, you!" Babel shouted. "I want a word with you! Big Mouth, Mr. Fancy Dan! Don't turn your back on me, you lordly fake!"

Maupassant came on in a crouch, like a dog scenting evil. You cannot come back from death as any one or any thing other than what you were when you were at your worst. Rule number thirty of the Golden Tablet.

The Frenchman's throat slit but still able to summon his own insults. "You there!" he bellowed at God. "You scoundrel, you cur, you carrion of a Prussian!" – a line that suddenly slipped into his memory from an early success, *BOULE DE SUIF*, Ball of Fat, that dear woman made to prostitute herself for the sake of a stagecoach packed with corrupt imbeciles.

A John Ford film, 1939, no credit given Maupassant.

Too late to run.

God, waiting, brusquely shook off the offer of a fish sandwich. Expensive, I'll say. He hated fish. Fish was a thug's food. He was shaking. He didn't like any of this.

6

YOU WILL NEVER KNOW
MY MAKER'S BODY

Each morning about eight o'clock Egi Balduchi, with a wheelbarrow to convey his ledgers, sandwich board, card table and folding chair, plods along Toronto's sidewalks until he arrives at what he deems to be a suitable corner. Here he sets up shop, in winter hunkering down in his seaman's coat against the wind, in summer placing his chair so that his face catches the sun. Once satisfied that all is as it should be – the twenty-six ledgers alphabetically arranged, pencils at the

14

ready – he hurries into the nearest donut shop to pick up a takeaway coffee and muffin. Balduchi needs the shop not solely for breakfast. *Thamn-al-batn*, trouble with those insides.

While the counter person fills his order, Balduchi keeps watch over his goods. Nine years ago, before Balduchi knew unhappiness, a thief ran off with his wheelbarrow. He chased the thief all along Bloor Street West, finally losing sight of him in the brush and valleys of High Park. At the bandstand rag tail dancers said to be from Port-au-Prince had been performing Kafka's *The Metamorphosis*. Good stuff, Balduchi had thought at the time, almost grateful to the thief.

Balduchi's present wheelbarrow is painted green. He wishes he had bought a red one, because red would draw the eye better. He should have been more selective with the chair as well. The chair he now employs is a fold-up web job, light aluminum but hard on the back. The straps are going. He had wanted to use one of the throw pillows from the sofa, but Ula, way back when, had told him not to be silly.

Ula had never been entirely behind his project.

His breakfast in a sack, he hurries back to his corner.

Balduchi reckons the project will consume the rest of his days, although this does not undermine his enthusiasm. He worries he will not live to see the deed through to its conclusion.

Today? Today he feels pretty good, except for *Thamn-al-batn*. Together with balking hands, crummy knees, a stiffness in the neck so stubborn he can't turn his head. Drivers seem out to get him. A moment ago, crossing Front Street, the wheelbarrow hitting a pothole and wobbling, a taximan wearing a Blue Jays cap told him to put some pep into it, Dad. Pep? Where can a man of his origins find pep in these days of dwindling resources? His pipes are clogged. The old body needs a new transmission. Overhaul the engine. His left eye dribbles. Twice today the right knee has quit altogether, leaving him breathless. He's had to grab at lampposts. The sleep of the homeless, over vents and in doorways, has tantalizing appeal. But Balduchi knows people in worse shape than he is, dead people, Ula for one, so he won't complain.

Thamn-al-batn. He's paying the price.

He'd started the morning along Queen Street, without once finding a corner appropriate to his mood. So he pushed the wheelbarrow south, more or less allowing the wheelbarrow and the crowds to dictate his route. He was surprised to find himself arriving at Union Station, that indefatigable crossroads of human industry. A mistake. Prospects here were always dim. "Sorry, no time," the commuters told him. "Catch you later, Grandpa."

He tried to take the subway north from Union.

"No fuckin' way!" the toll keeper had told him. "No wheelbarrows."

But in the end Balduchi signed him up. In the "E" book. Wm. Eldore Edison.

"Workiholic," Edison had said, under 'Occupation.' "Always wanted to do tap dancing. Me and Gene Kelly. Now see where I am." Married, two kids. "They inherited my good looks. One's a horsewoman, lives in Sweden. Sweden's okay, I been there. Me and the wife abide. They tell us to curb the dog, we curb the dog. The U.S. of A. has two million people in jail. Rwanda, they didn't lift a hand. Good people, though. Gunslinger on every corner. But they give us Elvis. They give us Satchmo and White Bread and John Henry Barbee. You going to have pictures in that book?"

Threading along College Street, bypassing for the moment Kensington Market and the few steps home maybe for a late lunch with Frannie if she's in, Balduchi pauses. The hip now. A briny taste on the tongue. Fuck me, as the dear girl would say.

He sits awhile on the lip of the wheelbarrow. His stomach churns and sometimes, as happens now, the churn spurts through his insides like a kite cut loose to the blue. The world keels over. The line from a book now riding the wheelbarrow wriggles before his eyes like cut earthworms. He'd picked up the book from the vacant seat beside his own not more than ten minutes ago. Maybe an hour ago. The precise time escapes him. Approaching College Station this was. *"Gentlemen, Ivan Ilyich is dead."* The subway. A pretty young girl with a silver ring in one nostril, ribbon of azure stones over the right eyebrow, hair trimmed to the scalp, those clunky, what Frannie called kick-ass shoes, sitting beside him one minute, was gone the next. Her book, must be. Balduchi thinks he must have dozed off. He had been thinking of the last day of his official employment at the Department of Prisons and Corrections. The processing of an order for forty-six brooms at Kingston Prison for Women. In a dream – it must have been a dream – forty-six women in identical grey smocks, their feet bare, showing the backside of their knees and jiggling fannies, were sweeping a long corridor with blue-handled brooms. An endless rank of infantry sweepers. Got to order more brooms, a voice said. Where the dream became physically uncomfortable was when the brooms began sweeping the women. Into corners and under carpets, Persian ones at that, the carpets gliding in from an outer dark that descended slowly, a theatre curtain. Balduchi, half-awake, groaned. Someone said: "Mon, looki dot whilbarr bro I tink im sick e need helep." At some violent lurch in the train, Balduchi reached out to steady himself, and there in his hand was an open book, the type muddy except for a single line. "Spank my bottom," as Frannie would say.

"Gentlemen, Ivan Ilych is dead."

Me, Balduchi had thought. This author means me.

Helep, helep!

7

THEATRE OF THE EAR

"Don't glare at me," Babel shouted. "Crackhead! Alien roach-brain!"

God reduced His radiance to practically nothing. Why inflame the old Cossack? Why bait these hayseeds with trickery when they were as useless to divine purpose as draymen grunting among the stars?

"But look here," He said to Babel, dancing away from the smelly Frenchman's wild swats. "I heard you died in a Bolshevik concentration camp in... what was it, 1939, 1940?"

"*Both*," Babel declared hoarsely. "Twice, you fiend. Once by a bullet in the head, Lubyanka prison, January 15th or 27th,1940. I have witnesses."

"I had been dead forty-seven years," put in Maupassant softly. "Not that You had not made repeated attempts on my life long before."

God pretended amnesia, although he wasn't God for nothing. He remembered. Maupassant's syphilitic affliction, the madness that had struck him as a youngster. Babel's disappearance, the seven months of torture. Charged with being a spy for France and Austria, my word. His ratting on a fellow scribbler, that sodball Andre Malraux, the fervour to recant. *Lies! Lies!*

Ludicrous affairs. How could He be expected to concern Himself with such trivialities?

"Another time," barked the Jew, "March 17, 1941. Under 'unknown circumstances.' Ha! Unknown, my ass!"

Saliva sprayed God's cheeks. He fumed to his roots but retained an implacable, even cheerful facade.

"Check the records, why don't you!" yelled Babel. "One Isaac Babel death wasn't sufficient to Your Worship's needs."

Maupassant clawed at Him. Despite his condition he was quick on his feet, the long nails rooster-sharp. The Frog would have drawn blood had God possessed any.

Always the insults, God thought. Death and insanity hadn't mellowed these slagheaps in the least.

"I'm hungry," Babel relented. "I need a woman."

Ever the rake.

The trio toddled in a dervish up Pushkin's fair street. Limping does, they were. Babel with his two deaths, God with the many, Maupassant on the lookout for a stranglehold. The old scribblers haggard in the pipes, rotted by hard times, God thinking about tender mercy that never had caught on with Him. The fish sandwich had left a greasy taste in His mouth. Reminiscent of the thousand-and-one Whoppers He'd consumed in his time, no french fries, alas.

Cold wind assaulted them. The air was damp and murky, thick with the odour of diesel fuel, cabbage, fish, human waste. Me here minus proper Arctic attire, God thought. Odessa, better off when it had belonged to the Turks. The Greeks.

Odessos, Ordyssos, it had been back in those inelegant, more agreeable times. He was freezing, the thumbs numb, toes icy. He had come out without mittens, without mukluks, no woolly for His neck. This thin coat stitched together from hides, rags, the skin of birds. Fat chance He will not come down with something horrible. Bejesus Me, he thought, how'd I get to this place? I blundered, must have taken a wrong turn.

Some things God had given up on. Wind, rain – all the elements. They'd proved too difficult. You gave something life – gave it Your very breath – then what?

Run for the hills.

At every street corner Babel poked Him. Maupassant pinched and clawed.

"You son-of-a-bitch," Babel said.

"Asshole," echoed Maupassant.

8
JOSEPHIAS

Josephias has dollars. But timidity assails him. He's never had a woman, yet wants them. They would laugh at his acne and big feet. They would laugh at what he believes he wants to do with them. They would call him dim. So he has called again upon his old pal from childhood.

"How much?" he asks Frannie, much loved for her sliding scale.

Frannie is concentrating on the scratching of the bird in the ceiling joists and doesn't immediately hear him. All afternoon she has been in the deep with her twin obsessions, Isaac and Guy. She's rescued her heroes from death and taken them on an outing to the Black Sea. Odessos, Ordyssos, may God see the light.

Yes, Bro, Josephias thinks, Frannie Balduchi has time for everyone but me.

The Purloined Letter's rear door opens to a dark alley. A few minutes later, that's where Frannie is.

"You're a skeleton," she says to Joseph. "You really could do with some Eastern
cooking."

Joseph's hands are on her. What he brings to her always, and only, are his hands. Those hands swim and divide as do amoebae between two slides. So busy. Bees are busy but amoebae are silent, never having to pause for breath. That's what flits through Frannie's mind as he strokes her: high school and the science lab and herself with one eye shut, squinting through a scope. Trash. That flits in as well. She forgot this morning to put the trash out on the curb. Egi won't like that.

"You feel nice," Joseph whispers. "Love ya."

"That's good," Frannie comes back at him. "Good, lover. Tell me when you've had enough."

He never lets her remove any clothing. He never ventures below the waist. He keeps his body clear. Only those hands.

"Okay," he says. "That'll do me."

Josephias of Arimathea always has had enough before Frannie expects him to. It unnerves her. The back of her neck heats up. The heat spreads. A dog's tongue could be licking her. She feels hurt and insulted and would like to throw herself down on the ground, thrash her limbs like a child. It is all the worse because she has given Joseph the freak a bootblack rate. Exactly nothing. The few coins meticulously counted into her palm will be slipped to Gregor the insect who looks after Joseph's glass.

"Thank you muchly," he croaks, sliding away. He has the vacant smile of an ill-equipped traveller surprised to discover he's survived a night in the desert.

"I enjoyed it, honey," she calls.

She has one rule. Never insult the miserable.

9

GREGOR THE INSECT

Gregor the bartender observes Frannie Balduchi coming in from the Purloin alley. The bird in the rafters issues a small squawk. Is snow falling again? Is rain coming down? She looks a poor specimen, no question. You see a door with scratches around the lock, where thieves have gained entry, and that is the look Gregor's Frannie has. She's a door kicked in too often and now when the door opens the hinges squeak, the door protests, because Frannie likes to keep her door shut in fear that someone will notice the place where she lives has been ransacked.

Gregor would open the door, but he is only an insect.

10
GRASSES, WATER, AND SUN, THE BEAST...

People of Odessa gawked. They'd seen much – Mongrel hordes, angry seas, Monarchists, fiery whirlwinds, Bolsheviks – but they had never seen their Notable Son, an underfed Frenchman, and the Supreme Being lurching along like oxen roped to a cart. Even so. Even so, the faithful swarmed. Touch me, Lord, begged the many. But He would not touch them. Bless me, Lord. But He would not bless them. The sight of so many thrusting hands mesmerized Maupassant. In the author's youth Algernon Swinburne had frightened the wits out of him by stroking his cheeks with a severed human hand. Babel was delighted. He thought the mob had come to welcome him.

The climb up Pushkin's knoll was a wearing one. At Vasatyatava Square a swirling wind smacked them full in the face. Patches of fog drifted in the damp air.

God's imminence lit up. He had spotted a drinking establishment behind blooming apple trees. Instantly He felt mellow and loving.

"Unlike you ghouls," He said, "I still carry autumn in my heart."

Babel and Maupassant looked at him, aghast.

Autumn, God thought. Shouldn't have said that.

In the minds of these degenerates he was scarcely more than whimsy. A spark for the ignorant or barren of heart. A child's cat's eye thumbed eons ago onto a slanted floor.

"Autumn, is it?" Babel replied. "You see here two brothers who looked upon the world as a meadow in May until you painted our eyelids with blood."

God sneered. Patience had never been a strong suit. The old Jew's face glistened with sweat. The wire specs aslant on the Jew's nose, God only now noted, had cracked lenses. The flesh of both was as ashen as wet mortar upon a board. Together they would weigh no more than a pood.

But God's suggestion of drinks enlivened all. "I am the vicar of thirst," Babel declared.

"Drink heals the wounds of Christ," Maupassant volunteered.

A single room awaited them. It smelled of horses and gunpowder. Fishing nets and frazzled ropes lay in heaps like ancient drunks. Toasts were offered in the dwindling light. God sat on a broken chair, his legs splayed, the frayed muffs of a fur hat flopping down over his ears. He was a drinker of some repute. He could drink these two under the table. He made a sucking noise, then snapped his fingers at a slender figure standing still as a statue in a darkened vestibule.

"Vodka for these ruffians," God said to the woman. "Crimean muscatel for me."

The scribblers hooted.

A dung fire warmed the room. A blue sheen wafted up from the floor. Babel said it reminded him of the Rotonde Café in Paris's Latin Quarter when he'd visited there in the thirties. Maupassant found occasion to say he was homesick. A clock gave the time as 3:46. The hands had long ago halted. A gauge on the door marked the temperature at sixteen below zero, which seemed about right.

They soon were through the first bottle. God had His shoes off. They had the texture of gristle stripped from his feet.

"Would the gentlemen like a nice egg?" asked the waitress. "A potato?"

God, drowsing, barely registered her presence. A nerve plucked at His lips. Some kind of tick there. In the left eye also, which must have caused much confusion for the faithful along the way. A smudged tattoo occupied the back of one hand. He was a nail-biter. The eyes were blackened, as though He had a habit of walking into doorknobs.

You reap what you sow, Babel and Maupassant thought.

"He's been alone too long," the woman said.

Babel and Maupassant regarded her warmly. Her voice was honeyed in mystery. She had the attractive tenor of a dog which buries all its bones under the same rose bush. "Sit on my knee," Babel said, "I'll tell you a story." The woman laughed. They were a good sort.

Stories, Babel told her, feasted on his and Maupassant's brain like butterflies flitting through a field on a summer day.

His first reader, he said, other than Monsieur Vadon, was a woman of easy virtue named Vera.

"Veraushka," he said. "This was in Tiflis, a burg on the Kura River, known for its roses and mutton fat."

"Ah, Vera," sighed the woman, as though she and Vera had exchanged intimacies during a soulful migration in the long ago. "You have your Veraushka, while I have a giant who every morning crouches in my ear saying nice things to me. Things only a giant knows a woman must hear."

She smiled grandly. They could see she was no one's doormat.

Maupassant spoke up. "Tell her," he said to Babel, "the story of how you earned God's wrath."

God stirred in His slumber at mention of His name, but paid no more attention than He would have if anyone else had summoned Him.

"It was my story, 'The Sin of Jesus,'" said Babel. "There was this hotel maid from Tverskaya Street being taken advantage of by guests and help alike. She was always finding herself pregnant, ruffians and gentlemen going at her till they were blue in the face. So she went to church one day and gave God a hard time, calling Him egregious names. 'Old Fatguts', 'tub of lard', 'lethargic poodle', and such. God negotiated. He made promises and poor Arina went back to her employment, where she found matters gone from bad to worse. Beatings one minute, pinned to the floor the next. So she went to church again and this time showed His Divinity no mercy. So much so that she won His attention. He told her to go home and He would send her an angel. Which I'll say He did. But He had warned the woman young Alfred was delicate as a rosebud and she must be careful when sleeping with him or she might crush his wings. They were made of babies' breath, those wings. Scented with precious powder found only in the back rows of heaven and in embassy gardens along the Quai d'Orsay. That's exactly what happened. Young Alfred was a corpse before morning. This time the maid hauled off to the church fast as she could go. Her legs were chained, weighted by stones, she was made to run through invisible walls. But she arrived. She truly took a strip off Our Master. So much so that damned if He didn't prostrate Himself. On His knees He was. That's why God hates me. He ate humble pie, yet the woman wouldn't forgive him."

"That's a horrible story," the woman said.

"Yes, but funny. I was pulling old Dostoevsky's leg."

"Why does He hate you?" the woman inquired of Maupassant.

Maupassant sighed. He shrugged. He pitched about as though ants were at march under his skin, conveying his heart's last little pieces to a secret lair.

"I sided with my mother on family issues," he said. "That was a major sin. Mother smoked, ridiculed the clergy, and wore short skirts. Someone had to pay for that. My mistresses tended to resemble mother and favoured high-priced restaurants over sitting at home with a shawl over their shoulders. I was diseased, which meant I had earned it. I failed at suicide, a calumnious act. I died too young. I didn't suffer enough."

He paused, white in the face and panting like a fireman.

"It wasn't just me. God hated all of Paris. It was more beautiful than heaven and double the size."

He bent down to tie his shoelaces. Then realized he had no shoes. His shoes were in paradise walking on another man's feet.

Babel furiously wiped grease from his specs. "God only likes black and white," he said. "He likes no in-between."

They sat in silence for a while. A cold wind blew. They tasted salt on their lips and felt its weight in the air. Their thoughts flew one way and another, adrift as homeless birds. A ship in the harbour sounded three long low notes, which bespoke a timeless misery sounding from the sea's depths.

God gazed upon them with sleepwalker eyes.

A young schoolboy appeared in the doorway, dressed in the stiff black uniform of Odessa Commercial School. The starched collar buckled high on the neck. The shoes were new but the trousers had grassy stains over the knees. The horsehair bow held in the left hand looked as though it had been used to whip the violin carried in the right. His lips were puckered tight, as by a string. A military cap, smacked onto his head, perched just short of a stubby nose. His cheeks were puffed full. His face was turning cherry red. Miserable, he eyed the company. His stance widened and suddenly he let out his breath. The fat cheeks collapsed. "Auntie made me come," a pinched voice said. "She commands I should play for the gentlemen ethereal tones."

He tucked a napkin embroidered with red geese under his chin.

Scowling at everyone, he struck the fabled Heifetz pose.

The bow began a tortuous grind.

Babel wheezed. As a child he had succumbed to the charms peculiar to a sickly boy. It had been a means for avoiding such performances as this. Every parent in the Mol-davanka had driven their sons to the violin with scoldings first, whippings next – the promise of ice cream in other worlds. Thanks to Maestro Heifetz and other galaxy stars, sons of Odessa who had cast the city's eminence beyond the moons, the Moldavanka boasted snotnose prodigies by the cartload.

Babel rubbed his eyes. He opened them and the boy's grin stretched ear to ear. The thirty-second concert was done. The boy had routed the Czar's pygmy army, heated his sword with the blood of swarming anti-Semitic hordes, with Yiddling words had swooned crocodile Poles into eternal sleep, and now could dash to Okhtinskaya Square for Marseilles cook-ies and a hero's tea.

"Asthma is salutary in a writer," Babel said. "It makes for short sentences." Maupassant smiled. The woman refilled their glasses. "I'm not respected," she confessed to them. "Men want to lure me up back streets where they can talk dirty to me. They hover like crows in a dead tree."

"That's sad," lamented Babel.

"Appalling," Maupassant agreed.

Her eyes moistened. Tears rolled down the tinted cheeks.

"I collect my tears in a Venetian bottle and empty them nightly into the sea."

She extracted a delicately blown azure bottle from her clothing and pressed the bottle's lip to each cheek. The glass was so thin it barely existed. Tears inside the bottle flashed like tiny jewels, each one distinct. "Sometimes I'm convinced it's these that incite shipwrecks." All were silent, contemplat-ing the image which failed to materialize exactly in their minds. "In my dreams these tears become small children on yellow tricycles circling the globe."

Perhaps sentimental, Babel and Maupassant thought. But you can't say she isn't literatured in the faith.

More words fell from her mouth. They fell onto the table like knots in an endless rope.

They comforted her. They clasped shoulders and embraced. For a long time they sat as three heads consigned to a single neck.

Babel told her of a people who believed stars in the heavens talked to each other.

When one of the stars said something really funny the others would let loose blinding light. They'd flit about like crazed fireflies.

Maupassant told her falling stars are stars dying from a broken heart. Their hearts are broken because no one has said anything funny for such a long time.

Stars are dumber than fence posts, Babel said. They see themselves reflected in our oceans and swear our earth is a place where humour enlivens every minute.

They don't know what to make of our daylight, Maupassant said. It spooks them. They spend their days wrapped in gloom, sorrowful as spiders, asking where night went. Then night returns and they dash about like dogs at a picnic.

The woman was calm again. She was becoming more calm with each passing second. She was becoming cold to the touch. Colour was oozing out of her. Her eyes were sealing. Her chest did not rise and fall.

She lapsed into rigidity.

A moment later, she was again posed perfectly still in the dark vestibule where she had been when they entered. Only now did they notice a marble pedestal dignified her presence. She had chips in the kneecap, they noticed. The nose was broken. A chopped ear.· She carried a pitcher that would never hold water. An obscenity had been scribbled across the fine bosom.

Babel and Maupassant's eyes drifted unwillingly towards God. They remembered. He had made that disgusting noise with His mouth, snapped His fingers, and a living woman had come to them.

Was some kind of truce in the offering?

As quickly as that, Babel was crying. Not for his sins, however. He had loved Odessa, he said. Here he had endured the pogroms of the Black Hundred. He had a daughter in Paris who had never seen Odessa and rarely seen him. His papa's fine house on Ekaterininskaya

Street was not far from here. He had three children by three women, none of whom knew the others, or even knew of the others. Maybe the NKVD had put bullets in all their heads. Maybe the world had ended and this room and Odessa and a woman's desecrated statue were all that was left.

Drunk already, he thought.

Maupassant has come to the door. Curious events are unfolding down the hill at Odessa Bay. The bay is disappearing. Workers in black coveralls are carting it away piece by piece. Only a smidgen of sky remains, and the water, along with its ships, the docks, warehouses, the strut of people in the far distance, have been sliced in half. Hammers are pounding. Workers shout at each other. "Unplug the master board, for Christ's sake. Do you want to get us electrocuted?" "Rein it in! Rope the bastard!" "The flats are numbered, numbskull. I thought you knew your business." "Load it! Not there, you idiot, that's for the lights!"

Life is theatre, he thinks. If you can tell one from the other, you're one in a million.

11

RASSKAZY
(STORIES)

Time passes and where has Egi Balduchi got to?

Over recent hours he's been holed up in one and another washroom.

Embarrassing accidents have befallen him.

"Honey, you can't bring that wheelbarrow in here."

"I got no choice."

"Not in here, sweetheart."

"A wheelbarrow?"

"You look sick, baby. You sick, honey? I call 911, you say the word. But no wheelbarrow. You bring in wheelbarrows, where I'm going to sit my clients?"

The situation is urgent. Balduchi has veered into Sister Angelique's Palmistry Den.

"You hear me talking, darling? Where you going? You can't take no wheelbarrow in there. Honey, that's my private toilette."

Ivan Ilyich's ill health, Balduchi has discovered, began *with a queer taste in his mouth and a small pain in his left side.*

Balduchi has that taste. The pain too.

Thamn-al-batn, the stomach price.

It comes to him that he may not finish out the day.

"Jesus, honey, you gave me the jitters. I thought you died in there. What's with the wheelbarrow? What's them whataya call them? Them ledgers, that board? Hey, I got it. You the Who's Who man. Am I right? You the Who's Who man. Baby, you famous. How come you not ask me to be in that book? I'm a Who's Who too, baby. I'm famous too."

She sits him at a table. "Hold on," she says, "I be right back." She returns with what she announces is ginger tea. On a yellow plate are biscuits containing raisins, jam, butter. "You missing you nourishment," she says. "This fix you right up. Put zing in you step. What's that? Money? Honey, I wanted you money I'd been in you pocket the minute you come through the door."

Her mouth rarely quits. Though a big woman, she moves with the speed of a sleek bird. Her brown back is wide as a hayfield. Watermelon breasts. Her body bulges with the good intentions of a ten-dollar mattress.

"How old are you?" she asks. "Seventy-eight? Hell's bells, you a spring chicken. My boyfriend older than you. A bull between the sheets he is. Toss me round like a heifer calf."

In the meantime she's taken over one of the ledgers – the "L" book. Between gusts of speech, she's furiously writing in the book: *Angelique La Rue's very own Who's Who.*

"Nothing sordid," she says. "I got quite enough of that in my real life."

33

What I told my man D who was hot after me was that I was secretly engage to a man who did NOT want to marry me but had in mine a woman to work his fields & do what he want with me when dark come but D was fine with that he said Step over here in the shade & I stept & next I known I was looped into next week I was hot in love & soon walkin the peer to new found freedom in whatever lan would had us which is how I come to lan in this shop with money D claim wasn't his & was NOT as I later fine to be the case not that I had regrets with acception of my chilren left behine but now with me thank God & even growed up now & my youngest one pregnant by WhoKnowsWho yet doin all right though it was my oldest DeLona I'd been watchiiiin every minute when it was Flora my baby was the wile one but D still on the scene thank God never mine his crankiness his Don't Know What I Seen in You days the days the shade sit on you doorstep like a three headed dog somehow A WOMAN can live with that if …

"Uh-huh," she says, breaking off from the scribbling, "Honey, what you saying?"

What Balduchi has been saying, holding himself tight, his eyes on the floor, alert for the sound of leaking juices in his insides, the pitchfork that will make sudden thrusts in his belly and knock him flat, is that money, not health, is his biggest headache. His Prison and Corrections pension doesn't go far, frankly. Well, frankly, to make no beans about it, what he's still hoping for is government or private intervention. What they call transitional funding. Bridging money. Surely a foundation ought to be interested.

"Wait, honey, hold you goats, let Angelique throw the cards, see what they come out with, see what my better half wiccam Sister Bleed in the Golden World have to say about you case. You sweatin' some, some bit pasty-eye, sure now you don't want to lay down?"

He needs in place a nice travel kitty, he says, since the project, done right, requires that he cover the city. Neighbourhoods he has yet to canvas are pretty far-flung – North York, Toronto Island, the Beaches. His own pocket-book can't stand the pinch. What he hankers for is a kitty with enough cushion to allow himself a modest per diem, as is the custom in the corporate world. A small truck or van would be advantageous, although of course that would necessitate a driver, and Frannie, Frannie could be a big helep there. Yes a big helep, not that he's going to ask her. Frannie's got her own concerns. She's getting up there, get-ting along, and ought to be having babies. She's got a warm spot for the project, though, unlike Ula. Ula was dead set against it, Ula saw the project as a big embarrassment. "The looks I get," Ula said, "the taunting! Did I marry a crazy man? Have I worked my tail to the bone for this? So you can push your crazy wheelbarrow through every corner of the city?" Not that I blame her, Balduchi said. She was a good woman, Ula was. A fountain of gold, except she wouldn't helep.

"Honey, who's Frannie, who's Ula," interrupts Angelique. "What's this *helep* jive? You got to tell Sister everything."

"We had a fire. My daughter suffered smoke… smoke inhalation. Her lungs. And Ula…

Ula died. I don't mean in the fire. I'm hazy on the details… Forty-six brooms. Such a precise number, I hardly knew what to make of it. Straw brooms with blue sticks,

those grey smocks, they were all barefoot. I can't explain it…
Thamn-al-batn. God has put a flag by my name."

Yesterday, unknown to Frannie, Balduchi had telephoned
Ula's old doctor.

Balduchi was seventy-eight. He had been retired for thirteen years. His wife dead for nine. But when he tried putting
his mind to the task he found he could no longer recall what
she had died of. She had been in sound health one day, dead
the next. He recalled that much. To be of sound mind and
body one day and dead the next had raised his suspicions.

"Ula Balduchi," he said to the doctor. "How did she die?"

"Good God," said the doctor. "Egi? I haven't heard your
voice in years."

"Ula. Was it suicide? Did I kill her?"

The doctor kept him waiting a long time. Then said,
"Great guns, Egi, are you that old? Maybe you had best pop
in for a visit."

"If she didn't kill herself," Balduchi said, "and I didn't,
how did she die?"

Another long pause.

"A streetcar, Balduchi. She was getting off a streetcar, carrying a bag of oranges, bag of mint candy for Frannie – and
got nailed flat."

It was Balduchi who then was silent.

"I doubt that," he finally said. "I really doubt that. I
remember nothing whatsoever of that."

"Pop in" the doctor said. "You need help."

Helep.

Balduchi was fairly certain the doctor had given the word
an extra flip.

12
EXIT, TWO GHOSTS

"I owe my every success to my old teacher at Odessa Commercial School," Babel said. "Monsieur Vadon. Did you know him?"

Maupassant reminded his friend that he'd departed this world a year before Babel entered it.

"Monsieur Vadon instilled in me a love for French authors and the French classics which I recited by heart here in the Greek billiard halls. Yours among them, my friend. Monsieur had me write my first stories in French."

Quietly they talk shop for a time. Life. Books. Art. The pressure to hold off oblivion.

"Tolstoy kicked his desk into splinters," Babel said, "looking for the right word."

"Flaubert would wrestle a word to the floor. He would pound it with a shoe until it had precisely the sound and meaning desired."

The hour drooped. It had been a long, frustrating day.

"That story of mine, 'Guy de Maupassant,'" Babel asks, "what did you think of it?"

"Mine were as good," Maupassant says.

They roar with laughter.

Babel sinks into gloom.

"No, really now, what did you think?"

"I liked it."

Babel nods. He wipes his specs. He wants more.

"It was a fine tribute."

"And?"

"You were always funnier than me."

Both fall silent. Maupassant gazes out over what is now derelict space. Gone are the choppy waters of Odessa Bay, the tilting ships, the onyx sky. One whole summer he had sailed a yacht on the blue Mediterranean. Now the terrain is empty. If he held up a hand he would not see that either.

"Shall we be on our way?"

God sleeps.

The hands tremble.

"He thinks He's home," says Babel.

"In the palace of ice."

A cherubic expression rests like a mask over His face.

Exit, two ghosts.

13

FRANNIE

The moment Frannie Balduchi caps the InkSpeak pen, folds away the yellow writing pad, closes the Maupassant and Babel books, the reams of dog-eared research, daughter Nathalie's books, the lover-engineer's book, and is stuffing these in the backpack, saying to herself It is time to go home and fix papa his dinner, the bird in the rafter squawks. It squawks as though its tail is on fire. But Frannie is mistaken. It is not the bird but Gregor the insect who is calling her name. In a panic. Gregor the insect is racing out the Purloined Letter door, shouting over his shoulder, "Come quick, Egi don't look good."

She is running too. She is running with wading boots. Stones are attached to each ankle. Wall upon invisible wall must be passed through. Air is heavier than lead and a queer taste has run right past her, leaving bile in her mouth. Her sight is riveted on her father, the overturned wheelbarrow, the scattered goods: on her father collapsed on the pavement, clutching to his breast as many of those precious ledgers as his hands can reach.

Jesus God, she thinks, running, it's that *Thamn-al-batn* come all the way from Algeria, come from goddamn somewhere, this shitheel *Thamn-al-batn* is fucking us up.

"Papa, Papa!" is the scream.

Run, Frannie, run.

14

STOMACH PRICE

Egi Balduchi, down on the pavement, fighting with demons who want his ledgers, is feeling not bad. He's given the project his best shot, and for an ex-bureaucrat paper chaser from the Department of Prisons and Corrections putting in orders for forty-six brooms he's done, no, not bad. He sees that pleasant boy from the Purloined Letter who has been smitten with his daughter since age one racing his way, and Frannie behind him coming on strong. Somewhere in the vicinity must be that fine witchy woman Angelique La Rue, because he clearly remembers a moment ago she had hold of his arm. She was steering him home when *Thamn-al-batn* stuck a thousand pitchforks in his gut.

He's okay, though. He knows he's okay, because he sees everything so clearly. He sees, for one thing, those many who have entered their stories in his books. He could sense among the passersby those who needed, who required and warranted, entry in his Who's Who. They were curious about his table, they studied his sandwich board, they examined him as they would the growth of something unidentifiable emerging from questionable soil, and always something in their eyes, the faltering steps, the what-is-this? gave them away.

Someone should be paying attention to these people. That's why he did it. It was what he had told Ula those long years ago, what Frannie seemed by instinct to have recognized. In that *Thamn-al-batn* country one had to feed the friendly visitor four days. Share with them your scraps, if scraps were all you had. Sit them at your table, let them use your bathroom. Perform the public service, don't fit them out with brooms. Too bad you had to pay the host's price. A hell of a price, an injustice, but what could you do? He would see these people coming and almost instantly recognize the need. There's one for the book, he'd think. That one. Already rising, extending a sharpened pencil, extending his chair.

Take your time. Get it off your chest. Spill the news. Tell your story.

So he had got a good many shits, con artists and the like, so what, let a good editor cull the crap from the true.

He regretted he had yet to come up with a proper title. Something classy was required... zingier, more a heart stopper... than *Balduchi's Who's Who*.

He has another regret. The "B" ledger. He never got his own entry in there. Whenever he tried, nights at home or sunlit days when little was doing on the street, people at home futzing in their gardens or the whole city scooted off to cottage country, proper words to stand as his own mark flew off into the dark.

How strange, he thinks, that they left no trail.

Birds, Ula had often said – starlings and the like – could pick words right out of a person's mouth, fly away, and make nests out of them.

In no otherwise could birds come equipped with speech.

Robbers, she told Frannie, rounded up the Balduchi family ZZZs while Egi, Ula, and Franuchka slept. They stacked the ZZZs up like cordwood at their own house so the robbers' little robber children could be snug and cozy when winter hit.

Ula had ruled the roost with stories like these and when the roost was shipshape she went off and ruled Monsieur's Empire of Cheese.

It was a damn lie that a streetcar knocked her flat.

Balduchi's X ledger is the thinnest by far. It is in the X ledger that the statement of the two Arabic-type fellows who informed him about *Thamn-al-batn* is to be found. Xebec, the pair submits as the family name. Shabbac in the Arabic. In Algeria, this was. Balduchi has looked Xebec up at the Runnymede Library on Bloor West. Three-masted ships once used by corsairs. Plain pirates to you and me. Though in Algeria if you said Xebec you could be meaning both pirate and ship.

It was Frannie, reading the entry, who had pointed this out.

He feels Frannie's warm mouth arrive outside his ear.

"What's that, Papa?"

He hears her perfectly well despite the distress in her little girl's voice.

Her mouth is in the wrong place. The ear doesn't breathe. She ought to move her mouth to where it can.

15

IMMIGRANT CULTURE

An ambulance turns the corner, cuts a zigzag path through the shuffling traffic.

It roars right through Babel and Maupassant.

"That was quick," Babel says.

"Laudatory," Maupassant agrees.

"It's the Who's Who man."

"One of ours."

Frannie, down on her knees, clutches her papa.

"Will he live?"

"He's alive now. That's all I dare venture."

"What is that book?"

"Your old friend Ivan."

They drift rearward, out of the field of action. Maupassant studies the scene closely, looking to discover trees that are not trees, water that isn't water, a sky that can be rolled up like a rug and carried away on something called U-Haul-It.

"Your little Fifi seems done with us for the moment," Babel says. "What do we do now?"

"I don't know. It's a bit vexing."

"Where are we?"

"No idea. A city I never knew existed."

"Different, though. Lots of mix and match. A rainbow world. Let's explore."

16

LOVE LESSONS

Gregor the bartender will load the twenty-six ledgers, the sandwich board, the web chair, the fold-up table, and a paperback book into the wheelbarrow. He will study at length a single shoe abandoned on the pavement. Worn heel, missing tongue, paper thin in the sole. Egi wore rip-off running shoes, Nikes, that he knows. All the same, Gregor will pitch the shoe into the wheelbarrow. He will push the wheelbarrow to the Purloined Letter and stow it behind lock and key in the beverage room. The wheel wobbles a bit. He will tighten the nut if a wrench can be found.

The Department of Prisons and Corrections has seen fit to locate a halfway house for women three doors east of the Purloined Letter. The avowed purpose of this residence is to enable newly released prisoners, mental patients and the like, a dollop of grace as they re-engage the terrors of society.

Some, of course, claim the halfway house is a festering sore, a drug den, a brothel, that its presence not only undermines neighbouring property values but also offers full evidence of liberal left winger shit winder heart-bleeding socialist politicos' mindless coddling of the criminal element and by rights, say, in a decent democracy, ought to be burnt down.

Gregor the bartender is not one of those.

Gregor the bartender once lived in this house with his sick mother in those days when the city was known as Toronto the Good and every day was a walk down Sabbath Lane. The structure had been a two-bit rooming house back then.

Gregor's custom, these days, is to pass the house with light footsteps and a sad heart, an eye slanted to see if a light yet burns in his and his mother's former room. To glimpse, as he sometimes does, her weathered face behind the panes. His mother had hung a prism from the shade. Over the years, not one ex-prisoner, mental case, or dreg of society has found cause to remove the lovely bauble.

Still there today.

Hello, old Mother.

A woman is sweeping the halfway house porch with a quick broom. She is barefoot, wearing a grey smock. Green hair cactus-spiked tops the black face. A week ago there was snow and bitter cold. The apple tree in the yard is unaware of this. Already blossoms are sprouting. Shrubs by the walkway, however, remain covered in burlap. "Who you looking at?" the woman demands of Gregor. "I see your snake eyes slicing my way. You think I'm something you want to look at, is that it? Maybe you think you better than me."

Gregor stops in his tracks. The wheelbarrow, such is its nature, flips over.

"Where you going with that wheelbarrow?" the woman says. "I bet it's stole. It is, I bet so. You got the look. I see your kind every day. What you got in that thing? Come here, let me see. Come on, I don't bite. I know you. You work at that gyp dive down the street. Got that bird. That fucker-bird keeping us halfways up at night. What's them ledgers for? I seen you pick them up. They's the Who's Who man's. I see you hugging the Who's Who man's daughter. I see you talking to Sister Angelique also. Me and Sister cousins of the First Light. That's wiccam talk. I know everything about you. You can't tell me one thing about yourself I don't already know. I seen them ghosts too. Looking like two ends of the same dishrag. Bible salesmen from caves in the desert, they looked like. Cars run right through them, no need a driver even to swerve. Chatterboxes chattering away."

"Pardon me," says Gregor.

"No need to."

"Pardon?"

"I see all things from this porch. With my halfway eyes. My little view of paradise. Love, for instance, I see that. Come here."

Gregor uprights the wheelbarrow and pushes it along the path to the halfway house when the woman holds up her hand.

"Stop right there," she says. "Halfway is far enough."

Gregor stops. He's at a loss. The wheelbarrow has been badly loaded. It leans one way, he corrects that, then it leans the other. The wheelbarrow seems to have in mind dumping all its goods at this halfway woman's feet.

The woman watches his struggle with cold eyes. She has a cold face. He feels he's entered a field of ice.

"Love, I said," she goes on. She has a stern, reproving voice, one that will brook no dissent. She has a warden's voice, but Gregor knows the halfway house is self-regulated. Residents answer to no one because they answer to all. You can get your throat slit if you don't toe the line. So Gregor has heard.

"You don't say much, do you?" the woman says. "You the Mute Force or the Spent Force, which is it? Speak up. This broom's gittin' antsy, it's not got all day."

She swats the air with the broom. Gregor dances back. Dust motes swirl. The woman pokes out an arm at Gregor's old room.

"None of the girls will habitat that room," she says. "A ghost in there. She yours?"

Gregor feels a cold wind circling his neck. Chill bumps run over his flesh.

"No need to reply. A fool can see the resemblance. You making a business call?"

The woman points to a small sign nailed above the mail-box: LOVE LESSONS DAILY, 2 'TIL 5.

Another sign says, WE BURN JUNK MAIL.

"Let me have a look at you," the woman says. She studies his face, then takes a slow walk around him.

"Stop turning," she says.

She comes up close. She rubs his belly, nodding. "Not too much flab."

She crouches low, running both hands along his legs.

"But no muscle man either."

A hand flits across his fanny. It comes up between his legs and folds over his penis.

"Least you not maimed."

She rises, smiling.

"You'll do," she says. She pats his back.

She's no longer cold. She's warm as Sunday Baptists roasted on a spit.

Gregor's face is crimson. No woman has ever touched his privates on a busy street in bold sunlight.

"Bashful too," she says. "That's a plus. I hate doing business with tight-butt arrogant buttheads think their pecker is the Taj Mahal."

"I better go," he says. These are the only words he can think to speak. Yet his legs remain locked in place. His breath is locked in his chest, no escape.

"You can go nowhere worth going, in your present state. You are lost in the Land of Unreturned Love. Any step taken is shooting yourself in the foot. How many feet can a man in the Land of Unreturned Love afford to lose?"

"But…"

"But?"

"Sorry. You got me confused."

"Affection Denied does that. A man in Unreciprocated Love walks alone in a dark halfway house."

"What?"

"You're a dog yelping at eternal fog. Let's get on with it. Plain as the nose of my face, I see you love Frannie Balduchi. Love sits on you like a new suit on a dead man, plain to eye and ear as a wolf howling from a woodpile. It runs out of you like sap from a Maple tree. Lust, love, hunger. It's all need and need is big in a man of your scale. Your biggest need is Love Lessons. Today it happens I'm selling them cheap. Got my special on. My two-for-one Gigantic Spring Sale. Open your wallet. Let me see the green."

"Love Lessons?" repeats Gregor.

"Lesson number one. You get a fat Fail. Don't repeat everything a woman says.

Number two. Pull that tongue back inside your mouth. Makes you look dopey. What woman's going to fall for that?"

"Ma'am?"

"Don't 'Ma'am' me. 'Ma'am' is what us halfways had to call the screws. Not to fret, though, I'll shape you up, turn you into a topnotch Spring Lover. Spring forward, Fall back, that's our halfway house motto. See this Love Lesson contract? Glance it over… sign on the dotted line."

The woman thrusts papers into his hands.

"Nine copies," she says. "Never mind the small print."

She thrusts an InkSpeak pen into his hand.

"Page two you see my price chart. Fifty dollars to secure the love of a stupid woman, twice that if she's ugly, a further fee if the love object has webbed feet, ingrown toenails, B.O., and such as that. The less you get the more you pay, in other words. Plus VAT and GST. But you're smitten with the beautiful and smart Frannie Balduchi so I'm prepared to negotiate. I'm open to offers. Smart women cheap is my deal of the week. Smart women are a glut on the market, oversupply and limited demand. Your lucky day. You want her, she's yours. All coming with my Spring Offer Money-Back Guarantee. I don't fix it, you nix it."

"You're saying you can make Frannie love me?"

"Make? 'Unmakes' more the tune. First we got to unfix the damage already done. Love is a mystery, as you've heard, but I can lift the veil. Come on inside. We talk it over. You got the Who's Who man's wheelbarrow. Mr. Balduchi the host with the most, never mind he pays the *Thamn-al-batn*. Frannie? Her heart's a piece of cake. Insect, she calls you now. Few of my lessons, she be around you like bees in a field."

A hand fluttering in the window above.

Mom?

Anything is possible.

Inside they go.

17

LOOTED TREASURE

Babel and Maupassant are down at the Toronto waterfront, looking out over Lake Ontario's blue expanse. Twenty-seven miles of broken glass, as a local poet has said. A portion of Europe could fit upon this lake, never mind that this Europe would instantly sink and be no more. A movie would be made of the sinking and win all the Academy Awards. History would find and redefine itself, buoyed by thunderous applause. Glass on the water are shards of light slipping from the mouths of the innocent dead. Their very last breath. We walk under green lanterns and find ourselves at the end of green evening arriving at the sea's green edge. Dry seasons lust for winter's cold and the snows of yesteryear succumb to the same fever. Babel and Maupassant are speechless, under the onslaught of what awaits.

Beginnings are without end and something always does.

On the esplanade a goateed man in a ponycart hawks wares made, he says, in the azure heaven that is Istanbul.

Bones from the Azores.

Attila's hatchet.

Spices from Beelzebub's very table.

The sacred tears of the young bride Psyche.

Whatever one wants.

Get it here.

18
CRADLE SONG

High condominiums wall the city. The sun knows it has been betrayed. On a balcony in one of these, with mortar and pestle a woman wrapped in a golden sari grinds a thousand stones from which will be extracted one drop of precious tea. The tea is a cure for a sick daughter. Why otherwise would she do it?

THE WINDS OF CHANGE,
THE WINDS OF HOPE,
THE WINDS OF DISASTER

The Winds of Change boarded the Western Comet in Be-
ceuse St. Jour; the Winds of Hope came aboard the next
day in a small Ontario resort town sitting by a body of water
so still and blue people often forget its existence. Where
the Winds of Disaster joined the train is unrecorded
although a quick scan of newspapers dated May 18 has led
many to believe these winds took to the train at Neepawa
Junction on or about that date. In Neepawa Junction thousands had taken sick from drinking tainted water and many
died.

What is known is that the Winds of Change settled wherever space was to be found, that is to say, throughout the 14
cars constituting the Western Comet at that point in its journey. In the small Ontario town with the still blue lake, Point
Pigeon, for reasons best explained by railroad officials, 19
more cars were added to the train, and it was in the first-class
compartments of these 19 that the Winds of Hope secured
themselves, immediately falling into a deep sleep, and unable, therefore, to shed any light on the timetable under
which their cousins, the Winds of Disaster, operated.

It is understood that in Chiogga Flats, 700 miles west, again for reasons best left to railroad czars to explain, an additional engine and another 66 cars were attached to the Western Comet, 34 of these 66 conveying 510 new automobiles of the Nissan Motor Company, the balance of these 32 cars empty but the siding latticed in such a manner that one could be forgiven for thinking them to be cattle cars. Among the 99 cars now constituting the Western Comet as it made its journey westward were 17 chemical tanker cars containing as yet unidentified compounds of a highly volatile nature. Where and when the tankers became a part of the convoy, or their intended destination, has not been established.

The Winds of Disaster, naturally enough preferring to keep their own company, largely confined themselves to the cattle cars. They preferred the unadorned, outdoorsy character of these structures, the acrid smell, the bitter whip of undefined, indiscriminate winds about their shoulders, the wicked unrelenting noise of metal grinding upon metal. The night view through which they passed thrilled them with its phantasmic abundance, no less than did the daytime sight of a land so locked under hellish freeze that scarcely anything moved, the sky an uncaring blue so frosty and brittle in appearance it clearly seemed an oval made of the most imperfect glass.

A student couple from Orebro, Sweden, aboard the Western Comet since Montreal, were first to experience the Winds of Change. It simultaneously entered their flesh the third day of their journey, on the outskirts of a nondescript prairie city that some on the train said reminded them of a cribbed baby. The Winds of Change, in any event, rode with this couple along the slow rails curving about the city, intense in the breasts of this couple as a brigade of dancers, until the long train at last broke free of city life.

"What was that?" asked the young man, and the young woman seated beside him, clutching his hand, suddenly overcome with the desire for something achingly cold to satisfy her thirst, replied in a high singing voice, "The Winds of Change, my love, the Winds of Change!"

The young man, until that moment believing his body had sat apart from him in a wet, barren cave the entire length of his life, beheld at once that he was now cast anew into a world of wonders. Whereas the girl, who previously had slept on pillows of stone, her mother's jewels in pawn to the profiteers of sunny Orebro, her life restricted to the shallows, now felt as easy in the world as a feather afloat on air.

The second party to succumb to the Winds of Change was a woman named Ana Coombs. Ana Coombs lived in an outlying district of the town, an area known as the Forks Reclamation Project, through which at one time had run a span of rail tracks wide as Rainy River Lake, wide as Lac St. Jean of the Cross, wider than those, these tracks and the attendant buildings composing the now rotted terminal summoning in its heyday an array of trains from every conceivable direction on the continent. In recent times 68 of these 70 tracks had been removed, the land ceded by government edict to the Forks Reclamation Project, a development still after lengthy decades mired in its First Phase, with parkland, roads, electricity, waste disposal, and other amenities yet to come, but on the drawing boards let us say; in the meanwhile some 6,000 beleaguered souls, among them Ana Coombs, called it home.

Ana Coombs was at the kitchen sink washing in mild soap and lukewarm water heated on a wood stove three pairs of white cotton stockings. She raised her eyes to stare out the window at the swaying train. She saw a young man with blond hair and a thoughtful face. He seemed to be looking at her with an expression of sheer delight. It was then that Ana Coombs felt the Winds of Change shift through her like a tangle of birds in sudden plunge from the sky.

"Excuse me," she said, "I believe I must sit down."

The man seated at the table in Ana Coombs' kitchen said, "I don't know why O'Toole feels responsible for every thought your sister has."

"I would like more coffee," he added, "but so far you have not invited me to help myself."

Ana Coombs' face was flushed, her heart was racing, and she did not immediately reply.

The man walked around the table to the coffee pan atop the wood stove and refilled his cup, which was a cup made to resemble a grinning monkey, a slot in the curved tail for easy handling.

"O'Toole's a sap," the man said. "If he holds himself re-sponsible for every thought entering your sister's mind, then his will be a long, sad story."

"That's right," Ana Coombs said. "O'Toole isn't responsible for how she fixes her hair. He isn't responsible for the lipstick shade she wears. Maybe for her shoes. I am not sure about the shoes."

Ana Coombs or the man, or both together should they have chosen to do so, could have turned their heads and had a good look at Ana Coombs' sister, Mary Alicia Coombs, asleep beside O'Toole on the high double bed in the nearby room. Until a year ago the bed and the room, in fact the entire house, had been the refuge of old Mrs. Coombs. Mrs. Coombs, the sisters' grandmother, once they had finished high school, had packed off the girls into the care of the world.

Now they were back.

The cup of the grinning monkey had belonged to old Mrs. Coombs.

A coffee table in the adjoining room, constructed of blackest gaboon and so hard it had endured 99 years without receiving a single scratch, sat on a faded oval carpet in front of a lumpy Empire sofa, the sofa covered with a worn fabric depicting ancient sailing vessels, and it was here that Ana Coombs took herself.

"What's bugging you?" the man asked Ana Coombs.

She gave attention to her short, thick legs stretched out on the coffee table, refusing to look at him.

"It would seem," he said, "that someone has ruffled Ana Coombs' feathers."

Ana Coombs laughed, delighted with the vision of herself as a 48-year-old woman covered over with chicken feathers, rising with a rooster's crow each and every dawn, laying the odd egg, pecking at gravel, scratching here and there in the mecca of the Reclamation yards with her brood of utterly uninteresting chicks.

"I have felt the Winds of Change," Ana Coombs said. "I believe it would make me happy if this minute you went in there and waked your friend O'Toole and you and he left this house, never to be seen again."

The man said nothing for what seemed to both of them a very long while. Then he said, "Yeah, well, maybe your sister might have a word or two to say about that."

Ana Coombs said, "Why don't you go and ask her?"

So the man did.

Ana Coombs smiled as she heard her sister emerge from sleep and say to the man, in a voice astonishing in its petulance, "That was grandmother's cup. You are not allowed to use that cup."

A woman named Dora Bell, also living in the Forks Reclamation Project, was the third party to experience the Winds of Change. She had run fresh water into a goldfish bowl, the bowl itself in the form of a large fish. Dora Bell was returning the bowl to its usual table by the front window when the Winds of Change reached inside her, lodging like a cluster of grapes inside her chest. She momentarily confused the Winds of Change with the bouts of indigestion which normally troubled her each morning, and thus for some minutes remained on her knees watching the fish poke about in their new clean water and speaking to these golden fish in the softly bantering manner that Dora Bell believed to be perfectly normal. Then her sight shifted above the bowl to take in that view presenting itself outside her window. The train. A woman exceedingly blond in her composition was looking straight into her soul. Her mouth, Dora Bell saw, was wide open. She seemed to be frantically waving something, perhaps a yellow handkerchief. Then a young man's excited face appeared beside the woman's, and his mouth too was wide open. In that instant Dora Bell saw as if in a dream her front door blowing open, the fish rising and swimming paths of sunlight towards some kind of natural home in a distant sea. A split-second later it came to Dora Bell that she had been struck by the Winds of Change.

The first mission she gave herself was to wash out the empty fish bowl and leave it on the drainboard to dry. As her second mission, she spent some minutes writing down the precise details of the door blowing open, the flight of goldfish through the sky, the open mouths of the two Nordic beauties aboard the Western Comet, the drumming in her heart when finally she closed the door. She made no mention of the Winds of Change. When she was done writing she neatly folded the paper and carefully placed it inside a porcelain jar which sat in plain sight on an elaborately-stitched Cuban lace doily on her mother's old maple dressing table. Here were contained all her dreams, these dreams now and forever corrupted, altered, and yellowed by aromas peculiar to the jar, the jar being one presented to her by her mother long ago, at that time filled with a scented ointment sworn to stave off any and all unwanted pregnancies, the jar emptied of this ointment since long ago because Dora Bell in those days had been aware of her mother's thrifty nature and thus had doubled her mother's every prescribed dosage.

"There," she said in a voice she thought of as her mother's, "now go away and play and please do not soil your pretty dress."

When done with these and other pressing chores, Dora Bell hastily packed a small yellow bag that still carried store tags attesting to the bag's virginity, saw that all doors and windows were locked, with some agitation arranged a favourite hat on her head at the hall mirror, a Toledo hat triple-feathered above the ear and boasting in full-sized facsimile a luscious Gadaffi peach. She got into her Nissan Fury, and drove a weedy lane east out of the Forks Reclamation Project for the first time in so many years that she scarcely could find the way. She had to rely entirely on her instincts, which thankfully the Winds of Change had refined into a condition altogether unusual for Dora Bell.

A boy of twelve was one of the few other parties in the area succumbing that day to the Winds. For him it was neither the Winds of Change nor the Winds of Hope, but the Winds of Disaster.

Each day for the past year, usually around sunset, the boy had been visiting the sick old man who was reputedly his grandfather. The old man lived alone in a derelict house close to the railroad tracks, a house not yet within the embrace of the Forks Reclamation Project and one which the old man's wife and children, no less than his grandchildren, had long insisted he sell. He had refused through these many years, and through as many his wife and children, no less than his grandchildren, would have nothing to do with him. Repeatedly the boy had been forbidden to call upon the old man – he had been admonished, whipped, even shut away in one of the Project's abandoned sheds where broken bicycles, old kites, and bag upon bag of hardened concrete were stored. To avoid this punishment, a year ago the boy had begun lying, had taken to reviling the old man with his every breath, whereas in fact over the past year he had secretly visited the old man every day.

In warm weather the old man placed a stool outside his front door and sat on the stool throughout the day. In earlier times this or that party from the Old Forks, long before it became a reclamation project, would roll up one or another log from the log pile at the side of the house, and join him. Nowadays, all of these old friends were dead, and his sole companion was the boy.

During the year the old man had held the boy's attention through stories of the plagues of Egypt. He told him of the plague of the first born, of darkness, of hail and birds, lice, frogs, flies, the plague of blood, the plague of murrain – one plague for each day. Today the old man had told him of the plague of the 365th day, otherwise known as the plague of finality or the plague of the final plague, the plague of the last suffering.

"There are no more plagues to tell you about," the old man said, "so you can go home. You can tell my wife and daughters and grandchildren a plague be upon them."

The boy was distressed. It disappointed him enormously that there were so few genuine plagues, a mere 365, and he had told the old man in no uncertain terms that he was mistaken.

"I am never mistaken," the old man said, "as to the plagues of Egypt."

"Then there are other plagues, plagues not confined to Egypt," the boy said. "Tell me of those."

"The plagues of Egypt are the plagues of all places," said the old man, "the plagues for all eternity. "

"That's foolish," said the boy.

"There are 365 plagues, no more, no less."

"You are mistaken," said the boy.

"I am never mistaken."

Now the boy was walking home along the railroad tracks, sorrowful that he had no means of filling his tomorrows and irritated by the sum of life's affairs as reckoned by his teacher. He was convinced in his mind that plagues were innumerable and sick in heart at this year he had wasted in secret visits to this old man whose 365 plagues barely touched upon so many of those very plagues afflicting his own existence practically from the moment he emerged from his mother's womb. His parents were right, the old man was vile, a stubborn senile old fool who long ago should have surrendered his broken-down house to the great powers charged with the responsibility of making the Forks Reclamation Project a reality enriching to all who might be so lucky to call it home.

The old man's final words to him had been as follows: "If you are so keen on believing there is one scrap of respectable plague beyond the 365 I have enumerated, then you must go away and invent the new one yourself. But when you do, don't come and tell me about it – first and foremost because

I will be dead, and, second, because it will not be a plague in which I or any other person of any integrity would have the faintest interest."

So the boy was a ready recipient for the Winds of Disaster that morning when he stepped off the tracks to allow the Western Comet unobstructed passage.

He saw no Swedes' radiant faces looking to share their joy from behind a grimy train window.

He saw instead a tumult of winds whirling inside the 32 cattle cars of the Western Comet, obviously the Winds of Disaster, he rapidly concluded, since their enraged faces, their deformed limbs, the lethal manner in which they fought for dominion over each other and over each inch of space was exactly as the old man had described them in his recital of the 99th plague of the 365 plagues of Egypt, the plague of the Winds of Disaster.

"They gore and maim each other," the old man had said, "until they work themselves into a state of utter fury, and it is then that they enclose themselves as one howling entity and sweep through Egypt or wherever they may be, crippling or killing all living things within their path and only abating in this mischief when their limbs betray them and their throats have grown hoarse."

The boy saw this malevolent fury building in each of the 32 cars passing so slowly before his eyes, he saw the loosening latticework through which the Winds of Disaster were ever streaking, the black swirling Winds of Disaster shrieking above each of these cars black as the water of Lake Neepawa, black as the black waters of the Forks' own black waters of River Aryan, blacker than these, and when moments later the

17 shiny tanker cars shuttled by with screaming wheels it came to him in a flash that the Winds of Disaster were not mindlessly whirling, but assembling.

The Winds of Hope had in the meanwhile ridden the Western Comet since Point Pigeon in agreeable comfort, content in mind and body and in no mood to meddle. The long train-creep through the frozen tundra had scarcely triggered a twitch in their eyelids; the extended layover in city after city and in rustic wilderness where their transport sat idly breathing within the shadow of tall trees weighed down by ice had not tempted them to bestir themselves, and their entry into the prairie lands had only raised to new heights of noble contemplation their sense of justified fatigue. The Winds of Hope had in truth enjoyed a sound and restful sleep through much of what most of their kind beheld as yet another tedious, all but purposeless journey, one done for show, done merely, one might almost contend, to establish yet again their benign ageless presence within an undeserving environment. A few from time to time briefly snatched themselves awake, some arousing themselves sufficiently to note the fragile work done by the Winds of Change in this or that wretched little house or crumbling tower constituting, for instance, the Forks Reclamation Project. Such was of little concern to them, however, for they were inclined to view all such acts as frivolities of their weaker sisters, acts not at all in accord with those high-minded, dignified standards of behaviour that the Winds of Hope had long ago mandated for themselves.

True, the odd member of their group, slumbering beside you one minute, might be gone the next, but these were by and large untrained and undisciplined junior delegates or duffers of the old school, gone completely round the bend.

The work of one such renegade from these ranks might be remarked upon: Samuel X. Sleane, 17, the X that self-divined portion of name he had crudely carved upon his own arm, was set to stab a needle into the vein above that point where the X had been cut, when a gust of wind shook the abandoned Project trailer in which Samuel lived. The wind burst through each of the trailer's three smoky windows, gusted the door from its hinges, captured in a whirling pool each object from door, window, and wall, three times catapulted Samuel X. Sleane against the ceiling, slamming his body three times against the floor, sucked the needle from Samuel X. Sleane's bloodied hand, blew the hair straight out from his skull, snatched all clothing from his body except one sock, whistled through his every orifice... as in the meanwhile and for the whole of Samuel X. Sleane's own tumbling the needle spun in fixed circumference through the crowded air, finally, it seemed to find its true course and drive itself with absolute accuracy into the most hated treasure Samuel X. Sleane possessed: the miniature, much weathered portrait he carried in his wallet, a one-inch by two-inch grainy black-and-white machine photograph of his father and mother snapped one grim drunken day in St. Paul before Samuel X. Sleane was born or possibly even thought about, this pair being the party Samuel X. Sleane, in rare, coherent moments, rightfully blamed for his painful sojourn on earth.

When Samuel X. Sleane came to his senses he was flat against earth, naked in tall bulrushes by a blue lake, under a cloudless sky, in a place he did recognize.

The Winds of Hope, he thought. Holy damn.

The rippling of the Western Comet began just beyond the Forks Reclamation Project when a black funnel of wind engulfed the 44th car. The 15 products of the Nissan Motor Company on that 44th car shook and shivered, the 8 wheels transporting these Nissan inventions lifted as one from the rails, cars to the front and rear responded accordingly, these cars upending and touching wheels high in the air, like a macabre ballet, one might say, the very rails weightless as sticks, whipping hither and yon. Within seconds the 17 chemical cars sailed through the air, exploding moments later in rivulets of fire heard as far away as Wisperthal, Sarama, and Wennemucca. In the end, the Western Comet's full complement of 99 cars came to final rest within a score of fiery fields, coloured fumes surging upwards in duplication of giant rainbows, liquids uniting high into the air, into the very clouds, where explosions took place by the minute, a dense congregate of particles raining down upon the whole of the Forks Reclamation Project, through the whole of the district and beyond, as far afield as Wisperthal, Sarama, and Wennemucca.

Dora Bell stopped her Nissan Fury in the middle of an unkempt path. For some minutes her eyes fixed on a naked boy standing knee-deep in the water of a lake so still and blue it seemed hardly to exist in a real world. She had seen any number of naked boys and men in her time, and she appraised the form of this one with the same deliberation given those others. That he looked to her stringy and wind-blown, scatter-brained, even more than a little deranged, did not concern her. He had the dark, somber, smoking eyes her mother had warned her about. She was beyond such idiocy now – or thought she might be – and here was a boy who needed a mother.

"Come on," she shouted, and the boy came.

"Get in," she said, and the boy did.

In Orebro, Sweden, later that day, there would be cause for celebration. Singed hair, a broken toe, the telegram would say. Otherwise fine. Send money.

When spears of light shot above the sisters' house and the very heavens spun, the sisters did as their grandmother had always told them they should. Go below, she had said. Hide.

So here they were, crawling on a cool packed-dirt route that went on so long and deep they had never found the courage as children to follow it to its end.

"Old Mum always said there was an underground city down here," Ana Coombs said. "Keep going."

The sister said, "I can't believe that worm actually took our monkey cup."

Ana Coombs said, "I'd like to have been here when she died. She'd have faced death with open eyes, calling it bastard names."

The old man at his shack by the tracks, holding aloft a black umbrella, looking at the sky while composing his own raft of bastard names for what it was he saw, recalled a plague unmentioned among the 365 Plagues of Egypt, the Plague of All Plagues, the Plague of the Unmentionable. To escape this plague, infants of his ghetto during the time he was born were swaddled in blankets, tied and knotted by rag, rope, and mystery. Under veil of night, these cocooned babies one by one ascended by balloons into the heavens, the foremost hope of those below that the winds be favourable

THE UNHAPPINESS
OF OTHERS

Bed and I are at the window watching what is going on in there, which is mostly the men in there watching something else, this blue TV light flickering over their faces as they swallow beer and nudge each other, Daddy Stump among them though not nudging anyone himself, as he is hoisted in his usual fatigued manner against the wall, when Bed says, a little too loud, which is how she talks, "Who died in there, Royce? What are we watching, Royce?" Which are good questions, the very both of them good questions that I am having myself, but too loud, attention-grabber questions, so I go to jab my fingers into her eyes to shut her up, when what she is doing is already running, which is the one thing she does first-rate, like Daddy Stump does standing against his walls. That is when the overhead bulb flares in there, inside the room where we are watching through the window what goes on, and a mad scramble from the men in there washed under these blue flickers, because the old pigshead barrel Bed and I are standing on has decided to collapse because of Bed's takeoff footpower when I go to poke her, this poke intended only to shut her up from her speaking of the dead, which she speaks of right and left these days on account of Mama Stump's bedridden plight, like her whole mind these days is consumed with thoughts of how the earth covers you and you down there with your eyes closed and the earth's weight weighing against your closed eyelids, as I do myself these days, when it comes to that.

"Quick, the light!" somebody says in there, first the dive for cover and then somebody says that, one of the former nudgers under the blue flickers, then the next second all of us scrambling, me just catching a glimpse of Bed swooping away around the corner of the house, shouting back, "I told you that old barrel was rotten!" Me in pursuit of her now, since she's running the wrong way, Bed is, into a deadly trap, if you figure the men in there are sharp enough to head for the front door and not the window where we were looking at what was going on in there, and had been since the minute we'd noticed them steering one by one, over the minutes, into that scrungy, rundown, unused place, them furtive and decomposed as something would be furtive burrowing into a hole where, once everyone gets in there, a thing worth looking at might be going on.

But they don't catch us or see us, thank God, maybe because they are too decomposed to swoop outside, or at least too disruptured to exit except by the stealthy departure, just as they'd done one by one in the ingress, their heads slunk down that way, like a chicken will bury hers under wing, since if they swooped out as a gang intent on finding out who it was was sneaking their looks at them they could be identified and hoof-printed, anyone seeing them to ask what they were doing in there, it being condemned property with No Trespassing signs slung all over the yard and trees, along with the KEEP OUTs.

Next time they will throw up planks over the window like they ought to have done this time, and you'd think Daddy Stump, snagged up against that wall in that way only he knows how, with a clear shot at what was going on in there, would have thought to do that, him being as well-versed and schooled in spy work and subterfuge – especially since his truck crash – as anyone else in these parts.

But whoa-up.

There is Bed sprawled in a mud puddle at the side of the house, the three black slips she likes to wear all hoisted and scrunched up under her elbows, now whimpering a little, not because of the mud but because of the humiliation of having been caught by me for practically the first time since she learned fast-running was her excelling point in life.

"Hey, Royce," she says, but I don't wait to see what else is coming out of her mouth, I just snatch her up by her waist-bands and bootleg her through the fence hedge, and back home fast as we can fly.

So we can be there, in the front room with the TV turned up loud, vibrating the little glass shoes it sits on so as not to scar the floor, Bed down on the floor spread out on the dog's old newspapers, to save the mat, which for unknown reasons is prized around here, and me sitting eel-bent on the foldout smelly couch with my hands up over my face, honing rapt-eyed on that TV set, when Daddy Stump hobbles in. Like if I bat my eyes the whole show and the crate that holds it will plain disappear. Like if you don't concentrate fully on every second of your life then the whole ceiling, to instance one thing that will, will collapse.

When Daddy Stump comes in. This being about three minutes, or pretty soon anyway, after we have fled from watching what was going on inside that house with him shagged up against the wall, which is where he goes now, to his usual wall, his head at the very same grease spot, after first turning down the TV to a whisper you can't hear even if you crouch inside the thing.

"You kids look a tad out of breath," he says. "You kids look," he says, in his own whisper that you have to strain to make out or know he's talking at all, "like you been up to something you shouldna' been up to," he says. His voice rising now and getting more meanness into it, the tone getting more his own now, like the words have to gnaw up past his wired teeth. This for some reason making me relax a bit, though not much. Not for long. Because how he finishes his speech is with, "And maybe I'm going to have to strap you, both of you, give you a few knobs to think about. The thing is which first?"

He's slipping his belt out of his pants as he says this, in no hurry to get down to it, this slow way meaning he means business now, which I see with just the half of my eyes, just up to that belt and no more, just up to that buckle, for instance, where there's a dab of red that could be old bloodstains, mine or Bed's or his own leaking out. Bed no doubt glomming onto the same, though otherwise we have the usable half of our eyes glued at these whispering people on the TV set, like they are watching us and being careful to keep their voices low so as not to intrude or halt anything going on in here, and whose watching silent talking make me think of the last time he had that strap snapping his business, when the people across the road called the law, which is what got the dog started, the law's arrival, and ended up with Daddy Stump's disfigurement, if disfigured is how you'd describe the condition he's got himself in now, which I wouldn't, not to his face, and Bed wouldn't either, despite a natural talent inclining her to spit it out. That head of his still swathed in the white bandages, though them not white now, from the surgeon's brainwork.

This goes on for slow minutes, that belt job, and for me, slick with sweat, it seems that what the entire world has reduced itself down to is the three points of a triangle like was talked about this week in school, minus the fractions I for one didn't hunch up to. There's the TV, there's that belt of his now being checked out for its limber qualities, little soft smacks against his own hand, him liking that the same way you'd like spreading extra batter over a cake or licking the spoon, and there's Bed with the mud drying and already cracking into jigsaw shapes on her slung-out limbs because the heat in this house is up to a constant 85 because of the infirmed one's shivery condition in the Fatal Care unit.

"I think it was I told you to stay home," Daddy Stump says with those teeth.

Then he has this clump of my hair in his hand, and it's my clump he's twisting, while I squint my eyes tight, my breath flat, catching the odd wet blink of Bed down on the floor with her hand crawling up under the black slips to scratch at where chunks of mud are drying in her behind.

I get an "ouch" or two out, hardly anything else including my breath, as meanwhile Daddy Stump is pulling out my hair until he can decide which body part will be juiciest to his strap as he goes about finding out whether we know or don't know what it was he and his buddyroles were watching in there in the KEEP OUT house down the road, under their blue flickers, or whether we've been here the whole of the day glued to this dumb TV box, which it is how with not one spoken word the world can hear what's going on in here.

Which is a good thing, too, because what we hear in the absence is the tick of the kitchen clock, the bong-bong recitation of minute and hour. Which reminds us, and Daddy Stump too, that it is time for the nursing rounds, time to turn Mama Stump on her sheets in there in the Coma Room in her bedridden, no-holds-barred, write-off condition.

"You two Joes just hold on," says Daddy Stump, giving a hard belt-lash to my ankle bones as he hobbles off in that up-down, swaying way he hobbles since his truck crash.

Bed is still scratching, now rolled over to watch me rub both hands over my scalp in the soothing of the ripped scalp patch and figuring out how much I have left.

"Perfection!" Bed says, "Utter perfection!" Yelling this out, along with a big grin which comes out at the same time, which statement I guess is occasioned by the new delightful sensation she's feeling from all this mud drying on her, even those clumps lumped in her behind, which would worry me.

I crawl up and flip the TV channel, wondering what another place would look like when you can't hear anyone saying anything though the lips are moving like they think you ought to be able to.

"You stay off that mat," I tell Bed, because I see her inching that way for the comfort, like she's decided the newspaper is something you'd put down for the dog to do his stuff on, that being how we did it around here before the dog ended up on Daddy Stump's truck hood and came through the windshield into his lap, where she still wouldn't quit, all while he's revving the truck to shoot it by those law officers who have squared off their Plymouths up by the mailbox, and squared off themselves behind it, their holster belts up near their titties, those blue lights whipping.

Daddy Stump, in his truck that time, sees this. He views it and is considering the choices even as the dog comes through the windshield. He's got to carom off the rear end of that Plymouth, hit the ditch and take out the mailbox, take out a few scrub trees and part of the fence, if he's to make it. Which he likely would have but for the pistol shot and the dog which is up on his chest now in a blue of broken glass slobbering her licks over his face, her legs doing a jiu-jitsu over the steering wheel, so happy that this time that dog is getting to go with Daddy Stump where it is that dog thinks he is going.

"Oh, Swami," Bed says to me then, with these raw welts on her legs, which I guess is why she's taken to wearing Mama Stump's black slips that Mama Stump won't ever recall once wearing herself.

Those people on the TV go right on with their mute talking.

A bit later I hear the door open in the Intensive Care room down the hall where Mama Stump abides the hour.

"Water," Daddy Stump calls.

Which Bed purses her lips at, watching me to see if we have heard any words hailing our way from the Death Chamber.

A minute later the door rattles open again, him saying, "Didn't I tell you to bring your mama a glass of water?"

Bed grins, like she's saying she never heard of water and wouldn't know where to look for it in its pure form.

"And I mean now," Daddy says, while I hold my breath to see will he add, "And I don't mean maybe," or will it be, "I don't mean tomorrow."

But he just bangs shut the door.

Bed is now clumping stiff-limbed around the room, looking to see will her mud suit fall off or will she be able to wear it forever.

"Stay away from that mat," I tell her again, for that mat's precious and could be is all that's left from the Stump twosome's old bridal suite.

Bed clumps behind me to the kitchen, where I draw the water. She's saying, "Mama Stump gets out of that bed when no one's here." She's saying, "I've seen Mama Stump's footprints."

"Where?" I say, watching the water run over the glass and over my hand and dribble down my arm to the floor, so that pretty soon there's a puddle there Bed can squish her toes about in. "On the linoleum?" I say. "Where have you seen the stalker's footprints?"

"All over," Bed says. "Mostly on the ceiling."

"Hip-hip, hooray," she says.

She points up at the ceiling where the light bulb is hanging from the chewed up, fly-speck cord, which reminds me of the dozen or so light bulb spares we've now got somewhere in the house, from the time this woman came to the door wearing push-pedal leggings and with this lopsided face, selling "Electric light bulbs," she said, "of assorted wattage."

"Proceeds to charity," she said, to Daddy Stump who is there by the front door holding her at bay, saying, "That's us."

Bed says, "Excellent," watching the puddle spread out towards her feet which she steps back from, not ready yet to squish about and upset the status quo of her mud suit. "Excellent, excellent," she says, raising her black slips up over her waist and on up till the three black slips are over her head, maybe in the darkness of that headspace remembering what I am remembering myself, which is Daddy Stump at the front door talking to this woman selling electric light bulbs of assorted wattage and telling her that he will bet her a dollar he can illuminate any one of these light bulbs she's holding without even screwing that bulb into a socket of any kind but simply by putting that light bulb screw-end into his mouth. And the woman saying, "I never heard of that," but not saying she will bet, though Bed and I are searching everywhere we can think to find that dollar. Because if Daddy Stump can do what he claims he can do, and do it without any tricks, then he is a man mankind has been underestimating all these years.

A minute later, he's doing it. He's doing it without even the dollar. He screws the light bulb between his lips, screws it tight, standing there at the front door looking out at the dark night and the lopsided woman's face with her open mouth. He does it, nothing happens, then he crouches, grimaces, and gives that bulb a last extra twist. The light flickers, it goes out. "Uh-oh, pay up," Bed and I say, because Daddy Stump hasn't said anything about flickers. But he smiles. He gives that bulb a thump, and that light comes on. It comes on and stays on. About 40 wattage on, I'd say. It doesn't flicker any more, even as he says "Excuse me, Sweetheart," a rumble, but that's what it sounds like, and he strolls past the light woman and down the steps into the yard, where he performs these several little spins, these struts, his head cocked, like he wants us to observe that he is not attached to by wires or On and Off switches of any kind, except maybe his tongue.

Because later he tells us the tongue does it, gets the job done, but only if he's been drinking, which he was doing that night, running back and forth from the Intensive Care chamber where Mama Stump presides in her agony, to his hooch stash behind the corn meal.

So I am now bringing in the glass of water which he has called for and which he cannot get himself, the water that is meant for Mama Stump who is too infirmed to drink it or even to know her nurse has come with it. Daddy Stump is hoisted up by the wall where I expect him to be, near the head of Mama Stump's bed, and she is there laid out in bed with only her dark brow and her closed eyes showing, the skin of those eyes dark as pecan shells, these peach pit eyes which are always closed, not even breathing insofar as I or Bed can tell, though Daddy Stump claims she can hear and understand every word said, or others unsaid, so watch it, he says, if you don't want to get swatted.

But he does not say that now. What he is saying now, which is like he's inside a story he has been telling Mama Stump over the past minutes, is "Itu, itu." This with a kind of smirk, or laugh, on his face, the same as was when he was doing his 40 watts with the lopsided woman's light bulb. All around the four walls are these head-high grease spots in the past coma year he's put there. He is hootched up against the wall, the leg cast, which is all the way up to his fanny, covered by his super twill ratty-edged trousers, only his pink toes with the long toenails showing, his head scrunched down deep into his shoulder blades or collar bone, deep into the grimy, yellowish neck brace. That one rebuilt shoulder riding up even with his turbaned ears. This lick of black shiny sideburn hair, which he wouldn't let them shave when they were scraping his head down to the hide, poking out from the wrappings wild as a crow's nest. A shadow folding from him to the corner and shooting on up the next wall.

"Itu," he's saying. "Itu."

Laughing full-out now, and looking down at Mama Stump like he's sure she's laughing too, if only under the covers where no one will ever see it.

I lift out Mama Stump's hand, her arm brown as ginger, like a dead, shrivelled root you'd pull from the ground, and I wrap her cold fingers around the glass, though she'll never know it and pretty soon the glass will plop over and wet the bed, the same as Bed will me once we are sawing the logs on that open-out couch.

It's the asbestos, according to Daddy Stump. The asbestos in the walls, which has brought about this strange discoloration of the loved one's skin, and he will sue the pants off somebody, once he figures out who.

"'Itu, I'm going,'" he's saying. "They've got this scrawl down at the bottom of the screen," he's telling the patient. "This white print scrawl which is a translation of what these

Japanese characters are saying up in the working part. The picture's working part, where this little fellow is working all-out, on the top of this nice-looking woman. They been going at it, you see, and when he gets there, does he say, I'm coming? The way me and you would? No, what he's saying is 'Itu, Itu,' with this thrashing of breath, these grunts, with this white scrawl down at the bottom telling us what he's really saying is 'I'm going, I'm going!'

"'Itu, Itu.'"

He even comes down from the wall, Daddy Stump does, to slap his knee, his casted leg, he's enjoying his story that much, and now looking over at Mama Stump under her covers to see if she's got it yet, is she laughing yet, which she isn't and won't.

"That's what they say over there," he tells her. "What do you think of that?"

But Mama Stump doesn't care what they say over there, or over here, or anywhere else in the world. Mama Stump's gone to where she can't think about it.

So I leave her fingers wrapped around that glass, and slip on out, glad for the minute that I have not had to brush her teeth or wash her limbs, coax the pudding cleanser into her hair, salve her, spray her, switch her backside over to the cooler portion of sheet – do anything other than get that water – as he slumps back to the wall and goes on with that "Itu" business, or wherever it is he goes when he goes in there to tell her what it is he goes in there to tell her.

In the kitchen, Bed is splashing up water from the floor pool, all over herself, wetting down that mud, which she's got slung now from one end to the other, over the dirty dishes, the curtains, the windows and door, and chunks of it up on the ceiling and on that hanging light bulb.

"Stupendous," is what she's saying

"First-rate."

"Incredibly yours."

Now it's night. It is night, and bedtime, and Bed is getting ready for bed. Getting Bed ready for bed is what brings on my shivers, for to get Bed ready I have first to open the couch, check the wet spots, root out the pillows, see the rubber sheet is stretched flat, see she has her stuffed doll, raise the windows and fluff the sheets and spread the towels over the wet spots. I have to get her promise that tonight she won't.

"Oh, no, Oh Swami. Never again."

I have first to do with her as Mama Stump has said she once had to do with me. I have to sit her down on the potty, to seat her there and coax her, shake her, run water from the taps, from the taps and the coffin-box shower stall, and sing her ditties about little girls on leaking boats in the tranquil flow of rivers, and press and poke her kidneys, pour glasses of water down between her legs, into her crevices, and woo her, browbeat her, though in the end, whether she tinkles or doesn't tinkle it will come to the same thing: in the night I will feel her cold puddle, I will come awake to the feel of its icy widening, her puddle spreading, arriving on under us and around us in a circle wide as your backside will ever find you, then to hear Bed murmuring, "Excellent, excellent," as she drops back into sleep again, her hand still and soft in mine, just the way Mama Stump said mine was in hers in those days long ago, before we had a dog, or asbestos, or Bed, or a house that had, as Daddy Stump likes to say, walls we could call our own.

Mama Stump is beside me on one side and Daddy Stump is guiding me on the other, scurrying me down the hall, both of them shouting "Hold it, hold it, one more second now," Mama Stump with this white towel spun over her head and in her soft black slip, her red toenails, Daddy Stump with his hairy legs, and me with my little pecker poked way out, holding it, us scooting along. Until it starts whipping about like a running hose you can't catch hold of, it snaking each which way, on their dancing feet and over their legs, splattering the walls, as they whip me and my little thing over the toilet where maybe one last little spurt will spurt down.

Then back to the bed, though not my bed, in between them there in their big dry bed, Daddy Stump's hips about where my feet are, me leaning into his mattress weight as Mama Stump collects my hand over her warm belly and laces both of her hands into mine, then his hand there too and Daddy Stump complaining, "He won't never grow out of it," while Mama Stump sighs, they both sigh, and she answers back, "This is nice, so nice. So let's hush, let's all of us Stumps hush and go to sleep now."

HEIDEGGER, FLOSS, ELFRIDE, AND THE CAT

Lights that flickered, curtain at a certain pitch in the summoning, the rendezvous with Frau Blochmann now concluded, Heidegger clamps his trouser legs and bicycles home.

Floss withholds opinion on the Master's affair with the eminent colleague, which he knows will continue another few decades. What he wonders is what Elfride will say when the philosopher king comes through the door. *That Jewish bitch again?* Or will she say nothing, having just dispatched her doctor friend through that very door. This love business is a bit tiring, is Floss's thought. Get back to work, he tells Heidegger. Not that such is required. After swallowing a bit of Elfride's tasty stew Heidegger will be at his desk. *Being and Time,* thinks Floss, page 355. Quote, Resoluteness, by its ontological essence, is always the resoluteness of some factical Dasein at a particular time.

Floss, in his cramped library carrel, has no argument with that. Well and good. Floss and resoluteness and Heidegger, Floss believes, are one and the same.

They are together, he and the Freiburg sage, working the deep trench.

Heidegger now writes, quote, The essence of Dasein as an entity is its existence.

Without entity, no essence: well and good, remarks Floss to himself. Particles afloat in space, what purpose they?

Quote, The existential indefiniteness of resoluteness never makes itself definite except in a resolution. Page 346.

Here Floss wants to say Hold the phone. Floss wants to put his foot down.

Floss's mind is rapidly scribbling notes to himself. These notes are scratching like a dog inside Floss's brain. *Hold the phone* is but one of the dog's bones.

Floss's index finger is rapidly scanning the lines, speed-reading Heidegger as the master composes. Are not he and Heidegger that close? Are they not twinned with respect to *Being and Time?* Are they not brothers?

Floss can quote aloud, at any time, Floss can, any one of Heidegger's current or future thoughts. The text is spread open on the desk for company only.

Photographic. That's what Floss's mind is.

Never mind that he has scribbled into his notebook the erroneous page reference. His *hand* did. Floss's mind knows the difference.

Not 346. 355. Floss has jumped ahead. He always knows where Heidegger is going; often he arrives at the destination while the King of Thought is still clearing his throat.

Quote, Only by authentically Being-their-Selves in resoluteness can people authentically be with one another.

Ah! Floss thinks. Let's not get too, you know, personal. Like.

In Floss's view this statement is another Hold the phone. This is Heidegger fighting a headwind.

That someone has just this moment walked into Heidegger's study is radiantly clear to Floss. *Being with one another* is an untypical Heidegger sentiment. The Master has been thwarted in his goals. Ergo, the line's impurity.

Who is the culprit this time?

Excited, Floss thumps his knees.

Elfride, of course.

This is Heidegger being influenced by Elfride. This is the wife calling the tune. It is Elfride saying, If you are going to be with me, then *be*... with me.

Floss can see Elfride hovering over the great man's shoulders. He can see her whisking dandruff from the great man's shoulders with a tough whisk broom.

—Don't mind me, Elfride is saying.

Heidegger doesn't like any of this. Naturally, he doesn't. Her very presence fills him with distaste. She has destroyed his flow of pure thought. *Be with one another*? How has that monstrous phrasing got onto his page?

Four a.m. Heidegger never sleeps, that explains him. But must Elfride do her dusting at this hour?

Floss thinks not. Floss thinks Elfride must have something up her sleeve.

—Dearest soul, the great man says – can't you go away? Can't you leave the room and quietly close the door?

—You know what happens if I don't dust, don't you? Elfride says.

Heidegger doesn't know what happens if Elfride doesn't dust. He is pretty certain Elfride means to tell him.

—Can't you make a guess? Oh, go ahead. Go out on a limb.

Heidegger is thinking he has always been out on that limb. He was out there first on the limb with the Jesuits when he was a boy, then with Husserl, the so-called father of phenomenology; he was out on the limb with Elfride, then with Hannah, then with Elfride and Hannah jointly. And don't forget colleague Blochmann. Occasionally the Stray Other. Now he is back on the limb with Elfride. Elfride is dusting the limb.

—I do not intend to engage in your theatrics, dearest soul, he says. I intend to sit here and work on this passage on page 355 until I get it right.

—It's right, dear one, Elfride says. I'm here to tell you it is already right. You get it any *righter*, then I won't know what to do with myself.

Floss, hearing this exchange, leans back in his tight carrel chair. He crosses his arms over his chest. He closes his eyes. "Don't let me interrupt you," Floss says.

Heidegger spins his head. Elfride ignores Floss. Floss is a pest; he pops in at inconvenient times; otherwise, he is nothing to Elfride.

—Keep out of this, Floss, she says.

Heidegger sighs. These sighs are magnificent. They express his full contempt of those who would make the philosopher's already impossible task that much more difficult.

Elfride, normally the most anchored of women, is subject to flights of fancy. Now she's whisking her broom at vacant air. She has even given that vacancy a name: Time Being.

There was a time, Floss recalls, when Elfride was more besotted with Heidegger than some now assert is the case. It is all that Hannah's work. Months before Elfride and her future husband met Elfride had carried in her pockets notes destined for the magician of Freiburg. *Don't deny it. Yesterday I saw you looking at me.* Or: *Last week I blocked the doorway and without a word you swept by me.* Or: *I beseech you. Love me.* She still retains these undelivered disintegrating missives under lock and key in a wooden chest buried beneath the floor. They prove her love. They prove her love existed prior to his. This makes her proud. Not even the great can be first in every regard. These notes will be published after her death. The instructions are contained in a sealed envelope affixed with her granddaughter's name. Not in this envelope or in the locked chest is the narrative describing the gypsy fortune teller's role in their haunted lives. Well, are not all lives haunted, Floss, who has never loved, reminds himself. The gypsy said to Elfride, *On the first rainy afternoon, following your economics class, stand beneath the first blooming tree your steps venture upon. The lover meant for you will appear.* Cold rain dripped, afterwards she caught a cold that endured through many weeks, and periodically through each wheeling year, this existing as nothing because love's astonishing light penetrated the drooping boughs and stormed her heart. Heidegger, under a black umbrella, indeed appeared. Through wet lashes he imagined he saw a dying tree where nothing had stood days before.

—You. What is your name?
—Elfride Petri.

—Why are you standing in the rain?

—Waiting for you. I am your fate.

Heidegger believed in fate as he did in Plato, with suspicion, particularly with regard to the monumentally salient question What is truth, but he was impressed. She was also pretty, though with rain pouring over her face he would reserve opinion on that. Yet when this schoolgirl fitted her body against his, his heart which was three quarters stone fragmented and certain sounds issued from his mouth never until that moment heard by himself or by any other. Fortunately only children on a dilapidated school bus, there to witness ancient Marburg splendours, were present, and they were too distracted to absorb any image of the historic coupling. This was because rain had become sleet, sleet had become snow, which in minutes had blanketed the lovers, flakes ascending and descending a second and third time, and then repeatedly, in abstract harmony with their movement. Floss, who was there and could have sought the better view had he been that kind of person, was mostly concerned with Heidegger's black umbrella which the gusting wind ripped into sundry pieces, the cloth flitting hither and yon like unruly crows, if crows were ever to attempt flight in such weather.

Heidegger has put down his writing pen. He is leaning back in his chair. He is crossing his arms over his chest. He fits his tongue beneath the upper lip; he can see clearly his thick Führer's moustache. The sighting gives him strength, although he distinctly prefers his own. He is reminded that theirs is a nation-building task. The moustache renews him in the impossible goal.

He sighs anew, leaning farther back. He closes his eyes.

His sighs now, however, are obviously feigned. They exist merely as an admonishment to his wife. Feigned, they express his resignation. His disappointment with married – the assailed – life. The sighs are meant to convey to Elfride that he has given up. How can he work with a loudmouth duster in the room, chattering nonstop?

Gone from his head is that trail he was tracking re resoluteness.

But that quickly does his mind seize again upon the trail. His shoe soles hit the floor. His burden has lifted. The pen flies into his hand. Once more he is at work. He is already scribbling again.

He is scribbling, Floss thinks, quote, *The resolution is precisely the disclosive projection and determination of what is factically possible at the time.*

Hold the phone, Floss is thinking. The projection is termed disclosive only because the thought has just this second revealed itself to the sage. Ditto, factically.

But Heidegger is breaking his pen's point underlining this significant line. It is imperative that the line be printed in the italic. If the line is not set in the italic then readers fifty years from now, speedreaders like that dunderhead Floss, will fly right by it. They will be blind to its pertinence, as he himself is blind to the dust, the dandruff – as he would wish to be blind to Elfride's galling presence.

—That's good, Martin, Elfride says. I love *that factically possible* line. It makes me break out in a cold sweat.

Indeed one of them in the room is sweating, though it isn't Elfride. Heidegger is sweating because writing a new philosophy, bringing the axe to old traditional philosophical walls – that, mein Führer, is hard work. Plus, there's the *other* problem: the window, the cat. How hot and stuffy this room is. If he *raises* the window, he will be wasting heat. Heat the Volk must not waste. Only a Jew saboteur would waste the nation's heat. So he is stymied on that front. Yet – and now he is getting to the essence of the situation – yet if he raises the window, the simple solution *sans* heat, the loathsome cat which always plops itself down on the sill, will come in. Thus, he keeps the window shut. He sweats.

Architects, he thinks, truly are a repellent tribe. They can get nothing right.

Floss swings in his chair. His shoe soles strike the floor. He sees Elfride poised. Resolute Elfride is ever on the job.

—Were you saying something, darling? says Elfride. It isn't the architects, it's me. Don't blame the architects for your stinginess. Blame the war. Or better yet, yes, blame *me*.

She parades curvaceously around the sage's desk.

—Although of course, she says, you would be perfectly justified if you blamed the cat. I'm with you there. I hate that cat. That cat is the ugliest creature I, for one, have ever seen. Are you *for two* – if I may phrase the question so – in thinking that cat is the most frightful creature ever to walk on four legs?

—Three, Heidegger says. If we are to speak of the cat, then let's speak precisely. The cat has but three legitimate legs. The fourth, as you can distinctly see, is so foreshortened as to scarcely exist.

—*Fore*shortened? says Elfride. Do you mean to say the leg in question existed that way in the *womb*? Perhaps in the very

exchange of *seed*? Oh, I think surely not *fore*shortened, because I clearly remember that leg was perfectly normal until
you crushed it when you caught the cat coming through your
window.

Heidegger lowers his head. He kneads his brow. He is
thinking, I have stayed up all night for *this*?

He is thinking, Hannah, thank God, was not a chatterbox.
Her head was on my chest whenever I spoke.

—Yes, darling, Elfride is saying. As much as I despise the
creature, it is criminal what you have done to that cat. You all
but pressed that cat flat. Martin, I hardly know what to say. I
hardly do. I am speechless, listening to your infirmity on the
subject of that cat.

Floss sees the philosopher's eyes narrowing. He sees him
looking with utter hatred at this wholesome, proud, meander-
ing wife. Heidegger's defence collapses. Elfride has described
the scene exactly as it occurred.

"It was an accident," Floss says.

—It was purely accidental, Heidegger says.

Elfride snubs this excuse. She whisks it away with her
broom.

Floss has his attention elsewhere. He is focusing on the
sleeping cat. The cat, to his eyes, has altered itself somehow.
That the cat suffers deformity is true enough. But it is no
longer the bony, undernourished cat. The cat has been eating.
It has found food somewhere. The cat is fat.

As for Heidegger, already he is scribbling again. Quote,
When what we call "accidents" befall from the with-world
and the environment, they can *befall* only from resoluteness.

Floss forsakes his study of the cat. Hold the phone, he says. Hold the phone. Hello, hello. Bravo, my friend.

But Elfride's broom is stabbing the air.

—You could *kill* the cat, Elfride is saying. Yes, my lamb, you could finish the job. *Then* you could raise your window, if only for a moment. Surely not a great deal of our precious heat would escape if you raised your window for one mere moment. Our war resources would not be sorely depleted. Fresh air, Martin! Glorious health! With the window open, even so little as a tidge, you would not be forced to wrestle there in heavy sweat. You could be comfortable. Surely your work would go better if you were comfortable. Kill the cat, my good soul. With the cat dead, your *Being and Time* will be concluded in nothing flat.

—Enough, Elfride. Enough!

—Shall I kill the cat for you, Martin? I would be happy to kill the atrocious cat if you tell me you believe I should, and can morally justify my performing the act. Issue the cleansing command. Think! She is only a cat.

—She? That cat is female?

—*Oh master*, groans Floss.

—Yes, and rather resolute, by the look of her.

Heidegger sinks low into his chair. He hoods his eyes.

—Are you done, Elfride, dearest soul?

—Done?

—Yes, done. If you are not done, Elfride, then I am leaving my desk. I am leaving my house. I will walk this night all the way to my cabin in Todtnauberg, if that is what it takes to be quit of your tongue.

Floss, at his desk gnawing a fingernail, allows himself a smile. The sage is tempting fate with this mention of the cabin, of Todtnauberg. He has stepped with both feet into Elfride's trap.

—Todtnauberg? Elfride says. Your cabin? But, darling, the cabin is *mine*. True. I gave it to you. But quit my tongue? Oh, heavens, you can't mean I have disturbed you. I rattle on, certainly, but only because I know how much my rattling improves your mood. If I did not rattle, you would go about eternally under your famous black cloud. You would never be able to look *anyone* in the eye. Your students would hardly hang on to your every word. Oh, I think it is fair to say, Martin, that without me and my tongue, and my Nazi boots, and just possibly the cat's presence at your window, you would never get your work done. You would never write a line. Most assuredly your opus would never be completed. Fame would elude you. Not a person outside Freiburg would ever have the pleasure of hearing your name. You can admit that to yourself and to me, can you not? I'll not hold it against you. You do not have to prove yourself to me, not ever. Certainly not the way you had to prove yourself to that schoolgirl, Hannah Arendt. And to take her to *my* cabin in Todtnauberg to prove it, well, my word!

—So that's it, is it? That's what this eternal dusting is all about. This *mouth* disease. So you can harp night and day on my little Hannah fling.

—*Little*, darling? What would poor Hannah think if I repeated to her what you have just said? Did you not write to her that she was your life? Did she not reply that you were her every heartbeat? That your paths would haunt each other until the death? Oh, I think so, darling. I believe those were the two sweethearts' very words. 'My homeland of pure joy.' Was that not your latest encomium?

Floss applies a handkerchief to his eyes. His eyes are wet. They ever get so each time he sees Hannah and Heidegger together in the cabin at Todtnauberg. Strolling together after class under the singing trees. The decades of love to come. How thrilling it must be, Floss thinks, to possess these loves.

Still. Still, Floss altogether shares Jasper's view when it comes to that Hannah relationship. Resolute, yes, but messy, messy. Cataclysmic love: Hannah defending him at the French de-Nazification committee hearings: scrambling to hawk his manuscripts to Columbia: through the years never one syllable from the master's mouth as to the beloved's own work which he read in secret and secretly believed ephemeral if not deliquescent. Her head ever lowered to his chest.

Elfride is thorough. Not all has been said:

—Or perhaps the precipitation in your eyes has as cause your forthcoming tart Princess Margot of Saxony-Meiningen? Will your rendezvous signal this time be flashing lights or will it be your shades hanging at a certain depth, as was the case with banal Hannah? Which? Will she hand-copy your every hour's text, as I do?

Floss is astounded. He is giddy with excitement. He has not heretofore perceived that Elfride's capacity to see into the future matches his own. He sees her now, as one day she doubtlessly will, hands clasped in an unrecognized lap, confused by the vague sense of warfare between aching joints, an old woman of ninety-two awaiting death in a caretaker home.

Will she see her two sons on Russian soil, prisoners of war? Has she yet seen the Delphic oracle rescuing from rubble manuscripts housed in what previously was a Messkirch bank? Hiding them in a cave?

Not at the moment, in any case. At the moment what both Elfride and Floss are seeing is the Master frantically bicycling 16 miles to Todtnauberg, flinging off his clothes, now dressed only in an absurd Tyrolean cap, Elfride, Hannah, the Princess, and scores of other women panting in pursuit, flinging off theirs. For Floss, madness promotes the vision. For Elfride, a confirmation of enduring love.

A thousand letters, cards, over the decades, informing Elfride where his Divinship is, not one suggesting who he is with. What a challenge this marital devotion, these conjugal splits. Send in your party membersip, dearest soul, thinks Floss. In resoluteness is strength.

"Get back to the cat," Floss tells Elfride. Forget Hannah. The cat, after all, has meaning; it is both a real and a symbolic cat. In light of the great man's post-war silence on the issue of certain atrocities, personal betrayals, I could tolerate additional intimate details re his treatment of the cat."

—Shoo, shoo, says Elfride. Stop harassing me.

Heidegger is distracted. Once more, Elfride is communicating with vacant air. But perhaps this is good. Perhaps her nasty obsession with Hannah has for the moment exhausted itself. Elfride, he thinks, with her everlasting can of worms. Essence of spite. Why can't my two great loves, my sprites, be friends? I must see to that, however imbecilic it may appear.

He looks at the cat, asleep on the windowsill. Even curved like that, one can see the leg's deformity. The crippled spine. The cat should be killed. It is doing that cat no favour to let it live.

He would give Elfride the order. He would say to her, Elfride, kill the cat! Do it now.

But he and she are locked in this struggle. They are *irresolute*. The cat, if it is to die, must die under Elfride's own initiative. If he were to give the order, the cat would ever survive intact in his memory. Whereas, if she killed it outright, slicing its throat with a knife from the kitchen or beheading it with the hatchet on a woodblock in the backyard or merely trampling it to death, then the cat would be gone forever. It would disappear totally and entirely from his mind and from the world. Its essence would have been annihilated, its entity denied.

He thinks: what Elfride is hoping is that the weather will get extremely cold this winter – Freiburg under ice, the cat stiff as a rock in the freeze. Certainly there is not the remotest chance that she will allow the cat inside the house.

Unless she does so in punishment of me. Unless she does so out of revenge for my taking Hannah to Todtnauberg. Such a stupid impulse, despite its having led to excruciating reward.

One, it had led Hannah out of drabness. It had transformed her overnight into a bewildered passionate vehicle of sex. Wrought, her mind had unloosened, her brain cells uncoiled.

God forgive me the moments I even have wondered she wasn't the better thinker than me.

Heidegger is close to tears. The shame of this.

—Oh, she's bright, Martin, Elfride says. I have never denied you her brightness. But – she snaps her fingers – she isn't *you*.

Floss leans back in his chair. He removes his glasses, polishes them. Elfride's face is flushed. Always, with that flushed face, any wild remark is apt to burst from her mouth. He wants his glasses clean, that he may see her clean, when next she speaks.

"Tip the scales, Elfride," Floss says. "Show the great man how bright *you* are."

—Martin, darling, Elfride says. She is laughing. – Look what I am doing!

Martin has been cleaning *his* glasses.

Floss, putting on his glasses, sees Heidegger putting on his.

As for Elfride, Elfride is at the study window. She is poking the cat with a stick. Heidegger keeps the stick there for that very purpose. Enter a line in *Being and Time*, then jump up and poke the cat. Enter another, poke the cat. Day after day, poke the perfectly stupid, ever returning cat. That is how his opus is being written: Elfride's dusting, Eflride's interventions – but whenever alone he has been poking the cat.

So Floss figures. Floss has figured it out. Just as he has figured out – flipping the pages, speed-reading the familiar text – the nature of the breeze. He must wipe his fingertips of glycerine, that's how much speed he needs. He has learned the dark secrets of this book. Floss knows precisely each line, each phrase, where Heidegger has got up, flung himself across the room, picked up his stick – tortured the cat.

But today, to Floss's mind, there is something different about this cat.

"A moment, Elfride. Consider. In my view, that's a *pregnant* cat."

But Elfride is in action. Elfride has the stick. She is poking the cat.

—*Da!(poke) Da!(poke) Da!(poke) Da!*

The cat is squalling; it is meowing, hissing. Clawing the glass. It can't get in, it can't get out.

Heidegger, cannot, will not, look. He turns his back to this scene. He claps hands over his ears. Elfride is capable, reliable. When the deed is done she will dispose of the corpse. He need never be appraised of the how or where. Philosophy need not concern itself with a being's single specific fate. It has steered fathomless circles since the Greeks established the course. Well done, Greeks. Now those old walls must crumble. With certain exceptions, work to date has been rubbish in the wind. The ground is soggy, diseased, repellent: it releases a fetid odour. Original thought is now required. Already the cat's presence, Elfride's resoluteness, is slipping from his mind. The pen flies into his hand; it flies across the page. Quote, "Irresoluteness" merely expresses that phenomenon which we have interpreted as a Being-surrendered to the way in which things have been prevalently interpreted by the "they." Sweat pours down his cheeks. He pauses. He wonders if he may permit himself a footnote excluding Plato, Hölderlin, Nietzsche from this "they." Probably so. Why promote their cause?

He works on. He is unaware that Elfride's *Da! Da! Da!* has catapulted into shrieks. Something about the cat. Something about something *inside* the cat. Let her deal with the matter. The cat is a household problem. That's what marriage is for. For wives to deal with them.

Floss isn't fooled. He knows Heidegger's deeper thought: This wife, this hellcat, *distorts the providence of being.*

—Do you wish to whack the cat, Martin? Elfride is whacking with each shriek.

Floss cannot sit still in his chair. His every nerve is shot. He cannot witness any more of this. He is shouting at Elfride, *"Put down the stick! Filthy Hun, put down the stick!"*

Already she has dropped the stick. Blood has splattered on the carpet, on her lovely nightdress. Her hands are covering her face. On the sill the dying cat is wrenching its body one way and another. Gore is leaking from the torn fur. Blood pools on the windowsill. A slimy wedge of kitten protrudes beneath the crooked tail.

Never mind. Soon, reaching towards sixty, Heidegger will be out on the hinterlands with young and old, digging trenches to delay the advancing enemy. Floss hurriedly assembles his books. He hitches the backpack over one arm. Rushes down the stairs. The library is exceptionally well lit. Fluorescent tubes quiver and spit. In the entire building no other individual is stirring. The universe is silent. Dawn has arrived, an ascending quilt. His own cat will be crying. His cat will be saying, Why have you not been here to let me purr in your lap? What have you been doing? His wife and children will be in tears. Where have you been? Who are you? (Dearest soul), resolute being, explain yourself.

BAD MEN WHO
LOVE JESUS

Queening isn't what it used to be.

This king isn't easily fooled. Take the queen, today she's staying in for lunch, mucking around in the kitchen with poisons in the mixing bowls, dipping the odd finger. Tasteless, she says, not quite aloud, which means it is only the rhubarb old kingy will notice.

Any minute now he'll be shouting, "Feed me!" So few of his tasters have died this year, if less than ten is few. "Less than on the battlefield," the king likes to say.

"Here woman," he's saying now, "kneel, rub my feet."

Queening isn't what it used to be. "Out of here," he's been heard to shout of nights, upsetting the peacocks asleep in the trees, "Tonight it's lesbians I want!"

He'll have them too, and any way he wants. Who's king here?

Lunch, king?

"Not rhubarb again!" he says, "Is rhubarb all this kingdom grows?"

"Ah, but lad," he says, "take a decent taste, not finger dips as I see the queen is taking hers. That's it, lad, a full dollop of the stuff. Now let's give it a minute, see if your face goes blue the way mine does when I sing. Singing's good for a body, you know, ask the queen, the whole this morning these tuneful hums under her breath, so happy, you know. Well, who would have it another way, a smiling face, that's the thing."

"Hmmmm, that food's looking good. I find it so undignified, this having to wait, a tugboat anchor, you know? How're you feeling lad? A fast poison, a slow one, how's one ever know? Lad, lad, I say, lad, poke out your tongue, I'm told that that's the first place a true poison shows."

"No, queen, you go ahead, don't wait for me. I insist, truly, I insist, here, let me put this big serving on your plate."

Minutes pass, an hour, so much time passing, my word. The taster boy prone on the marble floor, the king's doctor, a good rep, better at bloodletting than most, fans a broom over the taster's face. There, see him, frankly the boy looks done for to me. Ah, now the old feather-beneath-the-nose trick, is such really needed, did you ever see such a blue face? Too bad, such a fine, stout lad he was, come all the way from Egyptland, I'm told, though it's true that turban bothered some.

Did the king eat? We know the queen did, the king insisting, insisting, going up on his shoes, even flashing that steel, "If you like the stuff so much then eat it yourself. Eat, goddamn you!"

Our poor queen, expatiated, no, that's not the word that I was looking for, expired, that's the ticket. It's a case of "an ovo," if you ask me, from the egg, right there in the beginning a wise party would have known those who were not going to work out. Yes, as you say, those rogues in Rome have a phrase for everything, "anguis in herba," that about covers the matter, there was always a snake in the grass. Those lesbians, for instance, there was one that split the camel's back, that truly got the s – t hitting the fan, definitely. If I had to put up with monkey business of that scale, I would have come unstuck a long time before our good queen did.

Such busy times around here, ye gads, I'm having trouble keeping up. Yes, Queenie's Little Sister is alive, she's definitely alive, she has been released from the tower. As I understand the matter, this minute fitters are in the drawing room with her, she's had a wash; put your nose to the keyhole and you'll sniff a heaven of exotic scents, some all the way from Arabia, I'm told. Hair groomers, cloth merchants, shoemakers, vocabulary experts, they've been run off their feet. In seven days the wedding, that's the news, a good old-fashioned God-fearing interval, that's what the king said he wanted. Oh, little sister had been well-fed, no need for concern about her being a bag of bones, toothless, the doctor looked her over, she's sound and solid, so he said, alert and all of that.

Not yet thirteen, yes, as you say, not yet thirteen, not yet, April the 26th, they tell me, the same birthday as our Lord, the same hour, in fact, many tell me, seeing as how she's our Messiah's very own twin sister, though Mum Mary denies it, unless you get her alone on a gloomy night, then the full story unfolds like hard rain.

Bless me, in this day and age, the world set to end soon, surely thirteen is old enough, half a lifetime, for crying out loud. Mind you, don't know what her old Pa will say, the tower business, that will come as a big shock to him the same as it did to me. I recall years back the state funeral we had for the poor girl, the processions, games and such, theatricals and the like that went on for the whole of seventeen days, a thousand poems scripted in her honour, those word boys never had it so good as they had it then. Bit by an asper, that was the word give out, the word told her Pa. He'll wonder now whose body it is has been rotting in what we've been calling her tomb, he may have a few thoughts about this rhubarb business, her Pa has got to be pretty big in the king world himself, hell, I hear he's just taken over Meshach and points west, not to mention Shadrach and Abednego. What I figure is we might soon be in for the war to end all wars, old Joe being a globetrotter who Loves Jesus and his own way of thinking, none of it nice, if you're asking me.

OH, NO, I HAVE
NOT SEEN MOLLY

Place: Downtown Victoria, a Saturday morning in 1980

Open to: A storefront space, filled with
some fifty children. The word has gone
out. "Take a break from parenthood, hear
ye, hear ye! Drop your kid off for an hour
or all day and let Kaleidoscope Theatre's
actors, costumers, make-up artists,
together with a handful of the town's
writers, entertain your children with
storytelling, games, skits, dress-up, and
other forms of merrymaking, all under
Kaleidoscope's reliable eye."

Yes, open just so. The curtain, please. It is
nine o'clock in the morning and already
fifty kids aged crawling to seven or eight are
assembled, some crawling this very minute,
some shrieking, more than a few at tussle,
others steeling themselves for the dreaded

overture — silent, guarded, distrustful, morose, you would think, taking careful gauge of these forty-nine other orphans for the day.

Liz Gorrie, Kaleidoscope impresario, emerges from the hubbub: *"Now children, now, clap-clap, don't let me stop you from what you are doing, no, no, we are here to have fun and we are having it, and those of you Polly is working with in make-up and costumes, you just go ahead with that if you want to — oh but hello! hello! here are more children coming through the door, say 'hello,' children, and aren't those boys and girls just in time because this nice man you see here is going to read you a wonderful story, so let's draw up in a circle, move it now, hip-hip! shake a butt!"*

So the curtain, let us say, opens to this scene: pandemonium, shrieks, sniffles, a few wa-waaas, even, and watchful eyes as the nice man drops to the floor, opens a book, a triple-tiered ring of maybe thirty guarded or eager boys and girls, others off in the background painting their faces, trying on false noses, parading in boots, hats, sashes, veils, wigs, gowns of olden times, feather boas that cascade as in foaming seas — as, outside, cars, trucks, buses, and bicycles swoosh up and down, now and again a raised voice from that world, the blare of a horn, the whine of a siren.

But in here all is relatively calm, serene: *"The sky is falling, the sky is falling, look, look, children, the sky is falling! Oh, cover your heads, oh, cover your heart, the sky is…!!!"*

The tale goes on: oohs, ahhs, exclamation and the drawn breath, the peal of laughter, plops of pudding on the gay children's text. Snatches of floating song from the costumed revel of others in the background, woeful cries from the faint at heart, a pirouette of the small child here, there, the tinkle of bells, the cluck-cluck of child dressed as chicken, the click-clack of bewigged child in high heels, hats a yard wide and high: all is going as it should here at the Saturday morning kids' call.

"Look up, look out! Oooch! Owtch! The sky, the sky is…!!!"

But what's this? For some minutes now, a woman with drawn expression has been

circling the room, peering into every kid's
face, and you can see this person's alarm
mounting – she's thirty, thirty-five,
wearing a simple suit and trousers, her hair
tied in quick-tie, scarf waving from her
throat – but we have children to attend
to, no time to ponder this anxious,
brooding parent in obvious search for her
missing child.

—*"Ooooch, owtch! Oooo, that smarts!"*

Half an hour passes, more… let's draw
this tale to a close, lest we fidget, lest we
moan. And indeed there are moans, and
much fidgeting now, because now it is
clear: a child is lost. This mother, after
probing every face, questioning every
child, cannot find her own.

"Where's Molly? Have you seen my Molly?
About this high, this lean, and very shy, oh
the quietest little girl you ever saw!"

We are all into it now, looking under
tables, inside broom closets and boxes,
under long gowns and wide hats –
looking everywhere – and Molly can't be
found.

"Have you seen Molly?" we ask. The mother asks, everyone asks: "Have you seen…?"

"Oh *nooooo*," the one child says. "Oh *nooooo*, I have not seen Molly."

And Liz Gorrie is seeing lawsuits, she's seeing her theatre go belly-up, ruination afloat, and a lifetime of guilt and pain.

"Oh *nooooo*," this one child says over and over, under her wig, sashaying about in pumps and long gown, leading a train of others with her in their game. "Oh *nooooo*, we have not seen Molly! Who is Molly?"

Police cars arrive in whining clutch at the curb – two, three, now a fourth.

"My daughter's been abducted, *do something*. Oh I can't face this!… *Molleeeeee!*"

The father arrives, more cops: none of us can face this.

"Have you seen…?"

"Oh *nooooo*," the same little girl says. "I have not seen…"

It is ten o'clock now, now eleven, and
Molly has been missing for three hours.
Fear grips the heart, the chest strings
tighten… when our eyes fall yet again on
this little girl in a surround of others
similarly garbed: the wigs, the lipstick and
rouge, the long gowns, and this one our
eyes light on now saying: "Oh *nooooo*, Molly
is a bad girl, Molly is. I have not seen Molly
all day!" And the distraught mother is
suddenly lunging at this cherub, screaming
"*Molly, Molly!*" – and ripping away the wig,
probing the little girl's sorrowful face,
which face now erupts into brightest smile,
the girl saying, "Hi Mommy! Do we have
to go home now?"

GO FISH

"The children are playing Go Fish," Edwina said.

Her boyfriend Edwards examined her the way he sometimes did. But his manner was otherwise acceptable.

"I love fishing," Edwards said. "Once I caught a blue trout
this long." Edwina waited to see how far apart his hands
would go. She waited and waited. Edwards' hands were busy
holding his Scotch. He had both hands wrapped securely
around the glass. Maybe he lost a lot of drinks. Maybe someone removed the drinks from his hands or said you have had
too much to drink or maybe they put a pillow over his head
and smothered every ounce of life out of his staggeringly
handsome body. "Now would you like another drink?" the
murderer would say.

Edwina only went out with good-looking men who
dressed superbly and possessed a sophisticated worldly
attitude about matters essential to the realm. Cash flow
was rarely an issue. It was true, however, that these handsome boyfriends tended sometimes to be arrogant beasts.
They were selfish beyond contemplation. They never
called their mothers to say, Happy Birthday to you, my
beautiful beloved mother. Those mothers waited and waited.
These men liked saying to waiters, "This wine has gone
off." Somehow they always found a way of telling you their

shoes cost in excess of five hundred dollars. "My humble slippers cost twice that," Edwina might find herself replying. Actually it took very little to impress these flaunting bastards.

"That blue trout was a ten pounder," Edwards said. He had deposited his drink on the blue table top, surely a Scamozzi, ca. 1580. His hands went out, and out, until they could extend no more. "I gave that fish to an old beggar-woman going by the name of Tripe. She was deeply smitten. She said I was a good man. She said I was a better son than her own sons. I was better than a whole pile of sons. She said I deserved the Iron Cross." Edwina preened. "Before my addiction to immaculately groomed devastatingly handsome men, I flagrantly consorted with beggars of besotted uniformity. I was downwind of smelly disinheritance. I counter-sued. Who in my league had not done worse? You likely read of my escapades in the tabloids." Edwards stiffened. "Madame, I do not peruse the tabloids. Tabloids exist as therapy for simple folk."

Edwina folded her hands in her lap. Her eyes took on the glazed look of one who has stared too long at the endless toss of seawater. Minutes passed. Finally she heaved a sigh, saying: "You twitch, you know. When speaking sentences interminable or brief, you twitch terribly. Cadence is disrupted. Is its cause the ageing process of which my phalanx of rogue doctors speak so indulgently? Good-looking people ought not to twitch. Unless they are striving to formulate an all-encompassing point about something touching the very brink of incredulity." Edwards' back went straight; his very façade brightened. "That blue trout twitched like the very devil," he said. "Bette Davis twitched. Yvonne de Carlo twitched. Even Myrna Loy did."

"Those were their hips twitching. Hip-twitching is allowed among the female corp."

"Myrna Loy's *lips* twitched. When she drank martinis, called her dog, or pointed out a gangster to her boozy Thin Man husband."

"Yes. Even the most witless savant should know to *bless* Miss Loy."

Both sat for a long time thinking about a wide world of subjects — Edwards, for instance, wondering… Was it Scarfi… ca. 1780?… That blue table?… That scrolled, gilded sidepiece? Queen Hetepheres, ca. 3rd millennium?… And why is that damnable *Blue Boy* hung so devilishly high? — until Edwina planted her slippered feet securely on the marble floor, saying in a rather maniacal voice, "Pertinacity is my favourite word in the entire universe of words. All those other p.e.r. words dissolve into a rotted heap of hogwash when humiliated by pertinacity's glory. I cite you notable examples: Perch. Peregrination. Perfidy. Periphrastic. Peripatetic."

Edwards hummed. "Pestiferous," he said. "Pestiferous is rumoured to be poetic."

"Balderdash!" exploded Edwina.

It took her some few minutes to settle down. "I will grant you this," she at last said. "Although one never notes its presence in the Halls of Justice, 'poem' is a sweet word which slumbers and slides and slips and tilts gracefully on the tongue. It readily summons, like a gentle narcotic or cooling breeze. It induces in me the dream of sleepy, heavenly afternoons in softly lit rooms scented with lilac, when one is curled up beside the dreamy other after one's every fluid has drained."

"I will thank you not to be so grossly specific," mumbled Edwards, staring at his glossy shoe-tips, which outrivalled the marble flooring.

"Whereas," continued Edwina, "the word 'po-etic' is harsh, vindictive, and not the least bit conducive to reflection."

Edwards snorted, without intending to, because a gentleman wouldn't.

"Be that as it may," began Edwina – but then she too fell silent. She was remembering that her father, in a pique, had declared her an unsalvageable twit, during that troubled time when he – "to the full resources of my being" – sought her disinheritance. Clasp her in irons, he had said.

A heap of rotted hogwash, he had called his fellow railroad tycoons and manufacturers.

My dear sainted father.

Conversation stalled, the two sat on, under subdued lighting, neither aware of the room's widening shadows. Scamozzi's blue tabletop deepened to a rare russet hue, as it always did at about this hour. Small lamps lighting the many family portraits adorning the four walls in tuneful progression clicked on, the *Blue Boy* among them. In the view of some who ought to know, and of Edwina most particularly, the Gainsborough *Blue Boy* out in California is a copy.

She had been dressed in smart blue boy suits as a baby.

In her youth she had often dallied with those rather nice Hunt boys.

Madame and sir, dinner is served. Be so agreeable as to tackle your chairs at table. The work force, a duo dressed in brilliant white, has put in an appearance. Edwina and Edwards bestir themselves.

"After you."

"No, after you."

"Take my arm."

"You are a princely man."

Several children now also sweep in. Edwards loses count after three. He does not know the proprietorship of these children, and Edwina gives no indication that she does. Aromas arising from dishes being settled upon the beautiful table suggest a French objective. Edwards approves, as apparently does Edwina, who, smiling warmly, is at the moment musically tinkling a glass with a silver rod designed for that sole purpose.

Victorian, Edwards supposes. Possibly once the Queen's.

"Do you children recognize the tune?" Edwina asks. "Do you not detect hints of Bach's *Goldberg Variations*? Did you children have a lovely time? Did you play Fish? I heard rapturous voices crying out *Go fish!* during my every sterling moment with Edwards."

"Yes, yes, yes!" sing the children. "We all cheated admirably!"

"Excellent. Will the champion-cheater now regale us with prayer?"

LAP, A DOG

A dog, Lap by name, trotting upstream along a narrow creek, snapping now and then at swarming gnats ever in glide above him, yet never of a frame of mind so focused as to suggest he found the gnats annoying, suddenly felt a sting in his ear. In the next second Lap was flopping tail-first into the cold water because another sting had got him there as well. The dog lay stunned, quite astonished, his mind reeling, since these stings did not vanish, as might a bee's, but indeed seemed to deepen in intensity until the pain embraced his entire body. It came to him that his body was dripping blood at both ends, and now, reconsidering the matter, he thought he remembered hearing two gunshots before he tumbled over. But how could gunshots, if such existed, involve him? He snorted water from his nose. Looked blandly at the water streaming over his fur.

Above the bramble and tall trees pale clouds floated through a blue sky. Awful high up there. Awful empty. A few birds gliding along. A hawk giving him careful study. Forget it, hawk, he thought.

He must have watched the sky, the clouds, the hawk and other birds for some while, unaware he was doing so, thinking a good amount of time must have passed, because now he was shaking water from his dripping head and the sky had gone very grey.

Maybe I nodded off, he thought. Maybe I was unconscious there for a minute.

His body felt kind of numb, especially in the rear quarters.

He still did not yet take his situation seriously.

The gnats were going on about their business. Thousands of them lazily circling just above him. What were they doing? What exactly was their business? Were gnats merely decorative? Did they have any function at all on this earth?

Enough of this, Lap finally said. Time to get going.

He found he couldn't. He stared in disbelief at his legs, which refused to obey their summons. Neither would lift the smallest token. How extraordinary. Can you believe it?

Come on now, he said. Don't be silly.

He tried again. Better. Yes, better. This was more like the Lap of old. He was up on his front paws, knees buckling some but otherwise holding steady. The back legs were taking their time about it. They didn't appear to like at all what they were being asked to do. They seemed to want him to drag them along. All right. He could do that. You want dragging, I'll drag.

To his surprise, the instant he made to do so an agonizing bolt struck his brain; uncontrollable spasms shook his body; he splashed back down in the creek. He was underwater, his eyes open in disbelief, dimly perceiving schools of little fish reassembling – minnows, tadpoles? – to drift scant inches from his nose. Beg your pardon, they were saying. Do you live here? Do you mean to eat us?

For a while after that all was dreamy. I am asleep, was Lap's thought. Asleep and dreaming. A good lovely dream. He and his hawk, a hawk of gigantic size, were in heroic battle. The hawk squawking and cutting, slashing, giving it his utmost. Over the years Lap had had a hundred battles with this very creature, and always it returned for more. But when could a mere hawk defeat a mighty dog? Not in your lifetime, hawk, he told the bird. Even as he spoke the dream was turned sour; it was becoming another dog's dream. He was upside down in a black sky, the ankles of his hind legs caught in the beast's talons.

The hawk was saying, "Thought you'd play dead, would you?"

That couldn't be. The voice was not at all that of his old hawk friend. Lap opened his eyes. He groaned. He shook with fear. The man he knew of as Ome, Homer, had hold of his limbs and was dragging him through slush and sludge, over rocks, up a mossy bank.

Now Ome was crouched over him. Running a hand up and down Lap's body. Laughing:

"I knew it," Ome said. "Both slugs got you, didn't they, dog? My, my. I'm satisfied. Now I think you can die."

Something crashed into Lap's head. He felt the man's boots slamming into him. Then he was flying through air into the creek. He was sinking deeper and deeper into cold black water.

Night passed and much of the next day. He awakened to find himself back in the creek the dream had taken him from. He was cold and hungry, more than a little benumbed in his hind quarters. He tried standing, laughing at the shivers in his hind legs. You dumb dog, he thought. He laughed harder, and fell over. Into the drink again. He lay moaning awhile. Soon, he became aware of a pussy liquid dripping at the corners of his eyes and that sting again. In his ear. Yes, in his ear. Hunger, though, was his deeper problem. He was glad about that. Hunger was normal. Divine providence was master over fate. Not that this mattered. Both had long ago decreed that the whole of his days should be marked, one, by thirst, and two, by hunger.

On the third day after Lap's captivity by the creek, he might have been seen stealthily poking his head through the dense edge of a clearing. Here was familiar territory, here was home. The sight that greeted him was a heartening one. Too bad the day was overcast, or his spirit might truly have lifted. He wondered why he was being so wary in his approach to the house. Had she returned yet? Were the children here? Where and why were they gone?

He first peeked into his own slatboard yardhouse. No one had been in grooming it, he saw. His blanket was there. It smelled of him. Well, it smelled of the old him. His water dish and food bowl were supposed to have been by the entrance; they were not there. After a time, he found them, or pieces of them, spread about in a weedy field. So. Well, one could not expect matters to remain the same forever. No one, not even the children or the woman, had offered any guarantees.

He was keeping a wary eye on the back door. He was trying not to moan. It was taking a valiant effort to refrain from barking. His ear hurt. He was cold and hungry. This was not one of his better days.

For a while, from beneath the car, he watched the lit window. The kitchen. There was food in there. He knew exactly where it was, too.

He must have dozed. Some hours later, head resting on his front paws, he was seized by panic. Shouts. Racing feet.

"You son of a bitch," the man was shouting. The rifle cocked.

Wassup?

Lap ducked down, and just in time because he heard the bullet ping into the automobile exactly where that same ear might have been.

Now the man was again running. Gone completely crazy. Well, whenever wasn't he? Lap slithered backwards beneath the car and out the far side. He heard other bullets thracking.

Lap took off. Around the house, around a tree, slithering under bushy limbs, up the back steps, down the back steps, around the house again, beneath the house, under the porch, scrambling. Dust in his nose, his hide catching on nails, his head bumping cross beams, crawling, dodging. The man huffing after him.

Afterwards, he listened to the man's footsteps on the floorboards overhead, the man cursing, smelled the man frying up an egg on the stove, throwing dishes into the sink, talking on the phone. Walking, walking. Walking those boards.

On the phone saying, "I don't want them back. They come back, it will be the last thing they do."

At last the frenzy subsiding. Peace at last.

Everything so silent up there. Lap thinking, what's he doing, is he asleep, can I come out now?

Is it safe? Is the war over?

Lap listening, losing his concentration as he licks a paw, wipes pus from an eye, then some little scratch of sound and those ears springing up again.

He's up to something, the dog thinking.

It was like this before he locked those kids in the cupboard. Nailed them up in there. No food, no water, they stay in there till I say different.

Hours go by. Well, who's to know how long, does a dog know? Yes, hours and hours, as Lap would say: a fucking lifetime.

And at last the man's footsteps are detected crossing the kitchen floor, he's chuckling to himself, he's saying, "*Now*, you son of a bitch, let's see how you like this." He's crossing the screened-in back porch, he's coming down those back steps. Ever so softly, listen to that sweet voice.

He's placing a white plate on the grass. Meat! Lap can smell it.

Whoa! Outta sight!

"Come on, Lap. Come on, boy. Come on now, come and get it."

His voice ever so gentle. Like honey, that voice.

The man waiting, waiting.

Saying, "Come and get it, old boy. What say, Lap. Lap it up, old boy."

Lap scrunched down in a nearby hole, staring at the man's muddy boots, his legs. At that plate.

Looking into his eyes as the man crouches down, peers for him beneath the house.

"No hurry. I know you're under there."

Lap drooling. Dying to jump at that plate.

And finally the man returning inside the house, singing himself a little song. Happy as can be, the mean son of a bitch.

Lap sniffs the meat. He circles the plate. He drops down beside it, his nose pressing one chunk after another. Drooling. His tongue lapping. But not lapping that meat. It looks delicious. It smells divine. His jaws tingle, his tail swings, just to see it there.

But the meat stays where it is. It will stay there for hours, until dusk, when a coon mother and her coon children arrive, eat it, and die. Lap already is long gone. He is on the road. He knows these roads. These roads, not a single field, no ravine or quarry or wooded area will long fool him. He's hungry, sore, has a stinging ear, a headache, pus in his eyes, but he knows the way. He'll find a way. Those children, that woman, they need him. They've gone to Grandpaps. It may take a month, a year. A lifetime. He'll get there.

"There goes someone's dog," people will say.

There he goes.

SIDEBAR TO THE JUDICIARY PROCEEDINGS, THE NÜRNBERG WAR TRIALS, NOVEMBER 1945

[The Speaker, in black judicial robes, reclines in an easy chair, occasionally sipping from a cognac glass. Behind him can be seen the flags of the victorious nations. Lights throw shadows from the cutout figures who comprise his audience.]

The craniologist who came to measure Heidegger's brain was made to stand in the rain by the front step while Elfride went to ask the famous philosopher would he be willing.

Heidegger was in his study, surrounded by a heap of open books. He told Elfride not to be absurd. He was not to be disturbed.

Elfride told her husband that the craniologist had said the task would only take a minute. At this Heidegger laughed a scornful laugh. "We shall see about that," he said. Elfride had to jump aside, so quickly did he exit the room.

The craniologist, no fool, had found partial protection from the rain under the roof's overhang. Heidegger, striding fast, was outside in the rain himself before he knew it – whipping his head about in search of the visitor.

He did not see the craniologist until the man spoke.

"Over here."

Already they were both drenched.

What the craniologist saw was a short, thick-waisted man with a heavy face, a large, squarish brow, jet black hair, and an untended moustache patterned after the Führer's.

The philosopher saw a stringbean mortician, astoundingly advanced in years, possessing an overlarge head.

Elfride had taken up a stance in the doorway, which Heidegger, as often was the case, had left open. The great man could not be bothered with closing doors.

She looked at the two of them standing under the overhang, and at the rain splattering their shoes and the cuffs of their pants, and did not say to them what it occurred to her to say — that even dogs knew enough to come in out of the rain.

The craniologist was explaining his intentions.

Heidegger took the visitor to be a man of bureaucratic dullness, inflated with a sense of his own importance. This made the philosopher impatient and rude.

As for the craniologist, Goebbels' office had told him the Magus likely would be difficult — aloof, brusque, opinionated — and that he should persevere and endeavour not to offend, as Heidegger was under consideration for an exalted position within the Party.

He had not expected a man of such small stature.

Elfride remained in the doorway, biting at a hangnail, but with an air that suggested she thought herself every bit as important as them.

"If you want anything," she said, "you will let me know. But I am not bringing my good china out here in the rain."

The craniologist stood up straighter. He told her that he had not come here to eat.

Heidegger told Elfride to stop bothering them with her trivialities.

After showing both of them – by a look that flooded her face – how horrified their comments made her feel, Elfride disappeared behind the slammed door.

"Women," the craniologist said, "have small brains."

Heidegger did not leap to his wife's defence. He was thinking that the craniologist had by far the privileged spot under the roof's overhang. Hardly any rain was falling on him. He was thinking that their shoes were wet and dirty and now Elfride was unlikely to allow either of them inside unless they entered in stocking feet. He could not abide the thought of having a stocking-footed craniologist walking over his polished floors and sitting in his chairs.

It began raining harder.

"Eva, I've heard," said Heidegger, "has intelligence."

Heidegger intended this statement as a test of the craniologist's own intelligence. He was not going to waste his time out here in the rain talking to an idiot.

Eva *Who*? *Which* Eva? Those were his two questions, and the stuffy craniologist would either know the answer or not know the answer.

But the craniologist was not aswim in the dark.

"Eva has brains," the man said. "I stand corrected."

Heidegger scrutinized the craniologist's features more closely. *I stand corrected* were not words he could ever imagine himself uttering, any more than he could imagine the Führer uttering them; it proved that the craniologist, however much he wore the mask of public esteem, perceived in his heart that he was very much an underling.

"Eva Braun and the Führer are properly suited to each other," the craniologist said.

Heidegger had the impression the man was suggesting he had dinner with the Führer and his darling every evening.

"Move a little," Heidegger said, elbowing the man.

But the craniologist did not move.

Every now and then the wind was blowing the rain's spray into their faces.

The Heidegger house was set well away from the street. Under the thick hedgerow by the street a deformed cat, refused by the neighbourhood, was trying to find a dry spot. The soaked cat, to Heidegger's eyes, had a slimy look. The cat had been tormenting him for months by hopping up on the outside still of his study and moaning at him.

"The effect this rain is having on our soldiers at the front is God's own misery," Heidegger said.

It had been raining in Freiburg and over all of Europe for a full three weeks. There were times when Heidegger felt he would never again see spring. He longed for his cabin in the Black Forest, at Todtnauberg.

It was isolated there. At Todtnauberg he could don Swabian peasant dress, brew tea on the stove, and think.

The craniologist had no comment to make on the war effort.

The craniologist had with him a leather satchel in which he obviously transported the tools of his trade. He seemed concerned that the satchel was getting wet. A moment ago the satchel was between his legs; now he tried stuffing it beneath his coat, though the satchel was much too large.

"How do you measure your brains?" Heidegger asked.

The craniologist looked surprised. He looked as though he thought this was information which should be under everyone's province.

"Various means," he said.

Heidegger snorted; he hated the vague.

"By eye, by feel, by—"

The cat abandoned the hedge in a run. Midway across the grass, it stopped, then it scurried off in a new direction.

Good, Heidegger thought. The cat had developed a limp.

A week before, the cat had given birth to a single kitten.

"A cloth tape," the craniologist said, hardly opening his lips.

"Cloth or wood or German steel," said Heidegger, "you do not have measuring apparatus of sufficient girth to measure *Heidegger's* brain."

The craniologist smirked.

Heidegger told him: "The time that lapses between one Heidegger thought and another cannot be measured any more than the content of the thoughts themselves can."

It seemed to Heidegger that the craniologist sneered. Someone, he thought, should report this man.

"I show you two spoons," the philosopher said. "One filled with lead, the other with gold. In the dark you would say both weighed the same."

"I beg your pardon," the craniologist said. "That is not true."

Heidegger's mouth dropped open. Not since old Husserl, whom he reviled with all his heart, had anyone spoken so to him.

Edmund Husserl, right here in Freiburg, had invented phenomenology; Heidegger, celebrated, had but scratched the bare bones of time and being.

The rain was splattering up as high as their knees now. His shoes were sodden.

The critique of words by yet more words, Heidegger thought. Before Heidegger that is all philosophy was.

"When I sleep my brain swells enormously," he said. "Elfride has noticed this. She has the visual proof not only of her own eyes but also in the wear and tear of my pillow."

The craniologist nodded. The statement did not seem to amaze him.

"When I am teaching, or talking to certain people — Löwith, for instance, in the old days — I can feel my brain swelling large as a melon. If sat on a wall you would think me Humpty-Dumpty."

Elfride would have smiled at this joke; the craniologist didn't.

"The Heidegger brain is the potentate of the metaphysical," Heidegger said. "How can you hope to measure the metaphysical, when Heidegger has himself grappled with it each instant of his life? Even if your cloth tapes could span the metaphysical the hand meant to hold those tapes could not hold the volume of tapes required. Your cloth tape could not even span so much as the Greeks who relentlessly toil inside Heidegger's brain. How could you measure the one brain in the world which alone in the world charts the scope of time and being?"

"I can," the craniologist said.

Heidegger laughed. He was unaccustomed to doing so. His laugh sounded like a snarl.

The cat was meowing in the rain. Heidegger could not determine where it was meowing from. The cat was skin and bones. What kept it alive was a mystery.

"You could set around me a ring of buckets and I could pour my strange syntax into those buckets but you could never bring enough buckets to hold even my syntactical leavings."

A tick had developed at one corner of the craniologist's thin mouth.

"Am I losing you?" Heidegger asked.

A phrase hopped into Heidegger's brain: *from me and yet from beyond me*. Later he would endeavour to sort out what this meant.

The craniologist closed his eyes, as though in pain.

In his research on Heidegger he had learned that the philosopher had spent the summer of 1918, twenty-nine years old, as a soldier in the Verdun district. He had hoisted and studied balloons. With data gleaned from these balloons weather forecasts had been made, necessary for the success of poison gas attacks.

The philosopher had not shown himself gifted.

After two months influential friends had finagled his release.

"Look here at this shoe," Heidegger said, removing the same from his left foot.

"I don't want to look at your stupid shoe," the craniologist said.

Stupid? Heidegger's eyebrows lifted. The man was insufferable. Even so, Heidegger persevered.

"Notice how the heel of this shoe has worn inwards. Now look at this other shoe."

He removed his other shoe. His feet sank a few inches into the wet soil.

"The heels of both of these shoes, and the soles as well, are worn to the inside. How I walk is a thing you can measure but what this means, the relationship between the walking habit and the workings of the brain, is a thing your cloth tapes cannot reveal."

Heidegger paused, tapping a stiff finger hard against his brow. He could feel his brain expanding, and wondered whether the craniologist would have the wit to notice.

The craniologist looked at him. Heidegger looked away. He had never with ease looked into another person's eyes. Something he saw in those eyes was disturbing to him. Elfride sometimes gripped his collar and shook him. "Look at me!" she would say. "Look at me!"

In his family they had never looked at each other; in that regard he was a victim of his humble origins.

"Also," Heidegger went on. "Also, look how worn both these soles are up in the toe area. You likely have never seen this before, not even in Eva Braun or the Führer. When Heidegger has a thought, a brain wave – about nothingness, to mention but one example – his toes dig holes through the toughest leather. Before he knows it his toes are leaving bloody imprints on the streets. Every other month he requires new shoes. It is driving Elfride insane. But that, my friend, is called concentration. It is called *thinking*."

The craniologist looked to the ground where Heidegger was standing. He looked at the wet black socks on Heidegger's feet, at his narrow white ankles.

At their feet lay a bed of empty shells, black walnuts left by squirrels.

The door opened and they heard Elfride say, "Put your shoes back on, Martin. There's a war on. I am not going to spend the whole of my life tending to a sick man."

The cat appeared from nowhere, streaking between Elfride's legs into the house.

Elfride screamed.

The door slammed.

The craniologist flattened his satchel, then tried buttoning his raincoat over it.

"In the cat world which has the biggest brain?" asked Heidegger.

The craniologist did not answer. He was listening to raucous sounds emanating from the house.

A week ago, the pregnant cat had assumed its position on the sill outside Heidegger's study. It had stalked back and forth and scratched at the screen, meowing ferociously. Heidegger had just scribbled in his notebook, *No shelter within the truth of being*. Then the cat had again showed up, a slick, black, ugly kitten, newly born, dangling from its jaws. The kitten's entire head was in the cat's mouth. With its claws the cat ripped a hole in the screen. It stepped through and settled itself down in that space between the screen and the window. Heidegger had just written, *Elfride's stomach was last night made queasy by wine.*

The ridiculous cat, fortunately, had produced but one very small kitten. Horrified, Heidegger had watched it eat a second one, or the afterbirth.

"How do the Jews fare?" Heidegger asked the craniologist.

The craniologist remained silent.

"Who sent you?" Heidegger asked.

"I am not permitted to disclose that information," the craniologist said.

"What is your name?"

"That too is confidential," the craniologist said.

"Goebbels?" asked Heidegger. "Or someone higher?"

The craniologist's face remained indifferent to these questions.

"The Führer sent you?"

The craniologist pressed himself flatter against the building.

"I have every right to know," said Heidegger. "The higher the office you represent the less reason I have to question your credentials. You will agree there are a lot of crackpots running about."

It seemed to Heidegger that the craniologist did agree to this.

For a moment they watched the rain. Heidegger put his shoes back on. The trees were heavy with rain. Rain was coursing down the street beyond the hedge and flowing in thick grey curtains down the facades of the facing buildings.

From his cabin windows at Todtnauberg Heidegger had a sweet view of the Swiss Alps.

The Swiss were a durable people but theirs was not a fated nation.

At Todtnauberg he could wear knickerbockers and his peasant caps. He could tread the slopes on snowshoes.

At Todtnauberg, until recently, he had enjoyed the company of Hannah Arendt.

Christmas time two years ago he and Hannah had unsuccessfully attempted cooking a goose dinner.

The craniologist was studying him; Heidegger caught himself licking his moustache. He had got into this habit lately, one infuriating to Elfride, whose own alienating habits were confined to those inflicted upon her by her father, the high-command Prussian officer. A dozen times each day he would hear her saying, "How did these crumbs get on the table!" She saw imaginary ants everywhere. She saluted the stove, the cupboards, the light fixtures. She could stand for hours on end mesmerized by the sound and sight of water running from the kitchen faucet.

Her taut body was accustomed to upholding her father's rigid standards on posture; when they made love her spine emitted cracking noises.

"I measured Einstein's brain," the craniologist suddenly said. "When he was in Berlin." The words seemed to spurt from his cramped lips. His eyes were blinking fast.

"I measured his brain twice. Once before his property was confiscated and again before he was born."

"In the womb?" said Heidegger. "You took his measure in the…?" The philosopher's tone suggested that not since his honeymoon had he been so amazed.

Then he remembered that he and Elfride had succumbed to two wedding ceremonies, Lutheran one week and Catholic the following. That had amazed him. He would have to think a while now, to recall why it had been so important.

He and she had prayed together in those days.

"Trotsky," the craniologist said. "Lenin, I've done them all."

Nietzsche, Heidegger thought. I'll bet the son of a bitch will next be telling me he's done Nietzsche.

"Nietzsche, also. Now there was someone a man could talk to."

"You conversed with Nietzsche?" Heidegger could not believe this. For years he had himself been conversing daily with Nietzsche.

"We were… intimate," the craniologist said.

Something in the sound of the rain must have led Heidegger's mind to wonder. He became aware suddenly that the craniologist had mentioned a dozen more names of those immortalized.

"Wagner?"

"Wagner, of course."

They were both silent a moment.

"Napoleon, too," the craniologist said.

Silence fell again.

Heidegger stepped away from the wall. He didn't care how wet he got. He was excited.

"Who didn't you do?"

"I don't do Jews. Einstein was the last."

"I hear Julius Streicher is insane. Is the insane mind larger?"

The craniologist rolled his eyes.

"Have you done him?"

"I have done the highest echelon of Reich officials."

"Whose is biggest?"

"I am not permitted to divulge that data."

"Hölderlin? Our greatest poet! I would be curious to know whether you have done him."

"Too much decay."

"Hölderlin? Decayed? Our greatest poet!"

"Unlike Napoleon. Perfectly preserved."

"Jesus? What about him?"

The craniologist stared at Heidegger.

"Pardon me," the craniologist said. "But I would not walk in all that shit."

After a moment, Heidegger nodded. So here was another who had shed his faith.

"But I did Pontius Pilate. *Very* impressive." Clearly this craniologist, built like a scarecrow, as emotionless as history, was another time-and-being man.

The door opened.

Elfride stood on the landing, hands on her hips.

They waited for her to say something about the cat. But she did not speak of the cat. She had perhaps dealt with the cat as she had with its kitten.

She had dressed. She had done up her hair and put on lipstick. She had put on an alluring frock, with a silk scarf folding from a pocket, and had the niceties adorning her throat.

"Come inside," she said. "Both of you. Come inside *now*."

The two deposited their shoes by the door.

"Take off those wet socks," she said.

They entered.

"Your office called," she told the craniologist. "I had no idea this project was all so scientific. I had a nice chat with Goebbels himself. He was most gracious. *Quite* an enchanting man."

Heidegger stared at her red lipstick.

She was wearing stockings. Stockings were precious. Something of significance must have transpired over the phone, for her to put on stockings.

"Did he say anything about me?" Heidegger asked. "Did he offer any hints?"

Elfride was studying the craniologist's head. The heels of her hands rested against her slim hips. A cigarette burned there between two fingers, the nails still damp with red paint.

She seemed mesmerized by what she saw behind the craniologist's thick brow.

But a moment later she emerged from this state.

"The poor man needs a towel," she said. "Martin, get our visitor a towel. A nice one, from the guest room."

In one thin hand the craniologist was holding up his dripping socks. Elfride, her face flushing, the flush spreading to her ears, suddenly lunged, snatching them from him.

"I'll give them a quick wash," she said.

Heidegger was still by the doorway, holding his. It stupefied him that Elfride would wash another man's socks.

"What about mine?" he said. "What about me?"

But Elfride was already scurrying away. They heard water running in the sink in the kitchen.

The craniologist entered the living room. He looked about for a second, then settled himself into the room's most comfortable chair.

From the hallway Heidegger watched him cross his legs; he watched the craniologist dangle his naked white foot. The skin was hairless. Raw scabs, spots of blood, showed on the nubs of his toes.

Beneath the chair crouched the deformed cat. Its lunatic eyes were staring fixedly at Heidegger.

Heidegger felt a shiver steal over him. A thought had just come to him, bewildering and frightening.

Hitler would lose the war. The Volk would not claim its rightful greatness.

[The Speaker falls silent. He drains the last of the cognac in his glass. He rearranges the judicial robes, buffs the toe of one black shoe. A door is heard opening. A new shadow is seen. A soft voice is heard. "Gentlemen. It is time to reconvene."]

AARON & MAE

Dear Mae,
When you left me I was without Christ.
I never hit you, though, whatever you claim.
I was bad for the children, I remember you saying that.
The day that I was up on charges I said many bad things
to your face and to your backside later on.
Last night at the Bethel Street Church I accepted the
Lord as my Saviour. I tried this morning taking out a bank
loan to pay you back support payments said to be owed.
I was refused. I will try another bank, or there's a guy
I know. The past week I saw my oldest on the street
and he did not recognize me. Even when he dropped
a dollar in my hat. I am now living in the Good Light
rooming house next door to the church. You have to be
saved to live there. It's mixed, but I have left the women
alone. I walked by a room where a woman was ironing.
She reminded me of you. If you are not saved,
I pray that you think about it.
    Your
    Aaron

Dear Aaron,
Please do not write me again.

Dear Mae,

The woman ironing and me have established a
good relationship. Such is frowned on at the Good Light
and we are keeping it a secret. Judy is fighting the bottle
the same as me, only she's AA. She has two children,
the same as me. Do you have a copy of our divorce
papers? Judy won't believe me when I tell her I am
a single man. I'm sorry for that ruckus was made when
I come to your house. You ought to get rid of that
vicious dog. I could sue your pants off. The rock
through the window I see now was a mistake. It was
mean of you to put the law on my tail. They came
around to Good Light, asking questions, making
trouble. I am still saved, thank the Lord. I know
his love, if not yours.

Your

Aaron

Dear Mae,

I don't have money to keep throwing away on cabs.
A good Christian would open her door to her fellow man.
Judy and me have been kicked out of Good Light, owing
to a lot of tales. Drinking was not involved. You better write.
I want the kids to send me a note and pictures. I saw you
had a man around the place. I don't like that, and the Lord
wouldn't either. I am looking for another church. The Bethel
Street bunch can go to hell. I wasn't nowhere near their
tithe box. I put a brick through their window, the shits.
I will confess now it was me did it to your Dad's windshield
that time of our trouble when he come at me. Also, dear, my last

letter to you come back but I know you had steamed it open.
I'm wise to your ways and know the kind of woman you are.
Judy's the same. You can't take her out for a drink
without she's making eyes at someone. Her arm got broke,
don't ask me how. The car wash didn't work out, I only put in
two days. Judy is baby-sitting the Cloris woman's fat twins
and I am doing part-time roofing work these days
with a guy I know, Jerry, I think he come over
to the house once when we were in the two-roomer on
Darrell Street. Oh yeah, Judy's youngest showed up, he's 14.
He's the image of his mother and of solid mind. I told him I
wanted to be his daddy, and he said, Well, if so you'd be
the first one. So that got us going on virgin birth and the scripture
and we had a fine time. He don't smoke, drink, or cuss, and
has a bright fine Christian face. I give him a dollar or two, as
he's off to Utah. I carry the Good Book with me at all times.
I know my Jesus. I will be calling upon you soon. Your
injunctions don't weigh much with me, knowing as I do
your true heart. I saw your bumper plate sticker, Save Our
Wilderness, and nearly croaked. You'd best be looking after
hearth and home. It isn't right my children to be raised
by a heathen mother. They will fry in hell, that's guaranteed.
   Your
   Aaron

FAMILY QUARRELS

Young fella came up to me. Young fella said, "Old man, you're good as dead." I said, "Young fella, be polite. What have I ever done to deserve your insults?" He said, "Father, I am your son. Father, give me a dollar." I said, "Son, go to work. Earn your dollars the same as I have mine."

This made the young fella mad. He tried to take my dollar and anything else I had. He said, "Old man, father, surrender your earthly goods, or die." He tried scattering my brains with a tire iron, but I held him off with a thick board. I got him down. I said, "Young fella, son-of-a-bitch, here is a dollar. Buy your sweetheart a present." And I dropped the dollar in his face, now that he knew who was boss.

So that is how our friendship began. It is how our friendship got off to a good start. He turned out a pretty good young fella. He found employment, started thinking about settling down, raising a family, buying himself a good piece of land. I would give him a dollar or not give him a dollar, it was all the same to me. Blood is blood. You can't fault a child every time he comes up short. "Old man," he'd say, "thank you, father, you have turned my life around." "Bless you, son," I'd say, and we'd hug up to each other like lamb against lamb.

It was then the wife popped up. We hadn't seen her in some twenty years.

"There you are," she said, "the two thugs. All this time I been wondering what had happened to the pair of you. Wondering would you ever get together. Now here you are, thick as thieves on the Cross."

Then she got this cunning look in her eyes, and we could see trouble coming. We could see she had old scores to settle. What she did was take out this old dollar and flutter it up in the air. "Take it if you can," she said. "If you two snakes think you are better than me, then come and get it."

So we all three looked at each other and saw there a thousand scores never had been settled. We saw all these family skeletons rattling right there in that dollar.

We flung us all three into the battle. Him with his tire iron, me with my board, and her – to hear her tell it – with nothing but sober innocence on her side.

Don't ask me how it come out. All I know is the dust, to this day, has never settled, and every time I rehash it I've sunk lower.

DON'T COOK A PIG

We cooked a pig and fourteen people took sick. The wife said pig was wrong, we should have cooked a stallion. I looked at the stallion, and figured otherwise. Yet fourteen people took sick, eighteen if you counted the brothers, so could be the wife was right. Could be she is on to something.

The fourteen people who took sick have today received a questionnaire. Where do you think we went wrong? At what point did you begin to feel sick? Is it possible that your sickness had to do with mixing pig and strong drink, plus whatever else? What was the status of your health prior to your arrival? Were our actions, once you fell ill, all that might be expected? Would you come again, and how soon?

The wife hopes the responses will be in before this weekend, since this weekend we plan an even larger party. The invitations have gone out. We've hired Ted Oliver to sing and bring his band. Ted Oliver's band is a wonderful band, the finest available. As the wife says, you can't go wrong with Ted Oliver.

The brothers are coming, that's for sure.

The pig was smoked, maybe it was the smoke. Whatever the case, we went to considerable trouble, smoking that pig. This weekend we shall not serve smoked pig, even if it is not the same pig. We are laying cucumber sandwiches by, just in case. My wife will dance. She is an extraordinary dancer, especially when Ted Oliver sings, and I think we can assure everyone a good time. We will have hot tubs on the premises as well.

My wife figures twelve. I figure eight. We shall compromise on the tubs, just as we did on the Ted Oliver band.

Last week she tried to get the Ted Oliver band, but they were on the road. That was unfortunate because, as the wife says, last week's music was definitely not up to scratch. She hardly danced at all. Then everyone took sick.

This week the brothers will be passing out their usual leaflets.

Maybe the stallion. I'm still looking him over. But not smoked. I put my foot down there.

We hope you will join us. Actually, everyone we know is invited.

Know, too, that we have a backup plan in the event it showers.

Frankly, on this one, we are leaving no stone unturned.

FURTHER ADVENTURES OF A CROSS COUNTRY MAN

After the man say, "Get off my betrothed, I plenty mad, blow you straight to hell and then some," I get up and go that way myself with never the shot being fired. That a bad time all right, plenty worse time I ever been in before, but it nothing to what come next and I tell you now that story, the truth ever word or God in Heaven see me dead.

A man of my nature he always on the move, on the go to the somewhere he never been, headed for the somewhere he never get to in all the world. I think sometime the sun it will not shine on me another day but there it come, over the hill, over the meadow dusk green in the dew, above the trees on the far slope or rising up from the roof house or over the water, yes, there it come one more time, one more try, shining and so fat happy as the man with the full stomach and the tamale dripping from the mouth – there, one more time, pretty you please and pretending like the fool that it never shine the day before.

But before it is the day get worse it have to get better.

Mal, mal, hoy es muy feo, the man with the shotgun say, he blow me straight to hell, he say, or his name is not Fernandez Brown.

I get up, please, right away you bet, I say, and rise up from the warm skin of Chlorine to my trembling weak knees as the two barrels of the gun stare me in the nose.

Oh, Fernandez, Chlorine fast to explain, tugging at the North the Border stretch pants which have snag on the tree, I so glad you come, I not know how I survive another minute. This man, she say, I never see, he come up from the nowhere and throw his fat arms around me and wrestle me to the earth where he lay down over me and all my struggles in vain oh my Fernandez I call your name but he stuff my mouth with his tongue and I think I about to die till you come oh Fernandez shoot him sweetheart while he kneel over me breathing so hard with his pig face, shoot him sweetheart where he hurt, show the bastard amigo what you do to the man who violates the girl who love you with all her heart and who never been touched to this day.

So there she stand now between the two of me with not a stitch on her hide but as much as the truth in her naked heart and I am listening to her speech and saying to myself oh Mother of Jesus in what the name of hell I do now, save me Good God on High and I devote the rest of my life to your work, I work and slave and drink the milk of life and never use the name in vain or touch another woman with two legs, I do the duty where my heart is and find the woman I marry the three weeks before and give her a home in the Church and never stray the sheep no more, no sir. But never mind it is not the use, I see that soon. I see Fernandez his eyes over the wet bosom of Chlorine and looking at her body over the hips and the good strong legs brown as the summer sun, and he wet his lips and smack his tongue in the mouth and I see the two barrels of the gun begin to drop from where he have it aim between my eyes and that Fernandez Brown with his eyes hungry on the girl as the disease of man ever go and I know now anytime he going to throw the gun to the soft earth and take his bride to be and throw her flat back down on the ground as I have done myself, and I think to myself you a good man, Brown, you a man of my own heart, do it quick, forget I here. But what he do is he whisper, "Chlorine I never see you like this, I never know." And in the daze he gently stretch the gun out to me, he say, "Compadre, hold this please," and I say, "Thank you, sure." And then he touch the bare shoulder with his finger and with his hands he feel the shoulders of that Chlorine and cup the breast and pinch the nipple between his thumb, and he bury his head then against her neck and bring her into him, and he begin to breathe so hard I think his ears going to carry him into the air, and Chlorine she say, "Ah!" and they go on with their love in the fields of the clay for the pots standing straight as the tree but with the wind snapping at the leaves, and while I look I see the smile on the face of Chlorine and she open her eyes and with one of them winks at me and then she closes them again and yank the husband to be right off the ground onto her.

And so that is how I get away, one more time to roam, I back up, back up, away from there, and at the ten pace I turn and run for the life that is mine to keep, to run until the muscles in the legs about to break from the skin and the breath so hot inside me I think I destroy myself, with the ache in the chest and the terrible gnawing in the side and I think I die from so much running, to and from the love I never to find for long. And I think as the day begin to fall oh blessed Mother save me from this running, this love, this ache, to let me lie down and sleep. And then I fall on the straw of the tree I lay and in the sleep that night I am running, twisting, turning, searching in the dark between the El Paso and San Miguel for the way out of and to this love which boil in the black heart of mine till it most deplete. O Blessed Virgin Mother of Love, I pray, save me from this trouble mine! But I go on aching in the sleep, trying to rise, dreaming, trying to grab hold of what it is hold me down, and sling it off, and then there is the stab of light through the dark and in that light the smiling face of Carmelitta, Roseda, of Chlorine and in my sleep I am back to the clay field again and it is hell.

"Who?" I ask of the man in my ear, "sure thing, this woman yours? Please forgive, a common mistake, so sorry, I presume she not spoken for otherwise not touch her for the world. Not happen again, please excuse, here, you take her back."

But Chlorine, arms noosed around my neck, will not let me rise.

"Up!" the man in my head say, "Pronto! Be the gentleman once in you gringo life, quick, I count to three then I blow the brains straight out you rear. One... two..."

"Wait," I say, "I try, I try —" But something is pulling the other way and it is Chlorine, his betrothed, one track of mind she got, her hands on the back of my head pulling my lips down to hers and her two legs locked over my own there with the knees bend, holding me so that to move at all I cannot except to wag my toes, and I beg, I sweat, I plead, I say, "Hold the horse, Mister, I doing the best I can," but Chlorine she whump me in the back and my voice break as I hear the man with the gun say "Three!"

Goddam, goddam. I think in the last second before the shot pile into me of Carmelitta the bride of few weeks who I been such rotten to and who I never to see again, and who when next she hear of me her bastard husband it is she hear he have his backside blowed off while he straddled one more woman, the new chick, and I whimper unto my breath *mal mal* bad way Gonzalez Manuel to go, he never have a chance, all the time the pull and the push, I try to do better in the next land to come. The shadow of the gun move over me and I shut the eyes and wait for the death to come, and the hammer click in the bolt and the second of silence fall between the prayer and the answer and then the silence explode in me and the pain nor more than a whistle in the dark for I done gone to where I due.

In the morning I wake like a man done been to sleep in the sea. But I a man and one who learn from what he do, from where he go. A man of my nature he not get far if not the nature change. Theretofore it is that I say: so long so long, to Carmelitta, good wife of three week; to Roseda of the Marketplace, goodbye, so long, adios to you all, I now a man redeemed, know thyself, take care yours truly, cry none the more or roam the street for your feel the touch, I a man of new girth, me, Gonzalez Manuel, on my mother's breath I swear never to look again at the woman another day. No sir, *Amo a mi madre, padre, hermano, hermana* – sweetheart, bah!

And so I get through the first day.

And wake to the new spirit in the heart and the sun on my face and there is the goat grazing at my chin. Good morning,

I say, *buenos dias*, so far so good, and I shake the horn of the nice beast and pull the whisker and say, *Ba-ah-ahhh!* I know how you feel, goat-friend, I not much the same myself.

But I not moan the spilt milk for long, I steal the chicken pretty quick soon and wring the neck to it go pop, and then I hit the trail once more and pluck the hide of the bastard ugly bird while I march along without the care for the one first time in all my years. When the sun straight up over the head in the sky I look sad at the plucked bird and say, *Algunos legumbres, chicharos, espinica, caldo espeso, ah! Sorry son, now the time*; and plop his sagging yellow hide through the stake I drive in the ground, and then I go back under the tree, lie down, wait him cook. I catch the wink, forty times, I think, to it wake myself snoozing through the nose, and I get up and eat the sorry bird, and then I lay down the body, mine, to sleep off more the time. Night come on and I confess to the Father of my sins, as Carmelitta say I should, and I say to the Son, yes, you right, brother, a man travel with the Cross he get not far but a man know how to go light with the heavy load there not be a river he cannot be cross. And I say a word for the Holy Cross too I say, Watch out, friend, Gonzalez Manuel, once of El Paso now from San Miguel, he not far from that point hisself.

And so it is I get with the good intent and the fresh heart and the one bird through the second day and night and into the third.

On the third day, Holy Mother of Mary, my luck change to gold. Or so I think. And in the heart I can say to myself without the bitterness hello Carmelitta, hello Roseda, you too that man's betrothed, I now find the one woman put you all to salt, the one woman in all the world who can to share the hour and the day with Gonzalez Manuel. No more the El Paso, pretty boy soldier town USA, no more the San Miguel, pig sty of the world, pig's snout and chicken's craw. In the summer both you stink and in the winter you freeze up but now I friend for sure with this new earth I find, and we beat the devil out of you, me and this woman here, if you don't watch the step and provide us with the what we want. We taking nothing off no one no more no sir, we give you the business, you try.

For she different, this woman, I see at the glance.

Her name Helene, she say, de Troy, and it is on morning of the third day with the chicken leg over my right shoulder for the luck that I have come upon her, travelling companion for the duration, clean-cut American girl this time, no more the half-breed south the border *senora* with un *poco* heart, *el poco poco* head.

Ah, Helene! *Claro, caloroso, bonito.* Ah! *Bien hecha,* yes!

For love of her I have to hurt myself, me *he lastimado, llame un medico por favor, estoy enfermo, mi baceza y todo mi cuerpo me duele.* Ah! Helene de Troy… I tell you now of her what I know.

She is fled she say from the tall stranger who make her to set up in the hotel room of the Two Pines all the night long yanking on the Duncan Yo-Yo with the finger, he who say his name is Bertha Cunningham, Vice-Pres of the USA Steel, with cash and the credit card. Pay her plenty, she say, nothing fancy required, just the straight stuff, but he never let her finger to rest or let the hand to switch and after few weeks she sees his attention go, he looking over other sweet girls in the street so in the daylight hour when he is asleep with the cover up to his head she reach over with the good hand and take the money belt from around the waist and get out, she say, of that one place fast. I see her first after the third long day of my travel as I pass over the ridge of the Two Pines, bathing, she is, the swollen finger in the creek that flow down from god-knows the place. I scout around the ridge and come up to the one pine and she is no man with her around there so I yell out over the dark ground, "Drop it," just in the case she have a gun, but she right off unbuckle her britches and let them fall, saying, "OK, Mister, if you must, but make it snappy, see, I got some distance to spread between me and this place."

"You some chick," I say later, to which she reply when the time come, "That is what they all say," and it some many evenings latter yet that she say to me, "Mister, you ain't no slouch yourself, excuse me for taking you for granted, that what happen to a girl who live all her natural life in the city of San Diego. But how come," she say, "some big honcho like yourself is out here wandering around in this godforsaken and who else will have it wilderness." That is the way she talk, with the words long strung out together, slapping around like the beads on the string, planned that way for effect, I think, so to speak, because she a short-of-breath chick and with them kind of talk her breast they bob and dip like the cork with the fish pulling at the other end which matter of fact and to put the fact straight is most often the case. Or was. But then one day of the hot and the *sol* in the sky, *tiempo seco* so much she say she parch in the throat and will but to die for the water, we come upon the sign which say POBLADO

PROXIMO and I say to her, sure thing, soon, kid, none the worry, *tengo hambre, tengo sed,* you too, but that change soon, be brave, the earth provide. Next is the sign which say DEVASCION, detour, CAMINO EN REPARACION, and we must to go that way, and so for the hours we do unto I have to carry Helene de Troy in the arms she so tired with the faint, crying "Water, water, my love!"

"Not to worry," I say, "We have the God on our side, I am man reborn."

And pretty soon quick there is the cabin in the nowhere which is call St. Lopete and this man who say, "Sure, go ahead, wet the whistle, take the drink, your business your business, who I to stop?"

"Yeah," I say, "sure," doing all I ever can to give the man his right, "but this your well here, it on your land, contain your water, it your place in the world to say who drink here and who don't, now ain't that not right? Once I to take advantage of the fellow man but now I got the peace in the heart and though we both stand here perishing of the thirst we not move to you say we do."

He feel that way hisself, the man say, and hug me with the neck, and do the same to Helene de Troy, all over, on the up and the down.

"Drop the bucket!" he say, "draw the water, best water in all the land!" And he stand back to smile like the man in the John Wayne, thumb hitched in the gallus, one cool number he, I think, do us the good turn with not once the ask to pay.

So we throw the bucket down the well, it go splash and wade around and sink to the bottom and we pull on the rope and draw up the bucket, it come up leaking in nineteen hundred holes like all the boys of San Miguel peeing at one time, and we lean on the board and drink the water and say, "Ahh! Ahhhh!" and the man nod and blink and smile and cry, "Drink more, drink your fill, no better water in all the land, you come to the right place, I fix you up dandy, mucho pronto. Now you want to sleep? Sleep, I give you the room!"

"*Gracias*," I say, "sure you are the *caballero* if ever one I see."

And we leave him grinning by the well and go inside the room to sleep.

But in the night I wake to the sobbing in my car and it is Helene de Troy who cannot be still. I am tired, she say, Gonzalez Manuel, I am cold. *Estoy cansado, siento frio*: I am myself sick and cold. And for the hours that is how it go, *poco, mucho, alto, bajo*, and it is next morning that my travelling companion for the duration is dead and cold in my arms as all the flowers of the world. Helene, Helene, I hold her in the arms with all the care crushing down unto it tie up the flesh in bones and I think the heart to cry out in fear and pain. For all the forgotten love she sleep and never in this world now to find, oh Helene; to slide so soon from me while I sleep and never to slide this way again. Through the hours I hold her in the arms and stroke her yellow hair and gaze into the quiet sleeping face that is screwed tight with her pain, unto finally I am not the strength to move myself and I fall back into the poison sleep with the finger on the dead, parted lips of my Helene.

Later I to find the man has fled the scene with all our clothes and the money belt he has taken from me in the night. He has gone.

That is how come I to know finally I done crossed over the line of Mexico into Texas, *Lo peor, lo poer, va de mal en poer*.

I in that place for two weeks before the strength come back to me to bury Helene de Troy, which I then do, out near the soft dirt around the well where I find seven other graves. It enough to give a man the American USA religion for sure, a thing like that, that he find on such a bright hot day that he still can find hisself among the living. For the moment though, throwing the dirt over her face, I got it nothing in my heart but hurt and yell out across the broken land, "Come back here, you sonabitch," the one who say, "Sure, take the drink." The blood run up my head, I slam the shovel against the house over the well unto I all but knock it down and I cry then for the little girl who drop her pants so fast you still see her with the clothes on before it come to you indeed that they ain't no longer on, a good, well-seasoned girl who have it in her heart to please, that now she dead is a shame, a pity, poor thing who never done nothing to that sonabitch who done it all to her. I get dizzy after a while in the sun with the anger, I sit down and rest the head in the arms and it on into evening before I wake up with the crazy bird all but standing hisself on my shoulders. When I stand up and shout and wave the arms the buzzard all but fall over hisself from the heart failure, he squawk and cuss and leap into the air and I aint seen him since. Serve the buzzard right, I say to myself, if he never see another human face.

But what with that I begin to think all the bad luck I done have had since them few months back when I marry Carmelitta, and I tear off a board from the well, and calm myself, and get me some tar from the roof that the sun done made so soft it drink like the Pepsi Cola, and I walk a mile into the desert and write on it with tar THIS WAY TO THE WELL and point it out over the footsteps I just come and then I walk back and tear off another board and write on it the same and walk back out half a mile and plant it in the ground and point it to the well, and come back again to the grave of Helene de Troy and say to her, "Sweetheart, bet your ass, the next son-abitch come along, he's for you," and soon after that I strike out from that ranch of the St. Lopete for more of the parts unknown, naked as a body can be, with the sun baking the skin, but what to care I about that, who can feel a thing at all after he have the good buddy die like the snap of the fingers and comes so close to it hisself?

Donde esta mi Carmelitta? Gone. *Donde esta mi Roseda?* Gone, gone. My Helene de Troy? Gone, gone gone. In all this world sometime a man not want to go on – but he go. In the heart he cannot be made to lie down while in the legs he stand. Why? For the ace card somewhere must be in the dirty deck he dealt. For he like the dog which curl up when he fed and stretch hisself when he wake and bark the mouth when he see and howl the night when he lone and march the land when he must the need come to do. Ah, me! Life, it is like the shepherds of Lasteenkens say, *un mal negocio.* I say that to myself over by the grave where Helene lay deep in the earth with the dark pain on her face. The trouble, Helene, I say, it all come from the first mistake a man to make. All the others the child and grandchildren, niece and nephew of the first – abnormal, backward, scrawny-neck, mindless children bastard of the first. A man, Helene, I say, if he go back to the first mistake to stand a man forever make the more. Yes? He

153

not do that he remain *un tonto, un ass, un ignoramus*, his life *mezclado con impurezas. Vine al mundo*, Helene de Troy, *me meuro*, a man must to live smart between. That Carmelitta a good girl sure, I find her now again, start the life new.

I go now, Helene de Troy. *Adios*, mine *amiga*.

And so I do. But it hard to get back to where you never been before. And the days latter I no nearer to where it was I go.

I walk for all the day and the night and then the days and nights to come, with no mind to time or where I go, with the head like it in the frying pan and the sand gritting between the legs and the hot earth done eat all the soles off the feet. After a while it like I got so light the wind, when the wind come up, blow me along, and when the wind die down I fall down and sleep. And it rain the rain pour over me, it drip down my face and slide the hair in my eyes and it fall over the body and sit on me in pools, and the sagebrush slap against my knees and the dust crowd my eyes and once with the eyes wide open I walk slam into the big cactus tree and think for a minute I have arrived in Dallas Texas.

I go on, go on. Through the rain storm and the dust storm and the howling yellow wind. On the feet and then the knees and then the hands and knees and finally I think on nothing but the head. *Socorro! Socorro!* I die of thirst, of hunger, of the rotting blood! But I only repeat what I heard in reply. Nothing, nothing, and the sun go down. Sorry, sorry, holy mother mine, *no tengo envidia a nadia*. For finally I see it is in envy of all the pleasure in the world that is brought me down. Through the night in what sleep I can to find there is the great voice in my head commanding *baja, baja, Gonzalez*

Manuel. Go down, go down. *When the skin has melted away to bone then you stand up again*. And so I struggle on, waiting for the day to come.

Unto it is one day I feel the earth change between my feet and looking down I see sure enough there it is, the highway USA, big trucks, shining lights, Howard Johnson and the swimming pool down the bend. But for the hour I stand and the nothing see – only the white highway swinging there. "Calm yourself, Gonzalez," I say, *evitar el olvido*. Think clear. Now the civilization you back, this way and that, but make no mistake which way to go. One way is Carmelitta, wife and first mistake to find, that the way to go for sure but how a man to know which is which. *Baja baja*, the voice say in the head, and I shake it and knock it against the hand till it come clear and I can shout above the trembling heart: no, no! Gonzalez Manuel, he is going *up*. But for the hours I stand and none the traffic come, one dead highway it. I sit down and nap and am led to wonder in my mind how a man can travel on, through the elements, so to speak, of flesh and blood, sand and storm, without no food to eat for days at end and how especial he can do such a thing when he got no cause at all to move one inch from where he stand. And only after so long and the day turning to dust do I hear myself say: "Get up from there, my friend, play the cards. When you die you die in the shade, not let the bastard crow finish you off where you sit. Rise and go." And so convinced I stand and go the center line of the highway USA and follow along the way it stretch forever with never the curve to take. Walk, walk, you trudge the walk, one two three four, *hup-hup-hup* the soldier way, down the miles, the hours, on to the morning come, *hup-hup-hup*, this America, USA towns the everywhere, some one come hup-hup, you had the good home but you left, you right, sound off, on two three.

But in the end with the morning light I find I come to the no place at all. There by the road is the sign which read to it I cry

PARDON THE INCONVENIENCE
ROAD ENDS AT THIS POINT
SCHEDULED COMPLETION 1972

OK, OK. I a downhearted, yellow *wop* but I a man no less. Play me the trick I play the one to you. In the matter of time I uproot the sign and turn it round and sink it in the earth again and pack it down and with the smut pot from the highway side write on the clean side for the travellers to see.

FULL SPEED AHEAD
NO LIMIT HERE

and tear down the barricade and stand back to admire the work I do. Good, good! Helene, one more for the you, maybe I get one too.

With enough of that visiting for one day I leave the highway myself and go off into the desert the other way and keep my course to I can not stand no longer or walk another step. In the night I dream of poor Carmelitta and how I could use the alligator shoes myself now and I dream that night that the mad wolves of Lasteenkens come up and lick my face clean and bring me meat in the jaws and the big dog come up with the little barrel around his neck to give me water to drink. In the morning I am not surprised to wake with the fever and the thirst and the bare legs trembling and the hot flashes. There is the burrs in my head and the red bruises on the skin like the road map to El Paso and the stink to my hide like I nine days dead. The sun shines and the earth bake and the body burn but after a time the fever it settle in like for the long ride and I rise and walk through the desert with the feet sinking in the sand up to the ankles and who knows how long I go that time, finally, before I come upon the monastery with the boys and men coming out from the gate and falling over the walls racing toward me with they hands in the air and they faces flushing, crying words like, "faith!" and "He's come back, he's here," and a dozen women I think then falling on they knees to kiss my feet and looking up at me with the face of love, more of it there than ever I see in my life, beating Helene de Troy when the fruit of the loins burst forth or even Roseda when she bite the orange and watch the John Wayne in San Miguel, or Carmelitta when she put herself in the alligator high heels under the wheel of the American-Detroit US of A car and drive off from me for never to see again. They look up at me and kiss and wash and kiss my feet with they lips and dry the feet with they hair and lips and stroke my bare hot legs and run they hands over my buttocks and generally marvel at my body like they can not wait themselves to get alone with the proper hold on me and I recall that moment with they hands on me all the faces of the women who done made up the choice spots in my life and I yield to they touch now and look down on them and say, "Suffer little children to be removed," and I think on that message a minute and then try again to get the thoughts straight and the mouth familiar with the sounds, and look on the excited faces once more, and have it straight this time and I raise the hands as I have seen it done and I say, "Children, children, I am come home," and that is all I know of the day for I fall in my tracks right on top it seem of the soft bed of sighs and weepings and body flesh of the soft hips and loose breasts of the men and boys of the monastery all at my feet and reaching with they hands to hold me there, I not knowing in all the world of my mind when a man can rise again from such a fall.

HERE COMES
HENRIETTA ARMANI

A. Three One-Sentence "Once Upon a Time" Henrietta Armani Stories.

1. It came to Henrietta Armani, once upon a time, that she was not the same person Henrietta Armani had been, once upon a time.

2. The sound of two hands clapping is not the same as that of two toes tapping, whereas, once upon a time, they were one and the same, according to Henrietta Armani.

3. Henrietta Armani wrrittes aa sttorry likke th'hisss & callls ittt "EEEro" bbbutt therrre iis nnno "onccce uppponnn aaa tiiiime" inn hherr stttory, only little apple trees.

B. A Two-Sentence Story in Appreciation of the Cinematic.

1. Henrietta Armani lost herself in the movie, eating popcorn out of a box held between the knees of a second person Henrietta Armani refused to call by name, this arising out of principles vaguely formulating in her head. She did not think of him as a pleasant companion.

C. A Three-Sentence Story, One of Them Foreign.

1. When Henrietta Armani arrived home from the movies some dark person seated in the darkened room Henrietta Armani was forced to pass through in order to find herself in her own room said to whoever it was the dark person in the darkened room he (or she) thought it was (or might be) he (or she) was saying this to, "Who goes there?"

¿Quién va ahi?

D. A Multi-Sentence Story in Which the Key Word Is "Door."

1. Henrietta Armani was intensely distressed and embarrassed that the room she entered possessed a doorway but the doorway possessed no door. It seemed to Henrietta Armani when she entered her doorless room that a darkness entered with her, which was darker than the darkness already in residence; in daylight this did not happen; i.e., the light did not brighten when she entered the doorless room – which failure, Henrietta Armani reasoned, must have something to do with the kind of person she was.

Yes. Henrietta Armani thought this even as she piled heavy boxes in the doorway, these boxes held together by baling wire which she now had no more of because the baling wire had vanished from her room while she had sat in the darkened movie theatre with an unnamed person.

Why did the house in which she now resided have no electricity? When she had rented the room a radio had been playing. She distinctly remembers. The room may or may not have had a door.

E. A Henrietta Armani Story Composed of Brief Declarative Sentences, with Footnotes.

1. Henrietta Armani, alone in her room, says, "I will."[1] She says, "I will not."[2] She says, "Why are you pestering me?"[3] She says, "I hate you."[4] She says, "I wish you would drop dead."[5] She says, "I am such a lunatic."[6] She says, "Don't tell me I can't, if I want to."[7] She says, "This carpet is filthy."[8] She says, "That is the strangest thing."[9] She says, "I am eating an apple."[10] She says, "I applied today for three jobs."[11] She says, "What went with my money?"[12] She says, "Do you have a parakeet?"[13] She says, "You are an everlasting pill."[14] She says, "I refuse to tell you where I live."[15] She says, "I did not like it either."[16] She says, "Tomorrow I will try again."[17] She says, "If you do not like it you know what you can do with yourself."[18] She says, "Don't you just wish that was so!"

The footnotes:

[1] "I bet you will change your mind."

[2] "You always do."

[3] "Why don't you calm down?"

[4] "Did I ever say I wanted to marry you?"

[5] "Be nice."

[6] "We all have troubles."

[7] "What does *that* mean?"

[8] "I suppose that's my fault also."

[9] "What? What is the strangest thing?

[10] "I distinctly heard you say, 'What is that noise?'"

[11] "You won't get them."

[12] "You are always flying off somewhere."

[13] "Don't be silly."

[14] "Ditto, sweetheart."

[15] "Who wants to know?"

[16] "The movie?"

[17] "The doorman will not let you in."

[18] "I could have the police lock you up.

F. Another Henrietta Armani Story Beginning with "When." The Saddest Story.

When Henrietta Armani went to the bar on Amsterdam Ave. she sat first at the bar and then in a booth, with no action at either. She sat at the bar again, and the barperson who of course was interested in her said, "You again." After saying pour me another of what I had the other times, Henrietta Armani said, "What is the saddest story you ever heard?" To which the barperson, a decent sort who had been deserted as a child, of course said, "My own."

"Tell it to me," Henrietta Armani said, and the barperson would have done, each night of his many nights behind the bar had been waiting to do so. But the pool players wanted coins for their tables. An officious person on another stool at the long bar wanted a scotch and soda. A beer keg was foaming over.

In the absence of the barperson's sad story Henrietta Armani told herself her own story, which was not the story her brain wanted to hear, although her body was content to have Henrietta Armani struggle through it. "It will have you in tears," Henrietta Armani said to no one.

"Everyone I know is dolefully waiting out the hours."

She did not know who said this.

Afterwards, the barperson appeared again, saying, "I do not like to see your head on the table."

"Which table?" asked Henrietta Armani. She was again in a booth, and did not know how she had got there. The barperson's voice was a nice voice which conveyed no malice.

Henrietta Armani said to this nice voice, "I do not wish you to think I am alcoholic," being quite amazed to discover that not a single person was paying her the smallest attention.

"What is this?" she asked, and when she turned her head to examine the one thing, which was on the table beside her two hands along with the other thing, the other thing of its own volition lifted up and dribbled its contents down her throat, which was both a magical and an exasperating experience.

"Since my divorce," Henrietta Armani said, "I trust no one. But I trust you."

The face she said this to, someone passing, said, "You should eat something."

She was sick for a great while and did not in the least mind.

G. A Continuation of Henrietta Armani's 'Saddest' Story

Henrietta Armani walked down a long hall covered with grit and through another door marked with the notice DO NOT ENTER – only to discover behind the forbidden door a deserted kitchen containing two stainless steel tables with numerous gleaming objects of a practical nature hanging above the tables.

That is what she saw once she saw them.

Before this sighting she had to determine which of the many switches on the wall on this side of the DO NOT ENTER door worked to illuminate such gleaming objects, since, until that moment, the room, her head and its body, had all been wrapped in total darkness.

She switched this one switch off and on for a good many minutes, out of purest pleasure, because her own ex-husband, Mr. Demented, had once hung perhaps this very sign outside the door he went through each day or evening, after saying to the still air, "I must go and compose myself."

This had transpired in a certain house, one vividly locked in her mind, which she believed had been located in the country. *Willow Run* were two words which seemed to her to sound familiar.

If she had on her person now a road map, she bet she could find it.

Each evening she had driven a car, the blue car, with her daughter strapped into the daughter's back safety seat, to meet the 6:15 train from the city. Where she had parked there had been a sign which said PICK UPS ONLY. Her daughter in the back safety seat would throw her toys and she would retrieve them and return the toys to her daughter to throw again. She could hear herself saying things like, "We must not spoil our supper," and "You must be a good girl." Sometimes, "We must be good girls." One thing she often had said, and sometimes still did say, was, "This weather, I don't know, it is so bucolic."

It would be nice, she thought, and a composing thing to do, to hang a sign around her own neck, to hang it as that one had hung around his doorknob or as that other one did, not hanging, but nailed to a stick in the grass. Inasmuch as this sign hanging around her neck would be a thing which people must pay attention to. The sign would say, HERE COMES HENRIETTA ARMANI.

Her mother had only been comfortable with strangers, which was another thing she told herself she must think about this evening before she gave up the ghost and took a taxi home, assuming a taxi would take her there.

In her purse was the address, but where was her purse?

For that matter, where were her shoes?

On one of the several gleaming counters was a bowl of soup, Chicken Godiva, which someone had left for her, the note beneath it saying, "For you, Bubble Head."

Henrietta Armani, far from being offended, drank from the bowl with relish, wishing she could bother herself to seek out bread or crackers, but finding herself altogether too famished.

With Chicken Godiva soup the chicken was supposed to ride about naked, but in this soup the chicken had its clothes on.

Whatever, it was a very tasty soup.

There was a phone on the wall, with a stickum tab saying, *Trudy, call Travis*, but she was not either of these people, only wishing she might be so that she might hear what one said to the other, and advise them on the more effective alternatives.

The father – was this in a film? – had said, "Go ye and do likewise." This to her mind did not sound like the sort of thing her father would say to her, or say to another father, although he possibly could more than once have said it to her mother.

Why were they not inquiring about her, by the way? They had not inquired about her in a long time, months, although they knew her number, although it was the wrong number.

The *wrong* number would be the number of the old house, the family house, *her* house, though it had always been the wrong number. The new house did not have a number any more than it had electricity or a door to her room other than stacked boxes.

Who had packed those boxes? She certainly had not dirtied her hands packing boxes. Packing them with what Mr. Degenerate said was to be *her* things, not *his* things, not their daughter's things, nor those things which were so ambiguous they seemed to her to be the things belonging to no one on this planet.

Which she had told him – words to that effect – their daughter crying, but he had said, "You are not making sense."

He had said, "Go and take something."

Which she thought had meant, "Put something in a box," which she had done, a picture from the wall along the staircase, to which he had said, "Why do you want that? Why in God's name do you think I am going to let you have a picture of my *grandmother*?"

To which she had said, "God in heaven, *that* is your grandmother? I thought that picture was *my* grandmother!"

To which he had said, picking up and holding their crying daughter, "You are out of it, you know. By God, you are out of it today, you know!"

To which she had said – in a place called *Willow Run* she had said this – "Well, they were both *ministers*, you know!" Which made no sense to her now, although it had then, and it was certainly true that on both sides they had all been ministers of one kind or another, as proved by the little crosses each held up in the one hand, in whatever old sepia photograph existed of them.

"I'd advise you to go to bed."

Him saying that, and their daughter struggling to release herself from his arms, saying, "May I go too?" And then saying, or someone saying, *"Daddy, why are you hurting me?"*

H. More of the Henrietta Armani 'Saddest' Story.

In the bar, the lights off, Henrietta Armani looked for other light switches, and could not find them, although of course there had to be switches.

Her new room had switches but these were not switches that turned anything on. The first evening, that person in the other dark room watching her through the doorless door, breathing on her, a machine beside him (or her) that breathed for him (or her), she had clicked the switch off and on, saying *"Off,"* saying *"On,"* and everything happening, like there was power in her fingertips if only she would keep on exerting herself and not sink into the desuetude, where she customarily – since *when?* – had been sinking.

Her room in the new place had a loose board in the floor. She must remember, when she got home to the new room, to be wary of the loose board. Well, really, every *other* board was loose, but loose boards were better than having to walk in her naked feet over a carpet so filthy you could see the diseases in the fibres bumping heads with each other.

I. A One-Sentence Story Describing Henrietta Armani's War with Rug Diseases.

Wwwhiich offf yyoou bbad ttthings ddidd ttthis tto mmmeeee uunnder the little apple trees?

J. A Longer Henrietta Armani Story Filled with Action.

She poured herself *"a dring, a drinkie,"* the finest, and sat first at the bar, then in the booth, then again on her favourite stool, where once upon a time she had been dangling a leg, smoking, when a man with bigoted intentions had said to her, "You are such a honey. You are such a sweetie. You are such a tomato, I am delirious."

Then the man had sang *"Set'm up, Joe,"* which he said was a song someone named "Frankie" had made famous during his, the man's, youth.

The man flirting with her had a big paunch which he called a beer belly and he left the change from his drinks on the counter, all those dollars, while she lacked the courage ever to be so blatant about the amount she meant spending.

The men and women passing on Amsterdam, a few now and then, night owls with slumping shoulders, their bodies sinking into their shoes, all looked to her like people she had known at one time. Which was why she was sitting at the bar and not in the booth, so she would know them.

It did not alarm her *in the slightest* that they did not know her. More than once she said to herself, I am the Queen of the Planet, and each time she voiced this thought she would wait in silence for someone to issue denials.

She had her own answer, *You may be, but you are no better than me,* but she was waiting for an answer better and more spiritual in nature than that.

Another reason Henrietta Armani was sitting on the stool and not in the booth was because of what was behind the bar, on a shelf beneath the cash register under a wet J-cloth. Under there was a pistol which she had already explored. She had explored its handgrip, its black, snubby barrel, and the little twig of metal which anyone in her right mind would know was the trigger.

The pistol weighed, she estimated, about the same as three full drinks. In the movie she had seen with the man she was now so furious at there had been a weapon called a forty-five. She did not think this weapon, which for a while she had slid back and forth along the bar, was that weapon which, when you write it, is written point45. That is neat, she thinks, because these are things that when you use them you point them at someone, or at your own self, in the extreme case. "Like," she said aloud, "such is more productive than a sling shot."

K. Henrietta Armani Thinks She Would Like to Feed the City. Not the End of the Story.

Once three men shook the bar's door knob. Henrietta Armani was asleep on the stool when this happened, and knew nothing of this. Otherwise, she would have let them in and might have enjoyed herself.

Around five in the morning, daylight breaking, she went into the kitchen, breaking open into a gigantic crock every egg that could be found in the cooler, both the brown eggs and the white – close to two hundred. She was going to stir up eggs – bacon, if she could find it – for everyone.

The front door, however, would not open. It would not open from the inside. To open these grilled doors, they had to be opened from the *other* side. Which really was, to her way of thinking, a pathetic situation. People, clearly, would want breakfast. Already, gauging by the assemblage, there was an interest.

Henrietta Armani decided she would stir up the eggs in any case, since, otherwise, life had no meaning.

Home fries, bacon, a sprinkle of – the red stuff. Yes, not anise, not chili, but the red stuff. Not coriander, not thyme, not oregano or curry powder, none of which were red.

It amused and embarrassed her that she could not think of the name of the red thing.

Henrietta Armani had been known as an exceptionally gifted chef at one point in her life.

Because she couldn't remember, she took the eggs off the grill and went and made herself three tall drinks, lining these up on the bar, better to do the weight test again with the pistol which was not a point45 that was to be pointed at someone.

Cayenne.

Naturally.

The right word came when you were not thinking about what the right word was.

Cayenne, of course, was not exactly red.

Whereas "Bastards" was a word which fell off the tongue like leaves from autumn trees.

Which was another song – *the autumn leaves of red and gold drift by my window* – that man with the beer belly claimed a person named "Frankie" had made his specialty.

She was not herself keenly interested in or much moved by romantic ballads, even in stereo wraparound at the movie house.

Dress the egg dish with clawed tomatoes, sprigs of parsley, why not watercress? She had done this all her life, bibs for the three of them because bibs seemed so attractively old-fashioned and certainly the baby required one.

"Oh, yes," she said, "you are right, I stand corrected, that was ages ago."

To grow your own watercress, if you have not a river or spring or pool of flowing water, prick sizable holes in your tub, fill this container with black earth, install and tamp your seeds, then bring your hose to the tub and leave your hose running for the balance of your years on earth, to thence awaken each day of every year, your tub overflowing with an abundance of the finest product.

Which was what she had done in her marriage, precisely as instructed.

"So sit yourself down and partake," she told herself, seated at the bar with a plate of rock-hard eggs, the pistol, and the two remaining tall drinks.

Which was how Henrietta Armani was found when at eleven a.m. another barperson opened the Amsterdam Bar doors – another decent human being, whistling, tinkering with the heavy chains, then entering, thinking to himself as he saw her slumped there in the dead, shadowy air: "Why, there sits Mother!"

L. Mr. Bottle the Neighbour.

Mr. Bottle the neighbour built ships inside bottles, which ships each had the name, Mrs. Bottle.

Henrietta Armani was eight years old when Mr. Bottle invited her to forego her cartwheels on his lawn and experience the greater joy; to wit, to venture inside his lovely tract home and he would show her his bottles.

Mr. Bottle's bottles were all arrayed upon a white mantle, each sailing along splendidly inside the glass, although Henrietta Armani was more interested in Mr. Bottle's dress code.

She said, "Why is all that hair on your chest?"

To which Mr. Bottle responded by showing her his newest bottle, inside the bottle what he said was a ship known as a Shapper, invented by a Mr. Shapper, Esquire, of Birmingham, England, many many years ago, the special attribute of Mr. Shapper's ship being that it possessed virtually no leg room above deck, save that needed for wrapping sails and coiling ropes and something called the "Grig." While below deck, in that space Mr. Shapper called "the hole," in agreement with other ship designers, there was immense space for the oars, the oarsmen, the slaves, plus a chapel where a good man would preach the Africans' conversion.

Mr. Bottle told her all this and more, apparently having the highest opinion of Mr. Shapper's attributes.

"My dear, you see here all my ships are named the same name, Mrs. Bottle, not even employing numbers, as you see, because all women are exactly the same, they are all Mrs. Bottle insofar as Mr. Bottle is concerned, which I recognize as a gross exaggeration although it still seems to me to be the straight-out gospel truth, the Christian truth, although I will ask you to leave now, my darling, because you are such a nice girl, so lovely doing your cartwheels, before I or Mrs. Bottle decide that we must hurt you."

The truth being, as Henrietta Armani decided later, that Mr. Bottle, while deluded, was the first gentleman of her encounter, and far more advanced in the decorum of his thinking than any of those others with whom she afterwards had a relationship. Most of all inclusive in this her relationship with the man who said "I do" to her face, and kissed her, and from that moment turned inconceivably evil.

You do not have to go through with this was a phrase which all her waking days post-marriage existed as a plague in the mind of Henrietta Armani.

She had not shown *pluck* in removing herself from the worshipful courtship of the man suing for her affection.

M. Husbandry: A 'Sadder' Page in Henrietta Armani's 'Saddest' Story.

Give me your poor and your disabled, he had said.

This, on their honeymoon. He had been quoting, imprecisely, the script on the plaque in New York City harbour. Henrietta Armani had believed he was addressing, personally, certain shores of herself that had not yet surfaced.

She had thought his words addressed her essence, which essence his quotation was meant to sincerely applaud, and thus she could now share her secrets with him, as soon she would share her body – provided *she went through with it* – and Henrietta Armani had welcomed the degenerate into her bosom – into her arms, spectacularly.

Not that this, her body, had seemed to make an impression on him.

N. Henrietta Armani's Daughter, a Child Prodigy.

Her daughter, in conversation with grownups, would say, "I am not a conversationalist."

To illustrate the point, she would then spill something on something precious.

There were hack marks on the furniture, which wounds in the fine wood pointed the way to future serious problems. Had Henrietta Armani been psychologically or psychically attuned to take notice.

Not that she *didn't*, of course.

The question was what to do about it, other than have a seasoned restorer of fine wood come in and restore the fine wood.

Or drape their surfaces with cloth.

Both of these measures, as a matter of fact, were measures taken.

When Henrietta Armani first saw the child carving holes in the furniture, gouging the blade of her knife into the polished wood, the child had both heard and seen her, *looked* at her, but had gone on with her ruinous work on the elegant furniture.

Much later, several years, even though Henrietta Armani saw their dog being run over by a perfect stranger, when she saw the dead dog either actually or in her mind, she had been overcome with suspicions.

She said to her husband, "We have a disturbed child."

In answer to this he had settled his tableware all but silently over his Beef Wellington, crossed to her chair at the opposite table end, and struck her.

Her daughter said, "Why can't I chase cars too? Who is to stop me?"

O. Other Ingredients in the 'Saddest' Part of Henrietta Armani's 'Saddest' Story.

"If you want to speak to me," the child would say to her father, "why not speak to me? I like listening."

The trouble with Henry – how odd it was, Henrietta Armani often thought – to actually say his name – is that when he stopped to think, he stopped entirely.

The trouble with her, with Henrietta Armani, is that when she stopped, the last thing she wanted to do was think.

When she stopped she wanted *it* to be over. Therefore, often – wherever she was and with who and whomever it was she was doing whatever she was doing, Henrietta Armani stopped abruptly. She stopped what she was doing.

The man she went to for help, who had been her friend and who loved eating buttered popcorn in the movies, would say, when she stopped, "What are you doing?"

They would have their clothes off, at his place or at her place or at the place of a third party, and he would say that. The air would be cold on her skin because of the sweat. Her flesh would be pebbly.

She would not look at him at such times, because of how he was looking.

At the movie, the popcorn between his legs, she had sometimes, to be playful, allowed her fingers to clutch like claws where the popcorn wasn't.

He had made it clear to her that he did not find this amusing. Yet he also was not amusing, because often when she got home she would find butter stains on her skirt where he had wiped his hands. Which was not a friendly thing for him to have done, which was not a thing he would have done had he not believed, as he frequently was saying, that she was eating more than her share of the popcorn.

So there were these times but also those other times when he did not like it at all that she had suddenly stopped what it was she had been doing. He would glower at her, and say hurtful things, if she stopped. So Henrietta Armani stopped stopping. She also stopped seeing him at all, with precisely that same abruptness. She did agree to this much. "I will see you outdoors. I will see in such places where we can be publicly seen, seated."

He said, "Why should I want to see you publicly? Why should I be interested?"

Which provided her with a revelation as to his character, which she found interesting.

"But I thought you went to him for help," another friend said. Which was such a silly thing to say that she stopped seeing this other friend, who in a score of ways had proved herself to be a False Friend.

When Henrietta Armani passed this False Friend on the street she was inclined to say, initially, "Hello, False Friend." Later on, she learned to keep her tongue silent. Banter, insults, the tight expressions, she was finding disagreeable.

She would try secretly to wave at the small child the False Friend carried, to be sure. A child, her own included, was an innocent party. It hurt her to hurt innocent parties, such as her own child who was as innocent as any, despite the ferocity with which her child remarked on things.

Such as, "Why did you smile at that stupid baby?"

Over a long period afterwards, when one of these False Friends called – there were so many – and her innocent daughter lured her to the phone, the phone she held in her one hand as she listening to a familiar voice on the phone saying, "What are you doing," she passed the phone over to her other hand – to the hand that was doing nothing until that moment – both she and her daughter then looking at the one hand that was now the new empty hand doing nothing except twist the cord, as if both she and her daughter were thinking that surely that empty hand – something – must have the answer.

Eventually these people stopped calling.

The pain of those days so amazed Henrietta Armani that when she looked back on them afterwards it was as though her skin was crawling with venomous lizards.

Her husband said, "That sounds like a bad dream. Please know that I find all dreams boring."

P. Henrietta Armani's Wide Scholarship as This Relates to Her 'Saddest' Story.

Henrietta Armani read in a magazine that the answer resides in the heavens. In the molecules, the dust, of ancients who are in sojourn on their endless journey. A journey into nothingness, which goes on forever. There they are, she can sometimes see them, see their faces, their mouths opening, but these ancients have no answer either. They speak platitudes. "There, there, my girl, it will be over soon." Because time for them has now become nothingness. Two o'clock, ten o'clock, the day, the month, the year, means zip to them. They say to her, these ancients do, "You are making too much of something that is essentially trivial." By which they mean her life. Where they have arrived at, disembodied except when they speak, all existence, including their own, is without meaning. They are lucky because they no longer have to search for it.

If particles of dust contain the souls of her ancestors — where's the joy in that?

They are people in strange form, in strange solitudinous journey, but otherwise they are as lost as she is.

St. Paul in her dreams says to his brethren, "Put to the test, all of you would say you abhor women."

St. Paul — on both sides of what had constituted her family — was a gentleman that family had been fond of quoting.

One evening she said to her husband, "Excuse me, but to my mind your St. Paul was something of a bastard."

She had thought he would rise from the table and strike her. What he had done instead was to say to their daughter, seated between them, "Release your fork. Put down your napkin. Rise from your chair. Now go to your mother and slap her hard as you can."

When Henrietta Armani painted her lips during those days, she painted them outside the borders of her lips' natural formation. She did this out of nasty intention. When she spoke, if she decided she would, she wanted people who knew no more about the issues than she did to listen to her.

Similarly, her eyes.

Sometimes her daughter would say, "Why isn't Henrietta wearing her pearls?"

At times we were shockingly close is Henrietta Armani's view.

Q. The Inspirational in the Unhappy Life of Henrietta Armani.

What Henrietta Armani most sought from life was the inspirational. It delighted her, its common occurrence. Always, even at her lowest ebbing, she saw things that were utterly amazing. Which is to say, inspirational. Sunsets did amaze her, although sunsets were not so much as even in the realm of what it was she was talking about when she talked to her daughter about life's abundant marvels.

On evenings not that long ago from the back door, Henrietta Armani saw gypsy wagons on a road. She saw this where no road existed. The gypsies were so robustly singing that her daughter, upstairs in her room, shouted down, "Who is that singing?"

Henrietta Armani, one day, saw from her kitchen window a wild boar. The boar was leading one of its young up to her back door. She opened the door and the boars ate all that she dropped to the floor. Then the boars returned to the forest, where there was no forest. Her daughter, entering, had said, "What did you feed them?"

Henrietta Armani had only to open the door, to stand by a window, and the inspiring would find her.

It was not required that the inspirational be spectacular.

Hippos immersed themselves in muddy streams by the side of the house.

On a fine Sunday, Charlie Chaplin in hobo attire knocked at her door. She invited Charlie inside. She made Charlie a nice breakfast. Charlie sang and danced for her. He said to her, "Venture down the road with me. This little trick I do with my big shoes, my cane, my hat, I will teach you. Come. You will find the method useful."

R. The End of the Henrietta Armani Story

Ended, bang, just like that.

The bartender entered, saw the form draped over the bar. An indrawn breath as he said in full surprise, "Why, there sits mother!"

Henrietta Armani had not got far in composing what was to have been her final message.

On the floor he discovered Henrietta Armani's purse. Inside the purse a message and telephone number scribbled on an empty envelope: Here comes Henrietta Armani, Call this Number.

Over the coming days he would try this number, the telephone always ringing, no one answering.

He devised innumerable alternatives, none rewarded.

A ROUGH CUSTOMER

"My stomach is so flat," Orillia said gaily to Mr. Wriggley – to *the* Mr. Wriggley, lately of the mainland but now seeking improvement of his fortunes along the island's lonely, bemisted, strangely beautiful outer reaches – which Ucluelet certainly was – "It is so flat a person could shoot marbles on it... on my tummy," she said, laughing all the more.

Mr. Wriggley, swaying back against the door he had, against his better wishes, just entered, could think of nothing to say to this nonsense. The room, for that matter, was dimly lit, and some seconds went by before he succeeded in locating the speaker. Even then, he had to have her help.

"Down *here!*" Orillia trilled. "You're looking too high, Mr. Wriggley. I'm not up in the rafters – not up in heaven – *yet!*"

She lay stretched out on the living room sofa to her full awful length, merrily blowing on her fingernails and laughing up at him with her wet red mouth.

"Flat," she said. "So flat!" And she patted her stomach, riotously giggling. "Marbles, yes you could!"

Mr. Wriggley wanted nothing to do with her red mouth. He wanted to have nothing to do with women, period – just as he had, in no uncertain terms, told this one's husband. He shuffled his feet with what he thought of as a workman's vigour, and briefly, resentfully, hooked his gaze on Orillia

Peterson, much as if he were considering for himself personally the practicality of her insane suggestion. Yes, her stomach was remarkably flat. It was mostly uncovered, too – obscene is what it was – but so what? So what? That is what Mr. Wriggley asked himself as he shifted his weight from foot to foot, patiently awaiting his instructions.

"Now don't deny it, Mr. Wriggley," she said. "I have the flattest tummy in all of Ucluelet. You would have to go" – here she paused to kick up in his direction one of her naked, absurdly long legs – "to go as far as the Northwest Territories to find a woman with a stomach nearly the match of mine. The Northwest *Territories*, Mr. Wriggley!"

The foot was white – it was vaguely luminescent among the dim surroundings – and Mr. Wriggley wished he could break it off. He *hated* this. He hated having to listen to *any* woman, for *any* length of time, but to have to listen to *this* one rattle on about her ridiculous stomach was almost more than he could bear.

Vile, he thought. Oh, vile. She makes me want to do sump'n terrible.

"Speak up, Mr. Wriggley!" commanded Orillia, fluttering her nude, crooked little toes towards his face.

Mr. Wriggley thoughtfully regarded the fireplace – softly glowing, a bed of red embers – and let his gaze rake up over the crowded mantle, over the menacing shadows on the wall, and on down again towards the coal box, though he remained firmly fixed in place. No, he was not moving without instructions.

"The *cat!*" laughed Orillia. "That nasty cat, oh it has your tongue again. I have told and told that cat, Mr. Wriggley!"

Mr. Wriggley found his voice. He spoke gruffly, contemptuously, as if what he wanted to do was pelt her with rocks or drop her body down into a deep dark pit. "What do I do with this here bag of coal?" he asked.

Indeed, he had a large, lumpy bag hefted over his left shoulder. His hands, face, and neck were smeared with coal dust – in fact, he was smeared all over, for he'd taken numerous tumbles on the coal pile.

Orillia saw no reason not to continue enjoying herself. "A flat, *lovely* stomach!" she sang, arching her back. "I am immensely proud of myself. Aren't you proud of me, Mr. Wriggley?"

Mr. Wriggley groaned as she drew up her naked knees and lolled her head back on the crimson pillow. He hadn't yet determined what kind of indecent garment she had on. It was wine-coloured and airy, flowing up with every movement she made. Mr. Wriggley was thoroughly disgusted.

"It is no mean accomplishment," Orillia said, "after what I have gone through."

Mr. Wriggley had no reply to this. He hoisted his bag higher, casting a long look at the coal box and the empty bucket on the hearth. The lumps were grinding into his back, though he didn't mind that. He could bear physical pain, indeed was accustomed to it. He was accustomed to people making his work harder. What he minded was Orillia Peterson. She *irked* him. He *disapproved* of her. He secretly believed that all such people – people with wet, red mouths, people who shook their ugly white feet his way – those who stretched out on couches in dark rooms – ought to be rounded up and sent *East*! Sent somewhere, God knows, so a man could get on with his hard work and not stand around all day listening to nonsense about stomachs, for godsake.

He looked down at the small throw rug on which he stood, holding himself very still. "Where you want this coal?" he asked stolidly. "I brought you this here bag of coal."

"Oh *did* you!" cried Orillia delightedly, with a fine flutter of her hands. "Well, wasn't that sweet! Aren't you the sweet-est person!"

She smiled warmly at him. In Mr. Wriggley's view she was the spit and image of the total imbecile. He wiped a black-ened sleeve across his mouth and glared at her, at the room, and at what he took to be the presence of some aloof, immo-bile evil alive in the room. Women and that sense, they went hand in hand. Where there was one, there was the other. Near enough alike as to be twins, was how he thought of it. This morning he found her high-pitched, noisy, irrepressibly joyful voice particularly infuriating. Some people might call it pretty, even melodious – a pleasure! – but not Mr. Wriggley. How her husband – a nice enough fellow, if a bit slow – man-aged to put up with, to coddle and revere, this deranged piece was more than he could imagine. Her "sweet this" and her "sweet that" – it was plain disgusting.

He shifted the bag on his shoulder, looking wanly at the bed of red coals, and groaned loudly. Loudly, *yes*! Let her take note of the labourer's mantle. He ought to put down this bag right now. On the carpet. Let her contend with it. It beat him, it surely did, how an employer could refuse to give hired help their proper natural instructions.

Something in Mr. Wriggley's aggrieved expression must have been communicated to Orillia Peterson, for she now lifted her head from the crimson pillow, turned her body, flung both arms high, and exclaimed in a perilous, despairing, childlike tone: "Oh, don't be so harsh with me, Mr. Wriggley. I am recuperating, you'll remember."

A faint moan escaped Mr. Wriggley.

"No, dear sir," she went on, her voice more tremulous, "it isn't every day a woman gives birth to a child!"

Mr. Wriggley's head slumped to his chest, as if in his view she'd touched upon a topic grossly indecent – which, as it happens, was not far from the case. Mr. Wriggley felt precious little warmth for mothers; he stoutly affirmed that birth, being a mean, inconsequential affair, was no excuse for goldbricking, and that a woman should be back on the job within the hour – as his wife, and squaws he'd heard about, had done. His *former* wife, Mr. Wriggley meant, in as much as – to his mind – he was not currently married. He stood taciturnly dwelling on this. Babies – *the* baby – had been his ruination. Or marriage had. Or women. It was hard knowing where to fit the exact blame, for it was a chicken-and-egg proposition. One thing was certain: his wife's screeching, while producing the infant, had contributed powerfully to his disappointment with her. He could have tolerated a sob or two, but her howling was totally unnecessary. Respect had gone right out the door.

Orillia Peterson, however, was a horse of another colour. Compared to her, Ula had been a saint. It had been, as he understood the matter, a full month since the vile woman had dropped anchor.

Orillia sighed, dreamily.

Mr. Wriggley contemplated the distance between himself and the coal box.

Orillia's sighs lengthened and deepened.

"I know I am not so lovely as your divine Ula," she now said, in mock pout, teasingly: "But I do make the effort, sir. I do *endeavour*!" She stretched, preening, blowing on her nails, which over the past minute or so she'd been dabbing at with a red brush. She then pitched up both arms in a movement so unexpectedly swift that Mr. Wriggley, startled, yelped and fell back clumsily against the wall, knocking over a chair that appeared out of nowhere, stumbling down in such fashion that the coal bag looped his neck and came down upon him.

Whump!

Orillia seemed not to notice. "My Peter," she said, "claims I'm the most beautiful, gay, enchanting woman in all of North America. I'm perfect, is what he says." She lunged back prone on the sofa, momentarily closing her eyes and smiling with so much emptiness, smiling so eerily, that Mr. Wriggley forgot his pain. He watched her puckered lips time and time again kiss the air. Her arms criss-crossed her chest; she was hugging herself. Her entire figure seemed atremble with pleasure.

It was an orgy, Mr. Wriggley thought, that's what it was.

"Oh, I do miss my Peter," she said in agony, her torso heaving, her eyes flaring. "Oh, Mr. Wriggley, I miss that man to the entire compass of my being. I wish he would come sailing in this very minute and fling himself down upon me! I would invite it, even if he still smelled of fish, even if we had a thousand other things we should be doing. *That's* how deeply I miss him, sir. Am I not wanton?"

Mr. Wriggley did not know what wanton meant, but he too sincerely desired his employer's return. He *liked* Mr. Peterson. He could get along with Mr. Peterson. Mr. Peterson *understood* the necessity of giving a working man the proper instructions. If he told you to prop up a fence, or put the dog in the doghouse, or to shovel manure in the barn, you knew exactly what was expected. He never told you *why* these chores had to be done (that would be expecting too much), but *what* to do was plenty clear-cut. (This 'bring-in-the-coal-to-my-honey' business being a rare let-down).

If you didn't do the job the way he wanted, or not quickly enough to suit him, he would step in and take the shovel from your hands and scoop up the manure, saying, "No, no, no, Mr. Wriggley, you do it *like this*: you get a full shovel load, and you pivot about *like this*, and you throw your load over here on this pile *like this*." It was that *like this* part that endeared him to Mr. Wriggley. Any boss man with two cents in his pocket could hire you and say "Do this," but it was one who said "Do it *like this*" – and actually showed you *by demonstration* – who knew what the genuine employer/employee relationship was all about.

Like that time with the fence post.

"No, no, no, Mr. Wriggley! First you *dig* the hole. With this hole digger, *like this*, and down so far. Then you drop in your post *like this*, and pack the dirt down around it with this axe handle, *like so*. Then you sort of stomp the dirt level with your boot heel, *like this*. Got it?"

Good, clear, precise instructions, if a little vague on the hole depth.

Mr. Wriggley was thinking all this as he struggled to his feet. He had *told* Mr. Peterson it wasn't going to work out. He had *told* him he was asking for trouble. "Me and women, we just don't mix."

"No, no, no, Mr. Wriggley, now calm down," Mr. Peterson had said. "Orillia's a wonderful, gay-spirited woman and she will not give you a hard time. You look after her. Take in a bag of coal now and then. Do whatever she requires. Make yourself available. I'm confident the two of you will get along like a pair of kittens."

Mr. Wriggley's hopes of improving his fortunes in bleak, god-forsaken Ucluelet had evaporated the minute he heard this.

Mr. Wriggley now had the coal bag resting on the floor between his boots. He opened the bag and extracted from it a large lump of coal. He held the lump high.

"This here coal," he said. "Where you want it put?"

Orillia's abrupt, spontaneous laughter almost took the roof off. For some minutes – so it seemed to Mr. Wriggley – she lay writhing on the sofa, face buried among the pillows.

"There's the fire, Mr. Wriggley," she finally said. "There's the bucket. And there's the coal box." Her arm moved to each item in its turn. Mr. Wriggley's lips moved, nodding his head in recognition of each item named. This was more like it, he thought. Now he was getting somewhere.

"About five paces forward," she said. Then her face was again down among the pillows.

Mr. Wriggley advanced heavily across the room, wondering which he should fill first. If he packed the grate full, and brimmed the bucket, he doubted he'd have enough left to fill the box. That could mean a second trip. This was to be avoided.

"Mr. Wriggley!" Orillia suddenly screeched. "My *carpet!*"

Stooped at the fireplace, Mr. Wriggley spun about on his heels to find the woman deliriously pointing. "My carpet! My beautiful new carpet!" This distracted Mr. Wriggley, who yet held the single lump of coal in his fist. He considered hurling it at her. But before he could avert his eyes from her nakedness she had, like a maddened sprite, swooped from the sofa to drop kneeling on the rug, there to brush. Yes, they were black, he could see that. He could see the clear imprint of his boots in the golden fabric. But it was not his fault. She had not given him the proper instructions. She had not said, "My good man, you must lay down newspapers. You must remove your boots." But Mr. Wriggley was flustered. He knew where blame would roost. It was the working man who bore every brunt. He couldn't see why a few footsteps mattered anyway. Ula, confound her, had been the same. One knick-knack out of place and she'd fly into a tizzy. Women and the tizzy, they were as natural to her as soap to water.

Orillia had disappeared. Now she was back, towing a howling vacuum cleaner. She stuck the pipe in his hand.

"Clean it up," she commanded. "You vacuum every smidgen."

Mr. Wriggley's mind reeled. He was shocked. It was on the tip of his tongue to tell her *that* would be the day. A cold day in hell before you'd find him doing woman's work.

But Orillia was shaking her two fists. "Now!" she cried. "This minute! And I don't mean maybe!"

He could not believe a skinny, naked, feckless little spark-plug could display such fire. Or be so bossy. Her inconsideration of a working man's dignity utterly amazed him.

She yanked the pipe away. "Like *this,* Mr. Wriggley!" she shouted. And she shoved the nozzle back and forth over the befouled carpet. Then thrust the machine back into his hands.

It all happened so rapidly Mr. Wriggley could only stand in mute disbelief as she plopped down again on the sofa, squirming her body tidily against the cushions, pointing the soles of her tiny white feet out at him. "You exhaust me, sir," she raggedly intoned. "You exercise me to my very timbers."

Elsewhere in the house, a baby's unmistakable shriek sounded. Mr. Wriggley's expression mottled. His shoulders came up almost to cover his ears. The squall loudened. He might do a woman's work. He might. But never to that inhuman squealing.

Orillia bolted up, smiling. "Little Petey wants his din-din," she said. "Mother's coming, darling!"

She darted away, a witch on a stick.

Mr. Wriggley clenched his eyes tight. He straightened his arms and legs, his spine, his toes and fingers – he went rigid all over. It was a trick he had for composing himself. His hope was that his brain would go altogether dead. It would resist cranking. It might spit and sputter, emit ghastly fumes, but he'd be unaware of this. Such was his hope. Ula had come across him in this posture once, and when speech had not been forthcoming she's stuck an upholstery needle into his buttock. She'd struck a match and held it beneath his fingers.

The same then against his very eyelids. He had felt nothing. All Mr. Wriggley knew at such times was that the uneasy world was a far, far space removed. He'd arrived in a land occupied, if at all, by sniffing rodents, swooping loose-jointed birds big as dinosaurs, and him. It was some kind of strange working man's paradise, in that here *there was no work at all.* Everything had been done. He was as replete in that space as a minister on an old-fashioned Sunday.

He stood so now, anticipating a similar rapture. He'd come through galloping trees wide as rail cars and over hunchback snowcaps to this land's end, to this gnomed grove ghostly, maddened Indians had named Ucluelet – come to the very rim of the Rim. He'd come, seeking improvement for his fortunes, to this island's lonely, bemisted, strangely beautiful final edge, and mortal bones could carry him no farther.

Needles couldn't touch him. Fire couldn't. But a baby's lusty squawl apparently could penetrate Mr. Wriggley's potent armour. His left eye squinted open. Then the right. Both looked down, from oppressive height, with their owner's accustomed vigour, to the pinkish infant cradled in Orillia's swaying arms.

"Petey and I were worried, Mr. Wriggley," she confided, as though with a touch of pride. "You made our gooseflesh rise. We were wondering did your fierce vacuuming have you hypnotized."

True, Mr. Wriggley still gripped the whirring machine. True – and how oddly... how to explain it? – the carpet was now spotless! Not a footprint to be seen! He regarded with impolite suspicion his other hand: the lump of coal, carried all this while, lay in inert adherence to his palm, now a crumpled ash molded to that shape his fingers had pressed upon it.

"Goodness, Mr. Wriggley, you've *crushed* that coal. Petey, look at Mr. Wriggley. Isn't he *strong!* Isn't he utterely *fantastic!*" She shivered, eyes flashing, as though thrilled beyond endurance by Mr. Wriggley's awesome powers.

The baby, with its wide innocent eyes, rolled away from his uncritical scan of Mr. Wriggley's features, and buried himself chin, nose, and cheek into Orillia Peterson's exposed bosom. It sucked and kicked its legs and made such rash, thirsting, rapacious noises that Mr. Wriggley, his consciousness newly emerging, smacked that same hand which had flattened the coal up to his brow and through his hair and again and again over his face. Nothing made him shudder more than the sight of nursing infants. In public or private, he was strictly opposed. He dimly remembered that such had been his wife Ula's final undoing. This tit-sharing business indicated to him that God had forsaken all dealings with the female race. It indicated to him that females of every stripe should be kept penned up and only visited once or twice a month or as often as you had to carry slops and water to them. Ula had unleashed maniacal laughter when he said this to her. She'd then calmly, mysteriously, said, "How is it I have chanced to fall for such an unmitigated disaster? But you be on guard, Mr. Wriggley. As the Lord is my Shepherd, I'll uproot you yet."

"Eat, little darling," he heard Orillia Peterson say.

The baby's head flopped over and fixed its moist, doleful eyes on Mr. Wriggley – it seemed to him they did – then the head flopped back and resumed its gross suckling.

I shouldn't have come here, Mr. Wriggley thought. Ucluelet was the wrong place. The very edge of the edge was not far enough.

He wondered where otherwise he might have journeyed. Wondered whether there was any place left on earth, with its ramshackle tidings, where an honest labourer might stake out new roots, plant his boots, lay claim to decent fortune.

Nowhere, he thought. Nowhere. For a man of my burdens, less I have benefit of divine interference. Less I have a hamperful of proper instruction.

Ula hadn't had milk. She'd moped and moped. Wailed and wailed. *"Dry, dry, dry! It's how you look at me that dries me up like a desert bug!"* She'd twisted and spun and jumped about like a snake in a fire. *"Where went my mother's milk?"*

He'd liked Ula dry; she had some modicum of decency, as he saw it, so long as she remained dry. But she wouldn't let it alone. She'd messaged her breasties, poked and prodded them, coaxed and pinched and punched. She herself had swallowed milk by the bucketful; she'd swallowed pills and seaweed tea and gone to doctors and stood on her head. She swaddled her great breasties in towels steaming-hot to the touch. She said, *"You suck, Mr. Wriggley. I'd have milk to waste, if only I could get these jugs primed!"* And he might have, even then, even irked as he was, if she'd said, "Do it *like this*, my good man." If she'd told him *exactly* how she wanted it done: how long and precisely with what force and what he was to do once he'd wrested the first mouthful. For he took no stand against Ula's breasties as such, nor against fitting his working man's lips over her rosy, enormous nipples. It was the labourer's role in this madcap world – to serve. To broaden the knowledge, advance the method, refine the technique. To say nay to no task. It might be dirty, reprehensible work, but he'd never shunned that.

So he wasn't unwilling. No, it was the baby's part in the job that unhinged him. He hardly saw how Ula had come by having that baby in the first place. She was at a stove he recognized, in a room that was their own; she had a pan on that stove, with steam rising from it. She turned – inside Mr. Wriggley's head she turned – and stood a moment in cautious, unoptimistic study of him, her expression fixed, and faintly hostile. She had a blue bruise on her left cheek. He saw her shake drops of milk onto her wrist, and next saw her tongue come out and lick away the drops.

It was kind of peaceful... even pretty... nourishing... the way he was seeing it.

Then Ula was sliding away into darkness.

"You ought to know how I come by this child," he heard her say. *"You put it there."*

But he hadn't. He could almost swear to that.

⪦

Orillia Peterson was sleeping. The room was too hot; it made one drowsy. Mr. Wriggley was seated in a rocking chair, nearly asleep himself. *Do whatever she wants done,* Mr. Peterson had told him. Well, he was doing it. He'd never held a baby. He'd hoped he'd never have to.

Had it crawled across the carpet and climbed his legs to nestle in his lap? Well, why not? For the working man, shorn of instruction, the whole of life was a mystery.

The baby weighed nothing.

It smelled of soap and water and powder.

Its perfumed body was warm as a heater.

Its five fingers were up in Mr. Wriggley's mouth; one foot was hooked into his pocket.

Why was it smiling?

Mr. Wriggley was in the dark.

Ula would faint.

The working man is to his reward – was Mr. Wriggley's uncertain thought – as the mule is to his plough.

AT HEIDEGGER'S GRAVE

The finding of the proper
in the encounter with the alien
is the path of homecoming.
　　　　　—Martin Heidegger

Upon a time once in Poland, a thousand or so years ago, a boy named Tadeusz Benunito climbed a tree, chasing what he thought was a chicken. The cooking pot in the family clearing was cooking, though without a chicken and with what the boy considered to be little else. The boy went higher in the tree. So too did the bird the boy thought was a chicken. The supposed chicken took to the highest branch, regarding the ascending boy with what the boy himself considered to be a dolelful, somewhat sympathetic expression. It seemed to the boy that the chicken he was chasing was one scarred by the ravages of a hard life and the onslaught of old age. He meant still to have the chicken for his family pot. The white feathers could be put to good use; a few might go as a necklace around his neck or as adornment for his hair. A syrupy stain the colour of blood leaked from the bird's scarred beak but the eyes were fierce and bold; the bird seemed as unconcerned with this unsightly discharge as he was aroused by his imminent death. Perhaps – the boy thought – the bird had just eaten, although it assuredly lacked that plump fullness one associated with a steady diet. It was as poor and unsightly as he was himself. The boy had never seen a chicken with such a long bent beak, long almost as his head. But there was meat enough on the chicken's bones and the very thought of the bird bubbling in the family pot brought sweet juices to the boy's mouth.

Prepare to die, the boy said. The bird said nothing, tossing back its snowy, unkempt head in a scoffing manner that made the boy all the more determined. The boy reached to grab one of the chicken's scaly legs. The bird merely lifted that leg and the boy's hand closed on nothing. It was in that closing, in that moment when the boy's hand closed on nothing, that the boy fell. He fell, not dying from his long fall through the nothingness of air – only, in the end, as it turned out, breaking a leg.

He would be spoken of, in the days to come, as The Boy Who Does Not Walk Easily. Or as The Boy Who Stumbles. Sometimes, merely, as The Boy Who Fell. As for the immediate event – the boy's pursuance of what he saw as a chicken and his subsequent tumbling – the wiser speculation among those in attendance was that all the boy's bones would be broken. If the gods were merciful he would be dead before he hit the ground.

Lo, their wonder when indeed the boy survived with merely a broken leg. The boy was young. The leg would mend. Tadeusz Benunito – of a nomadic folk some attested had got here by way of Asia (no one else carried their cooking pots on their backs from place to place; certainly not from Asia) – would not always be known as The Boy Who

Stumbles, or The Boy Who Does Not Walk Easily. For years afterwards, many claimed – some of whom had been nowhere near the vicinity – that the bird itself cushioned the boy's fall. The bird swooped down – down, down, down. Time did not exactly stop, although for some seconds those assembled around the pot in anticipation of that moment when the bird would be tossed into it saw the boy riding the bird's wings. Riding those wide wings virtually to the ground, until, perhaps out of impatience and a sense of humiliation, the boy on his own volition surrendered his grip around the huge bird's neck and tumbled head over heels to earth.

Which is how the foolish Tadeusz Benunito, never known for his brains but a whirlwind when it came to bravado, broke his leg. Much swearing, chest thumping, religiosity, developed in surround of this incident – with particular attention given the act of the strange bird. By those on hand, as well as by those from miles around, who would later, and for many years, affirm they had witnessed the miracle with their very own eyes.

The bird the boy held to be a chicken was, by any standard, not a chicken. It was a Polish eagle, white as the driven snow in his original conceiving (so many ages ago), come down from the skies because of its bonds with the oppressed people of that time and place. This benevolent trait the eagle himself considered close to useless, a travesty, the result of some inglorious wrangling between two-headed gods, since he could no more fill the people's pots with chicken than he could sprinkle those pots with spices; he could only offer inspiration and hope – diversion, spectacle, aesthetic charm – and often precious little of that. Time's encomium, dolorous song, a bird's-eye view of ragged historicity. Winged Aquila's simple accounting.

The eagle-that-was-chicken was eternal Poland's symbolic bird and Keeper of the Grail. Its emblem. He had been so, the popular myth went, long before Poland existed as a nation, and in fact, in the intervals since, seemed most in evidence during those periods when the armies of other nations were doing their utmost to eradicate Poland's land-mass and people from all memory. That is, every few years over the past one thousand.

This seemed to be the eagle's fated mission. *Après moi, le deluge*, the bird would think, during more arrogant, fanciful moments. He could have been saddled with a worse fate. He could have been yoked with the never-ending miseries of the Poles themselves. An indomitable people, certainly, these Poles, though not without their flaws. Not least of which was the anti-Semitic legacy so many of their numbers embraced. *Untermensch*, subhuman, was a good German word that slipped easily over the Polish tongue.

The bird was very old indeed, so old that not infrequently, of dark nights when his head lifted in stark anger at the cold heavens, he conceived of – and into the hours convinced himself – that he remembered that time long ago when his body had opened and out of himself had come himself. Fully blown and already a thousand years old. That had to be, because at no time could the old bird recall having been a youth. But then he would shake his head free of this wizardry and acknowledge that this self-birthing was an idea born in antiquity and renewed with some regularity since; in, for instance, that pre-Christian era when the Agnostics in Persia, in Egyptland, over the whole of Asia Minor, out to find release from the void through which they drifted, concocted their creators and gods and saviours and serpents, more than one of whom had seeded his own womb and given birth to himself. Such insight made the bird miserable. He prided himself on being an Original Thinker, tending towards the hylozoic view, but in this concept of his own birthing he was no better than a common plagiarist.

Whence did I come? The question roiled up in the bird from time to time, and when it did he would tear at his nest, pull at his feathers, squawk at the daft Wawel custodians, spit blood at the workers trudging about with their barrows of heavy mortar, until his siege of insignificance, of meaninglessness, passed. Despair. Forgetfulness of being. Another of the great burdens placed upon his scrawny shoulders, arousing convulsions in his balding cranium.

A city bird, he thought, made moody and insecure by a cross word, a bad day, bad weather. He would berate himself while cruising the skies, reminding himself that he must keep a tighter rein on his emotions. He was childish, gross, a loony; these temper tantrums served no purpose.

Grow up, he would say. Act your age. Stay cool.

After all, fate could have ordained you a chicken.

Knowing itself to be an eagle, as far from a chicken as an eagle could get, the bird nested each night when at home in a corner tower in Kraków's ancient castle, known since the fourteenth century as the Wawel. The eagle had had its nest or aerie here for over five hundred years, in a south tower that boasted a numinous view of the snow-heaped Carpathian Mountains and the high Tatras within that chain – Tatry Wysókie – not to mention the fine vista afforded him of the Romanesque and Gothic rooftops, steeples, towers of the ancient capital itself. The forests of Ojcow and Niepolomice, from which the many small bands of resistant fighters had made their raids, were under his purview. He could see horses at graze in Bednarskiego Park, swans on Lublin Pond where the SS commandant had enjoyed his summer swims. The peoples' river, Poland's soul, the great Vistula, originating in the West Beskid range of the Carpathians, flowed through the heart of Kraków, directly beneath the Wawel's decaying walls on its long journey north through Warszawa, Warsaw, where it angled northwest to Torun and Bydgoszcz, there veering due north again to pass the towns and cities once the domain of the Teutonic Order: Chelmno (1223), Grudziadz (1230), Tczew (1260), until at last emptying into the Gulf Of Gdansk – Gdanska, Danzig – on the Baltic Sea.

Although the natural-born Polack might raise a fist in disgust at the notion that the old eagle was the spiritual symbol for the Polack, the Gypsy, and Polish Jew – Jews in 1939 constituted one-eleventh of the nation's population – the bird took his calling seriously: he was a Zionist-bird on September 1 of that year when the Nazi's invasion of Poland launched

World War II and five days later the armoured divisions of Oberstgruppenführer List rebuffed the small-arms fire of the Polish People's Army, thundered over Kraków's Podgórze and Kosciuscko Bridges on the one flank while roaring down Iontelupich and Deluga and Mickiewicza Streets on the other. Installing in the very Wawel where the old eagle nested, the National Socialist Party's Governor General of occupied Poland, Hans Frank. Within four weeks of Kraków's fall, a forced labour edict applying to each of the city's fifteen thousand Jews would be in place; before November's end each of these fifteen thousand would be registered, their food allowance be at half-ration (half that allowed the Poles), the yellow star affixed to each breast, with the ghetto of Kazimierz, just by the Old City, soon to come.

Nowadays, from his aerie, the bird could awaken in the mornings to shouts of skiers as far away as Zakopane on the Czech border, scarcely one hundred kilometres as he would fly it. Without lifting wing, he could see on clear days the mountain's highest peak, Gerlachovki, at nine thousand feet and by lifting wing scarcely a feather's token, might allow himself an indulgent float over the glaciated region's countless hanging valleys, lakes, streams, moraines. Nearer at hand was the ring of parkland gardens known as the Planty, encircling Kraków's centrum in close delineation of the town's original Old City walls. Here beneath the bird's nest lay Ryneck, the city square by St. Mary's Cathedral, Staszewskiego Street rimming the Planty before pouring its cargo into Starovislna Street leading down to Podgórze Bridge and the ghetto where fifteen thousand Kraków Jews had been driven from their homes, shot on the spot, removed to Plaszów labour camp three kilometres along the road, or shuttled onto the Otobahn's cattle cars bound for the Oswiecim-Brzezinka (Auschwitz) death camp sixty kilometres west. In those days, to lay claim to a five-hundred zloty reward, all a decent Pole had to do was inform the SS, (*Sicherheitsdienst*), their own OD, the Field Police, or any earnest Rottenführer, of the whereabouts of any Jew hiding in a forgotten attic or behind a fake wall. Kraków was to be Judenfrie, a concept scarcely less attractive to many Poles than it was to the occupying force. This, of course, was before the Poles came to understand that their destiny too lay with the forced labour camps, the Zyklon B ovens at Auschwitz or elsewhere. By the bird's calculation, which coincided with that estimate of the Pole's post-war Commission on Nazi Crimes, eighty thousand had perished from starvation, disease, and by mass execution at Kraków's camp, Plaszów, their bodies burned by the Waffin SS or buried in mass graves on the piney slopes of Chujowa Gorka. Ash of the burning dead floated over Kraków, settling on the rooftops and streets, the Vistula waters, the backsides of the horses in Bednarskiego Park. As ash settled on their shoulders in their glasses, officers of the Third Reich headquartered in Kraków, gathered for drinks at the sidewalk tables at Krakovia Hotel, would have to move inside, cursing the Jews for their nasty ashes as they went.

During whimsical, melancholy moments, when weighted down with incipient senility, plagued by mange, ticks, lice, a bad case of the hives, or while tucking head under wing in acknowledgements of a paranoia or manic depressiveness of exhaustion so severe suicide seemed the only recourse, the bird liked to think of his aerie in the Wawel as civilization's last remaining Abode of Truth. *Menschheit's* final outpost.

The nest, this abode, over the centuries had evolved into a vast assemblage of smelly, decomposing sticks, mud, twigs, feathers, rags that extended to the very depths of the Wawel tower. Which explained why the castle's wardens were ever having to go to immense expense in the shoring up of that one tower's blackened limestone walls.

At the Wawel, the bird was not and never had been a favourite. Included in the nest's decomposing muck was an assortment of relics, artifacts, mementos, curios, for somewhere along the way a deep sediment of sentimentality had seeped into the bird's bones. The plunder of forgotten missions. *Nyet, nyet, prashoo*, the bird thought. No, don't tell it, please don't. Leave an old bird his little hang of dignity. Here in his nest, then: a precious gem from the Sandomierz crown of Casimir the Great, which one day he must remember to return; a hinge from St. Leonard's twelfth-century crypt; a bolt from that same century's famous Gniezno Doors; a lamb's ear belonging to the statue of St. John the Baptist at Wroclaw Cathedral, 1160; a stone from the *Monument of Three Eagles* at Majdanet in Lublin; the right thumb of the Madonna of Kruzlowa, 1410. And more still: stained-glass slithers, sarcophagi detritus, fossilized bones, warrior anklets, chains, marble fragments, a yellowing, once white robe with red cross and shield worn six hundred years ago by a Livonian Brother of the Sword; worm-eaten woodcuts, gold-threaded capes worn by kings, hair from the very head of Ladislaus the Short. A thousand buttons, a dead soldier's rags, a dead gypsy's sweat-scarf, a kit bag, a peasant's formless shoe — a disintegrating page from Goethe's diary, blown from Germany, the bird supposed, by an uncaring wind.

In that part of the aerie where the bird was likely to defecate, to leak his bladder dry, to storm and rage and puke his bile, were scattered more recent acquisitions; he had lately been applying the eagle-researcher's eye, following leads. Roaming afar, smitten with a collector's zeal. His holdings now amounted almost to a specialty — his holocaust wing, as he thought of it. Nazi paraphernalia, anti-Semitic tripe, by and large. The racist tracts, books, diatribes, memorandi, doggerel of the true cartographers of bile. Chamberlain, Gobineus, Stöcker, Bernhard Föster, Julius Langbehn, J.F. Fries, Alfred Rosenberg, together with the urine-soaked, rotting words of Dr. F.K. Günther, Hitler's major theorist and apostle for racial purity. A tooth from Mengele's jaw, taken by force from that silver-haired merchant of death. Calcimined pages of the *Protocols of the Elders of Zion*, purporting to be the proceedings of a Jewish congress in which was plotted an international conspiracy meant to overthrow Christianity and terminate with the whole civilized world under Jewish control. A 1905 work of the Soviet secret police, but since revised at irregular intervals by Aryan legionnaires for dispersement around the globe. Hitler's favoured paper *Volkischer Beöbachter*, complete with doodles.

The city bird at the moment, however, is not in his nest in the Wawel's high tower. Today he has taken to the country. An excursion borne out of despair and fatigue and pure fancy.

He has come here to Messkirch – this little burg in Germany – on a whim, and against his better judgement. Call it, he has said to himself, a dare. Tell me I have not lost all my marbles.

He has arrived in Messkirch, where Heidegger, the famous philosopher, is today being buried.

Immediately upon arrival, the bird has invited trouble. The moment he entered the German skies, he cried out in full voice: "Poland! Eternal Poland! You Volkspeöple! Psssst! A plague of boils on your house!" And laughed so hard he all but piled into a haystack when a pair of German civilians – farmers, from the look of them – tooting along a road in an open car, shouted a slew of obscene Polish jokes up at him.

Humiliating, these three-point landings.

Hard on an old guy's beak.

Someone on his way to the philosopher's funeral, spotting the eagle nursing his wounds by the haystack, had given the old bird a second glance and yet a third. Is that a chicken or is it an eagle? It came to this person how appropriate it would be to bury the bird with the old Nazi in his coffin. After all, Heidegger was something of an eagle himself. He had pounced where others did not, had invented his own language, recast his field's traditional laws, founded new schools, flaunted his powers – had flown above all others.

Come along then, this person told the eagle, if you've nothing better to do.

Meanwhile, not far from the crowded site where the old philosopher would soon be lowered into the cold ground, a dog – certainly a Deutschland dog – was moving through the cemetery, stopping to piss upon every leaning stone. Marking, in its daily way, its territory, and gradually expanding that terrain in graduations befitting its own imperialistic doctrines. With faint regard for how many other dogs, or lesser infinities, might have pissed there. A thinking dog, even a philosophical dog, aware, perhaps of its own mortality and destiny.

Moss. Moss, the dog found, was so attractive.

The bird watched the dog, feeling a kinship of sorts. The eagle knew the dog's eventual destination. It admired the dog. The dog took a similar trail each day, often twice a day. The dog must visit her dead master's grave, being that kind of dog. So in this way at least, at some level, the dog was aware of her own mortality, though without setting any great store by it. The dog nosed the stones, paused to hike a leg and splash its water. The eagle understood this. The dog was his kind of dog. The dog did not return each day to her dead master's tomb in the expectation that the old fool would be risen from the grave, to rub the dog's head and thump the dog's belly. The dog wasn't a fool herself, but a creature of habit, and habit, in this instance, was but the route to her ultimate destiny.

The dog, in turn, regarded the eagle. This big, ugly bird. And eyed the streaks of – what was it, red gravy? – that leaked from the old eagle and dabbled onto the bough of the tree where the bird now rested. Aromatic stuff, I'll have it *à la carte*, the dog thought. *Garçon, a table, please!* Yes, it would be nice to lap at something. Essence of Pole would be what that was. On second thought, maybe I'll pass. Essence of Pole might be asking too much of a Deutschland dog's fickle stomach.

Ah, me.

Another long boring day.

The dog took a quick 360-degree turn in place, swinging her tail if only for the hell of it. Swish, swish. Then plopped back to her haunches – nosing, licking the grass. "That *dasien* fellow's passed on to his reward," the dog suddenly said. The wind wrinkled the dog's nose. *A-choo!* she said.

"What? What's that? Speak up."

Up at the funeral site affairs were moving along. Work in a eulogy or two, the dog thought, yeah, yeah. Bow-wow. She flicked her ears, hearing a cough from her old master below. Ten years under solid earth, ten years with the rot in him, and still her master had that ragged cough. Too many cigarettes, too much *schnapps*, too much coffee and cake. Too much *stress* hiding his Jew origins, the dog supposed. "Yes," the dog said. "That *dasein* rogue who put this burg on the map, he's gone." Stillness, silence, from below. The faint whisper of creaking bones. The old coot was listening, sure enough. It would take his mental powers a while to come around. A lot of rot in that brain.

The dog didn't know why it was that she seemed always to address her remarks to her old master's feet. Maybe because in her lifetime she'd seen so much of them.

"That philosopher fellow, you know," the dog said. "Not much else worthy of report." There was a great deal more she could say, but the master's interest was confined solely to activities on German soil. That the Palestinian situation was heating up would make him snore. So, too, the military coup in Argentina, the assassination of the U.S. ambassador in Beirut, the South African police killing hundreds of blacks in Soweto.

"Who?"

Well, by God, at last the lump had got his senses sorted out.

This excited the dog, who jumped to her feet and took another complete turn, all the while barking at the ground. *Wake up, wake up, do you think I've got all day?* Then she settled down as before. She'd be slow to respond herself, locked up under wet earth for a decade.

"Who?" the dog heard. "Not that Nietzsche fellow?"

Oh, get your wits about you, the dog thought. In the next breath correcting herself. Manners, manners. Mind your manners now. Patience was required. No cause to be so querulous with the fool.

"I'm listening," the dead man said. "Give me the full details."

So the old rotted one was feeling good today. In his palavering mood, it seemed. It was *entertainment* his old spirit required.

"You do remember, don't you," the dog said, "what Nietzsche's dying words were?"

"Nein. Can't say as I do. You know how damp and cold it is down here."

"'I am sleeping,'" Nietzsche on his death bed said. "'Go away!'"

The dead man laughed. The dog licked a front paw contemplatively, grinning along with him.

"Hegel now… you know Hegel?"

The dead man snorted. Hegel? Of course he knew Hegel. Had Jewish blood, did Hegel. "All power to the state." Wasn't that Hegel?

The dog grimaced, gnawing dirt encrusted on a shin bone.

"Hegel's last words were, 'Only one man ever understood me… and he didn't understand me.'"

Chortles from beneath the earth. His dead master was having a good time. Others in their graves were lending their attention to this dialogue. Hegel's parting words had personal meaning for them, and why should it not? They would not be averse to having epitaphs crooned into their ears all afternoon. But she was a busy dog, much on her burners, for all her dandified posing of leisure.

The dog watched a butterfly, monarch it was, flit by indecisively, then settle on a nearby stone. A pretty thing.

"Or there was this dog I knew. We put this over his stone: 'Never young, never old, never smart either. Now just dead.'"

His dead master said nothing to this. Around him, the dog felt the rest of the dead relax back into their timeless comas. Dog stories did not interest them. They had brief attention spans. The wind blew. Damp. Likely it would rain before nightfall. The dog looked to find the monarch but the monarch was gone. Monarchs had no interest in dog stories either. They were interested in other monarchs and this one was likely caught up in the derring-do of the ten thousand mile migratory flight it soon would be induced to take. Such flimsy things. You'd think they'd hardly be able to reach the corner store.

There was wailing up by the funeral site. Elfriede at full-throttle.

Well, the dog thought, grief will out.

"*That's it?*" the dog heard his dead master say. His voice sounded like coins rattling in a tin cup. "*That's all you have for me today? That's all that has transpired of consequence? You're telling me I'm not missing much.*"

They chortled together for a time over that. The dog's old master, alive, had not been unknown for his garden-variety jokes.

"*How's the wife and children,*" the dead man asked. "*They getting along?*"

The dog shuddered, having no reply for this. His dead master's memory was memory of a convenient sort. He'd turned his wife over to the Gestapo for being a Jew. His children as well. He hadn't known she was a Jew, he claimed, when they had wed. They had all been ovenized at Auschwitz. For the husband's trouble, and his fidelity to the Reich, he had been fitted with a brown suit and, later on, sent to the front, there acquitting himself well.

"That's it," the dog said. "Not much bone in this day."

"*Yah. The same here.*"

The dog scrambled up, looking around. The wind was rising. Off to the North were storm clouds.

"My fleas are worse," the dog said. "If that's any news. On the flip side, my mange is on the mend."

"*Hold on now. It's Nietzsche who's dead, you say? God knows we don't need another existentialist in the cemetery.*"

"Nope. Heidegger, this one is. The Being and Time man."

"*Oh well. No doubt about it. Soon we all will be crowded out. But at least these hallowed grounds are Judenfrei.*"

"Oy! Only you," some dead voice said, "stinking Jew bastard!" A chorus of other dead German voices joined in the outcry. Even in the grave their racism persisted. But their rage was without steam and silence soon ensured.

"*Auf Wiedersehen*, then."

"Auf Wiedersehen. *Regards to your wife and children.*"

The dog loped away, heavy of foot. The old guy didn't even remember his faithful cur was a bitch.

Elfriede presented difficulties. Elfriede, with her clear vision, beheld at once that the bird was little more than a common chicken. A filthy clucker. The clucker was overly large for a chicken, true. And its arrogance was undeniable. Quite unlike a chicken. But the large size, the elaborate beak, was likely explained by the presence of a glandular condition. Since the war, nothing looked like itself any more, not even a chicken. The dear departed, her precious Martie, he had not looked like himself either.

Elfriede would not allow a common chicken, venerated though it might be in the eyes of some, to share the master's coffin; that the chicken thought itself an eagle, and some accepted this, did not soften her view. She examined the chicken, or eagle, closely, finding definite Jewish features in the bird's horny beak, the fractured eyes, the dingy coat, the filthy, monstrous talons. "Take it away," she said.

It was with this statement that the real trouble then started.

Her sons, arriving to remove the bird, looked up at their mother in alarm when the bird's beak spurted blood into the palms of their hands. Likewise staining their crisp white sleeves and dribbling over their polished boots.

Blood? Everyone crowded in, wanting a look at what the general cry said was blood.

A trait, only, of the Polish eagle. Ergo, what the eagle spewed was the blood of the Polish people.

This upset more than a few in the assembly, since a Pole's blood, to speak metaphorically, was on their hands. Or, rather, on Nazi hands, but who here (other than Elfriede, who still was) had been a Nazi? Were they not all innocent? Hadn't all the Jews, the Gypsies, the Poles, been carried off by elves? Still, they were German, so the charge could be scarcely viewed as theoretical.

"Just kick it away," Elfriede told her sons. "Your father was not overly fond of birds to begin with. I doubt he ever was drawn to note their existence."

The boys kicked, and in a show of temper the bird spat blood up and down their new funeral suits. The boys – adult men they were now – picked up sticks, swinging these at their victim, but the old eagle caught the sticks in its jaws, standing pat. They then tried stoning the bird. Despite the crusts over its ancient eyes the bird easily thwarted these attempts, somehow finding strength in its ancient legs, its deformed talons. Some in the crowd knew from this that the chicken truly was an eagle, and a force to be reckoned with, whether Polish or not. An eagle, to some in their number, was a noble bird deserving of respect. They wanted to save it from Elfriede who was scurrying away now, in the securing of a pistol she knew to be hidden under the church floor – having stashed it away there herself during the dark recesses of the war, after Hitler's death in the bunker, when she and Martin had discussed the benefits and disadvantages of a joint suicide. It had been determined at that time that she would fire the first shot, into his brain, and then turn the weapon on herself. They would do this in a closet, to minimize the mess and spare the children. She had in fact argued that the children should be included in the pact. Martin, on this point, had been clear and upright in his view. The present had less claim on the children, he said. They would mourn, but everyone mourns.

The mourners at Heidegger's funeral set out a cage, filling it with food, to lure the bird. The eagle gave the receptacle a contemptuous glance, then craned its neck to include everyone. It next spread what all agreed were gigantic wings, and flew to a high limb, straightaway, powerfully, despite its age. As it flew, those on the ground watching it were struck with a strange notion: this frightful fowl was a mythological creature. None knew how they knew this: the truth just came to them, and to all simultaneously. Nor was it here out of respect for the philosopher, no matter how tall he stood among other philosophers or how high his stature in the world. One by one they drifted back from the hole in the earth into which their luminous philosopher was to be interred. If they would be a part of these proceedings at all, they would be so from afar. From the safety of distant headstones, the slopes of adjoining fields. Better yet, delay the services until tomorrow, when perhaps the eagle chicken would be gone. Why wouldn't it go? Poles always went home sooner or later.

The animal kingdom was not a kingdom revered by the master, as was clear from his opus. Chickens, for God's sake, did not think. Perhaps not even mythological ones. If you wrung this bird's neck, it would thrash about on the grass for a good while, but these convulsions did not signify thought. Moreover, while the bird might indeed be the world's oldest bird, while it perhaps might be regarded as the essence of bird, of chicken elevated to its highest plateau, as the master himself had said, *To raise the question is to leave the question*. To answer the question is to have departed from the question as well as the self that responded to the inquiry. Thus does the present ever awaken the future, and thus is the question's answer of no significance. *The essence of being is the not-yet being*. Presumably, this applies to the bird as well, whether or not it is mythological. Basic phenomenological epistemology may deduce no otherwise.

Through all of this dialogue, the bird sat at roost in the bough of its high tree, chuckling. Discourse on such a plane had ever lifted his spirits. The search for truth, the bird thought, epitomizes, makes real, the darkness in which the seeker searches. Mythological creatures included.

The eagle spied the dog again, lying near another gravestone, rolling in the grass, scratching itself. A creature of habit, thought the bird, smiling to itself. That was the life. No random treks into time and nothingness. No stressful encounters with people who thought you were a chicken or wanted to stick you in somebody's smelly coffin. Just a lazy, relaxing stroll around the graveyard, a chat with the old, dead master who likes to be kept up on current events. And outside of that, few cares, zero responsibilities, no burden or being the emblem of a race of people who don't know what's good for them.

But after a while the dog's doggedness bored the bird; it held no curiosity for the bird, any more than Elfriede did, crossing the high ground from the church in her black dress, her hat, her red lipstick. The bird laughed, seeing the pistol shaking high in the woman's hand. A Luger? Yes, a Luger. And what, thought the bird, will you do with that? Do you mean to shoot me? Then have at it, my good woman. Take careful aim. But think twice, darling Elfriede, for with the smallest squeeze that Luger shall blow up in your face. The bird ignored the advancing Elfriede, and with dark eyes studied the philosopher's grave, probed the craftspersonship of the box containing the twerp. Being and time, it thought, time and being. Well, my good sage, what do you make of it now, eh? A waste, you would say? Death as unsporting game? Better you had poured your genius into something useful like *The Art of Cookery*, forsaking hyperbole and neologism, phenomenology, existentialism. Forsaking your war against nihilism. Or for that matter, and for what it's worth, your beloved Greeks whose civilization certainly had its nasty portion. Plato, if the bird recalled accurately, had not found slavery wanting. He, too, had less than sanguine ideas on breeding. The past flows in with us here, does it? Well and good. More power to it, my scribe.

The bird paused. A shot, still ringing in the bird's ears, had fanned the leaves nearby. The bird cocked its head, glaring down at the murderous Elfriede. No doubt about it, she was one for her age, as had been her sage husband. Another bullet whizzed by, stirring the bird's feathers. She was a better shot than he had supposed. She had a calm hand. So, alright, pull the trigger a third time and see if your Luger doesn't blow up in your face. The sun caught the barrel; the bird could see the shining coil inside the barrel, and see his own haggard image reflected therein. He could see his own grim eyes. Damn. The bitch had him dead in her sight; he would be the world's oldest dead bird any second now, if his calculations proved wrong. Fair enough. He was not a bird that knew everything. The Maker had not poured unlimited wisdom into his ears. Damn, wrong again, the bird thought, crouching on its legs to spring just as he sensed the Luger was scheduled to sound a third time. He had no business here anyway, just out on a toot. Just keeping up appearances, when maybe he should have stayed in Kraków. Confined himself to the Wawel's towers. Damn and double damn. The woman was determined; he'd have to be a whiz kid to make it. If he didn't, the Poles would be up Shit Creek.

The bird lifted, lifted off – just flung himself helplessly, blindly, into the oppugnant air. Swimming through jelly, was how it seemed. He felt ridiculous. As if he'd been reduced to an ignoble state where a bird had no dignity at all. Huff and puff. Flap, flap. Mush in his legs, lead in his wings, his brain leaded too. God help me, the eagle thought, where did my youth *go*? Did it just vanish? To have my youth back and not creak along like a dipshit, groaning *boat*! To have that old spring in my legs, that raw instinct, that killer mentality. Oh, the wonder of those infantile days when he had been the terror of all European skies. Now it was all serendipity.

The eagle lifted and as he stumbled, gasping for the heavens, his eyes pivoted over to where the dog lay on all four paws on its dead master's grave. Now that was the life! That was how life should be. Tongue lolling, the dog now snapping at fleas as she regarded his passage with envious – but, even so – not unsympathetic eyes. We are cousins, yes, the bird thought – lifting slowly (it's just that I no longer have that old get-up-and-go), hitting thumpy currents of wind as blood dripped from his mouth. No news there. He was a Polish eagle. He always had been.

The dog rose up on her front legs, contemplating the bird riding the air. Imagine, the dog thought, to soar like that, to be here and gone in the blink of an eye. But the life had its rub, of course. Imagine having to nest on cliff tops, to piss away your time in trees, to eat rodents, to sleep on sticks, to look *like that*! The frosty, cold nights you must endure rain, sleet, snow. The chilling winds. All in all, the dog thought, so much easier on a cur it was to be a dog. The solitude up there would get to him. What crotchety, oddball creatures they are, the dog thought, as the sound of the beating wings faded and the thing itself speared into the sky's nothingness.

WHY SO OFTEN YOU ARE
AT A LOSS FOR WORDS

A dark night. Two men meet on a street corner in Rusty Cove, Nova Scotia.

"Got a light?"

"You bet."

"One of these days you won't be able to smoke even in your own house."

"Like that in some places now. Amherst, Massachusetts, for instance."

"You don't say."

"Quite a storm we had. Blackouts up and down the entire east coast."

"Yep. Italy, too."

"One little twig. In Switzerland, wasn't it?"

"That's right. Hard to believe."

The men light up. Smoke.

"My name's Jack. What's yours?"

"I'm a Jack also."

"How about that! The two Jacks! What's your line, Jack? Me, I'm in divots. The divot king, you could say."

"The king, that's good."

"So what's your calling?"

"I'm in dry goods, you might say. Words."

"Words? How's that, Jack?"

"I'm what you might call a word terrorist."

"Well there you got me, Jack. Al-Qaeda, you mean?"

"Nothing like that."

"So what do you do? In the practical realm, I mean."

"Oh, different things."

"Like?"

"Like, well, how to say it? I place words inside tin cans, ceramic jugs, lard buckets, any common household receptacle, really."

"I'm mystified, Jack. Where does the terrorism come in?"

"A word terrorist plants a little bomb inside there with the words."

"Inside the receptacle?"

"You got it."

"Then what?"

"Then nothing."

"Nothing?"

"Well, you get a big explosion."

"I feel I'm missing something here."

"Take a word. Whatever word or words you've got in your receptacle. When your tin can – I prefer tin myself – when your tin can explodes, goes sky-high, there goes your word.

There it goes, gone forever. You've got a thousand little pieces, usually burning. I mean, if you use a fire bomb naturally those pieces are going to burn. It's the best way we have of killing certain words. Then there's the wind factor as well."

"Heavy work!"

"Stressful, certainly. A guy could lose an arm."

"I guess you'd have the odd little letter floating around, though. Say an 'e' or a 'y' lands in a puddle. There's that letter looking up at you, asking, 'What happened?'"

"I can see you've got a feel for the job."

"You think so? Gee. But, well, divots, you know. Not quite the humdrum thing some people think them to be. An open door into the world, that's how I see divots."

"Not quite sure I know what a divot is."

"Me, too, Jack! I was that *innocent*, when I went into the business!"

"The same here. But now… well, some words refuse to die, Jack. Explode that sucker a thousand times and there it is back in the morning stronger than ever."

"Yeah? Like what? Give me a fer instance.'"

"'Love,' that's the classic one. Man, that one is a killer."

"You're kidding."

"'Foible,' that's another. That is one tough word."

"Damn, I don't think I've ever used it."

"You hear it a lot, in my line. 'Foible.' That baby keeps me up all night sometimes."

"Foible. Who would have thunk!"

"Yeah, it's a zinger. Here, have one of mine."

"What's that brand, Jack? Gauloises? My goodness!"

They light up. Smoke.

"Packs a lot of memories, this Gauloise, Jack. Thanks."

"Good memories, I hope."

"Oh, the greatest. My first wife was… was—"

"French?"

"No, no, nothing like that. She was a Gauloises. Francine Gauloises. I'd fall into a swoon, just hearing her name. Music

221

to my ears, that was Francine Gauloises. So what are some of these words you've killed?"

"Pardon me?"

"You know. Some of those you got rid of."

"I can't do that. How could I do that? That is one crazy notion."

"You mean… because they really are gone? They no longer exist, so you can't tell me what they are?"

"Exactly. I wouldn't have a clue."

"You're looking a little uneasy. What's the matter?"

"Oh, nothing. It's just that lately I haven't been myself. Sometimes I stuff a word in the tin can, grab a handful, I'm not even looking. *Boom*, there they go."

"You're committing a 'foible,' eh?"

"You could put it that way."

"You keep that up, sooner or later you and me couldn't be having this conversation."

"True."

"If all of you word terrorists blindly stuffed in words, before we could blink, silence would reign."

"Yeah. I guess so."

"All over the earth, silence."

"Yup."

"And wouldn't that eventually kill all those words you say won't die? What was it, 'love'?"

"Yeah, that was one."

"Your sweetheart looks at you, she can't even tell you what's going through her mind. A kid wanting ice cream would have to point. Hell, you wouldn't even be able to call your dog."

"There's a responsibility, I couldn't agree more."

"I'm getting upset. You can't even call your dog, that's really rotten."

"We're getting it together. Try not to worry."

"How many of you word guys are you? How many?"

"In our language? A few billion."

"And I bet some of you don't even use the – what was it you said? – the common receptacle. Damn! I ask for a light from a guy, I share your Gauloises, here I am shaking."

"Calm down. Say silence did reign, it would have a plus side, wouldn't it? Think of all the benefits."

"Benefits, sure. But can a guy call his dog?"

"You and dogs! No need going haywire over a pooch."

"What, you don't like dogs? Look, here's a question for you. I'm in the dark on one small point. Why?"

"Why?"

"Yeah, why? Why kill the words?"

"That is a damned silly question. You know? That is damned silly."

"It's a good question."

"It's insulting is what it is. It's the stupidest question I ever heard. Do I ask you why you make divots?"

"Now who's being insulting?"

"Hold the phone."

"Phone?"

"Sit tight a minute."

"What's going on?"

"Cover your ears."

"What?"

"Ears. Long fuse."

The two men cover their ears. Small explosions go off nearby. Tin cans, fragments of burning paper, are seen tumbling high in the air.

"Hot dog!" says Jack the assassin.

They run over to where the paper scraps are falling.

"Total success!" he says. "A dozen or so, gone forever. Jesus, that was pretty!"

"Was whatayacallit in there?"

"What whatayacallit?"

"That word we were talking about."

"'Foible'?"

"No. That other one."

"Who knows, Jack? Who can say? Well, I'll just retrieve my tin cans, then I'm off."

The second Jack hangs by. He thumps out a – whatayacallit thing – from his pack, puts it in his mouth, then remembers he doesn't have a whatayacallit? Waves can be heard splashing against the pilings down at Rusty Cove. The entire east coast remains in the dark. Maybe Italy as well.

Me, too, Jack thinks.

Time to go… where?

Walk the… whatever it is called.

THE YALE CHAIR

One Foot and I and our beset tribe found ourselves on the lam through the Dakotas, and many yesteryears removed from those encounters here I am alone floating upriver on the Nile. The Nile? They said it was the Nile and took my passage money with nothing back. At night this was, off a black pier. You walked a shaky plank and hoped it was a boat at the end. Stay in line, they said. No bickering. Yes, princess, I will assist you with that trunk. You don't mind I drag the bitch?

The river banks were a dark entanglement, as I remembered, but in fact you do not see much when you are slung over the deck and sick to your very footsoles still from the crossing. Down below this was, where you could see nothing of what might be out there, including entanglements.

Some wondered what we would do, what would happen to us when we landed, and where we might land – the captain being vague, in fact silent on this issue, though I did not inquire myself, being more the willy-nilly type who goes where gunshots, fate, or romance decrees she must. My main concern was my wardrobe, and for that matter it still is, so long as I have my head, because my wardrobe with my tattered princess dress is all I have brought with me from my marriage to One Foot in the Water.

One Foot. Oh, One Foot! One Foot is in retreat from civilization's memory now, but once he was the famous leader of his people and husband married to the beautiful princess in her boned and beaded dress. I say this proudly. A certain dispersement of beings brought him all the way to Yale University on a professorship, which by one measure was that point in our lives where ascent and descent, happiness and unhappiness, had their bridge. A Chair this was called, the Jefferson Chair! But the hellhag bride was discovered aswim in her princess dress on the savage's arm and every weathercock and slubbergut mobbed the streets and we were shouldered back to the train. Scat! Never let us see your faces again! Or else!

Which was how we found ourselves again in aim for the Dakotas, our entire tribe in the meanwhile out there in a state of collapse and desuetude without their leader One Foot to harangue them or muzzle the extreme faction bent on the suicidal cause.

But all this trading of the aged news is discouraging to me now, as it might have been then, for we were both without our sap and listing in the wind after our long flight from the Chair zealots.

Our child arrived during the return journey from Yale and the commotion surrounding this natural event put great strain on every person in the six cars constituting that train, especially following an episode with a man who called himself Luther. This man flung burning fuel at my husband – this in the form of a torch that some attested appeared flaming from his very mouth – and did his best to slit our throats during the conflagration and hubbub, with everyone shouting and sliding fast as they could through the windows of the train which was hurtling at topmost raucous speed across the continent.

It was the swaying of these cars, I believe, and the constant clickety-clack, the heavy air, the stink of boots, which brought on our child's early birthing. I was already sore from the sticks hurled at us at Yale and hearing so often the Whiffinpoof song in rendition by groups of boys assembled on each street corner, and confused from the beginning by the endless talk of the Chair, the Chair.

Oh, I can make light of it now. Now that I am ten thousand miles removed from those shores and am beginning to breathe the sweet moisture of home. Usumbura we passed yesterday. Ruana-Urundi tomorrow. They can't fool me. It is something in the blood.

My husband, pursued by these Chair forces through the Dakotas over the span of three summers and winters, repeatedly had sent word to Yale's tireless posse that he had no interest in their Chair, or in the wealth that accompanied this appointment, as Jeffersonian democracy was neither his specialty nor a concept in total arrangement with his liking.

I would not recommend acceptance of this Chair, should the offer come your way.

I would be wary of any invitation to show yourself upon New Haven's public green.

Avoid the whole of this uneasy state, if you are able.

My husband told the Chair's emissaries that he under no circumstances could accept the Chair, even a Roving Chair, or ambassadorship, and in reaction to this sentiment we were ordered out of the Dakotas, advised that we must not set foot into any adjacent state or territory, nor think that we might take leave by water for that ocean was under sovereign jurisdiction as well.

So all right, I lie. I veer from strict truth.

But we were on the lam through the Dakotas for some many seasons, the Chair's supporters in hot pursuit and our tribe decimated and factions arising at every turn, since none of us knew that much about why it was that such hoards of influential and moneyed people were willing to sacrifice so many lives or effect such widespread deprivation all in order to bring about One Foot's ensconcement in the deplorable Chair.

A council of elders was called and in one voice, after but a few minute's deliberation, they summoned us before them and said, "One Foot in the Water, take the Chair."

Take it before all our people are dead and only our bones are left to rattle through these Dakotas.

Off we went to Yale for receipt of this honour.

Until our arrival that rain-soggy day, we had not known even of the existence of violent and powerful forces simultaneously at work to prevent just this occurrence.

Yet also at Yale, in the president's house where we were lodged in the initial days, some kind and consummately patient person sewed score upon score of roses onto the lining of my princess dress. These were of the old York variety, with each thorn carefully removed and fine invisible mending done on the hem, where my heels back in the Dakotas had time and time again caught the beaded and boned fringe.

Every bead polished, every bone wiped, our bedcovers folded back, and the pillows bestrewn with further displays of these blossoms.

Two bleached antelope shinbones crossed over my pillows, which sign made me tremble, for they spoke of home. Decades in the flow since and me but a nippling when uprooted.

I wore these petals next to my skin and wept, for it had been a long time since we had enjoyed privilege or mercy of any kind.

One Foot cried, to see me bathe, these lovely petals at float on the scented water.

Our bed and the floor about that bed ablaze with York blossoms, and the air afire with the airy petals as we loved. Us little expecting these times to be our last hours of bliss in each other's embrace.

At five the butler's bell rang and we passed down the stairs to a gay reception and dinner.

"Perhaps you will get accustomed to sitting in this Chair," I said to my husband.

"Good bed," he said. "I like beds." And went on to explain his view that the entire westward expansion owed everything to the presence of these eastern beds.

So I saw he was putting a good face on this Chair issue, and thinking better of Jeffersonian principles in the aftermath of our couplings.

A stone occasionally strikes the deck of this boat, and skids off into water. We are told black infidels are ashore in the bush, tracking our passage, and to be watchful for poisoned arrows, though I have yet to see any proof of this menace. Only these small bouncing stones or harmless splats of mud which a child might mindlessly fling.

A crew member sent by the captain stands solemnly beside me and after a long interval presses a warm glass in my hands. I drink its contents without inquiry, and return the glass to him. He does not quit my side.

"What was in the glass?" I ask.

He cocks his head indifferently, standing close by on spread legs.

"A soporific," he says.

"It had the taste of rum."

"A soporific, princess. With rum, to settle the stomach."

He smells of monkey. I have seen any number of these animated creatures at swing in the wheelhouse or scampering along the deck. But I will not satisfy him by stirring even one inch, and my little knife as always is at the ready. I have stuck it through tougher beings than this one man.

"The captain wishes I should report to you that your trunk is secured."

Although he smiles, I am not deceived. He would pitch me overboard and be done with me, without the smallest qualm.

"It is in the wheelhouse?"

"Yes, princess. Padlocked under heaviest chain." He bows witlessly and tosses the glass my lips have touched into the Nile.

"Then how am I to have ready bargain with my clothes?"

He does not reply.

I thank him and at last, reluctantly, he goes.

I hang over the deck again, retching into black water, as night-birds thrash and squawk in the trees.

Curiously, our train car had palest-blue balloons in dangle-ment from every inch of ceiling, these aloft at a level equal to the heads of those men and women standing in tight press along the aisles. Each few seconds a smoker's cigar would burst one or another of these, and each man in the vicinity grabbed for his blade or handgun. One Foot could not remove his gaze from this display of dancing blue balloons, the pres-ence of which puzzled him greatly and elicited endless whis-pered commentary into my ear. He sought to find messages in this armada of balloons as he did in the night's sing of stars, and was vexed by his inability to conjure same, although he laughed mightily each time a balloon popped from the ceiling and on its own accord shot at dazzling speed its wild orbit above our heads.

The child was coming; I was in considerable torment and retained my composure, I hope, although One Foot was sorely incensed that no one in the packed car would surren-der his seat or even squirm so much as an inch to right or left. But he was already hobbled in one leg from the fray on the public green at Yale, plus suffering a dog bite which now was festering, plus carrying in addition deep wounds in his side from his youthful wars.

He could do little to right the matter beyond arranging some little rope's length of comfort for me in that space on the cold floor beneath the gentlemen's feet. I lay on this slab of grit and boots and food spat from the travellers' mouth, shuddering with the clickety-clack of iron against iron and in the grip of deepest anxiety and pain, for this child was my first and coming early and my attendants all scattered in result of the fray at Yale.

Pity me, to have been so senseless as to wear my princess dress.

It worried me that my dress should not survive the ordeal, or that my child might not, and between bursts of pain and the dizziness of balloons, I had mind to consider my great wardrobe of seven steamer trunks long since reduced to the one, and One Foot's worry that he could no longer provide for me. It is a pitiful thing to see this recognition sap a prideful man, and I wept bitter tears for his misery and for my own and my labouring child.

These gentlemen pressed their boots about my head and chest and limbs through the entire birthing process, their cigars in ceremonious toil and their ash in steady cascade about my face. Their boots kicked and prodded my flesh at every turn, some perhaps unconsciously, to render them that justice. My floorspace smelt of pigshit and piss and the eastern civilizations enough to make me gag. Soldiers in attendance to see to our safety were at cards, or bent with drink and frivolity, or such obscenity as betokens handshake with the uniform. They lifted not the one hand, but instead inflamed the matter, which did not in the least surprise us, given the discord in surround of the Jefferson Chair.

Oddly, a gentleman sharing our cramped compartment sat in study of an Eastern paper through near the whole of my birthing throes, often kicking his boots against my head and body in his excitement as he discoursed upon the rights and wrongs of the Jefferson Chair, and its rich endowment, which investment seemed to his mind to exist in contrary fashion to the democratic ideals the Chair's very creation was meant to promulgate.

Mr. Jefferson had never been a piece of God's creation that he could champion, he said, and had Mr. Hamilton shot the rascal, as so often had been his desire, the country would have been saved much grief.

There was something cunning underway with this business, he said, and it was his guess that European monarchists were behind the whole of it; they had put up the coin, no doubt about that, he said, and duped the intelligentsia at Yale, which institution had sorely declined since its removal from old Saybrook. But what could you expect, given the tenor of these times. A great debauchment of the people's trust was in the wind now that the laws of entail and primogeniture were at lapse. Much claptrap, he said, was being put about with regard to the requirements of education for the poor and uncivil, with slave and redman and pickpocket rising to assail one at every turn. Women strutted in secret, arrogant rule up and down every corridor of power from the Potomac to Yale, and the country would suffer calamitously if the citizenry did not soon come to its senses and cast off the foreign yoke. Hang the scoundrels at home, who knew not where their bread and butter did come. Cast off this puerile exercise in free thinking, which rewarded only freeloading rodent, chimney-sweep, and slubberdegullion. The country must forsake its restless clamouring for art and the snooty ideal and the luxurious life for every upstart or field hand with tongue to flap or arsehole to fart it out of.

A great boomswell of "ayes" sounded in aftermath of this speech, and heavy trampling of boot where I lay in dire sweat, huffing and puffing, with thrusting pelvis, my water sloshing beneath me and the flesh of poor One Foot's palm between my teeth chewed into rag.

"Aye!" they said. "All the evils of this nation's business can be seen in this episode of the Chair!"

"Aye, the Chair, heaven help us!"

But now my husband forced some little extraction of space between my legs and slung my limbs high upon his shoulders, for he took news from my shrieks and thrusts that the child was in its daylight chamber and he must be my woman and my midwife now.

The gentlemen through some precious moment or two fell silent, and stayed their feet.

I shrieked anew to see my heels at lock about my lover's neck and to glimpse his bloodied hands at work between my naked legs. Sweat roiled upon our skins and the jolting pain now was without surcease. I closed my eyes and locked my teeth on whatever came between them, as for instance the toe of the talkative gentleman's boot. But he grappled this away from me, with a show of bad humour which found release in a stream of lurid comment upon the vileness of travel in this ignorant age.

With each new siege my feet thrashed against my husband's face and chest, my great belly heaving and my buttocks at slushy romp, until at last he was made to force them into the grip or brace of whatever man of quality would consent.

The men at crowd upon us, by and large, seemed bored with our activity, or assumed attitudes in antipathy with our goals, and soon went on again with their scholarly perquisites.

"Women should not ride the train," one of these said, "and there's the proof."

Another chorus of "Ayes" sounded, and much toasting to this chap.

The man with the newspaper announced that he held exalted status with the Halls of Transport and Railroads, and that he normally would be found riding in the owner's caboose, with mugs of hard cider in each hand and comely Chinee wenches in slit red dresses showing ample ankle or even garter belt to see to his every need. There followed a great tipping of hats and a flood of inquiries about the availability within that office of other exalted jobs.

On this occasion, the man said, the caboose had been turned over to that Chair savage from the Dakotas who had incited the riot at Yale and trampled innocent children underfoot. Yes, thanks to government intervention and outright laxitude, lawless, irreligious hoards could usurp a fine man's seat anywhere in the land, and it was high time a Cotton Whig took hold of the realm and hung this low-life from a tree, wherever they be found.

Yes, yes, the savage was riding this very train, he said, and likely coupling this very minute on the owner's divan with his black princess who, as was well known, had cavorted shamelessly with a thousand men away there in the Egyptland she hailed from.

"Aye, aye!" the others said. "'Tis well known."

There's some as should hold the line, he said, as to which raw whore they'll take aboard a good slave ship.

"Aye!"

Profit or not, there's principles at stake here!

"Aye! We ought to go ourselves and plug the bitch!"

But at this moment the vulgarian's attention was drawn to One Foot, as if he had but just noticed my husband's presence for the first time. He offered his fatted hand for shaking, and for some protracted seconds that hand hung at mean jiggle above my eyes, One Foot's own hands being at busy engagement between my legs.

"And what is your opinion on these matters, sir?" this magpie asked One Foot. "Do you have views, I mean, as a redman and savage, on this treasonable business with the Chair?"

At this very moment my child's head slipped loose of all encumbrances, sorely irritating this unsavoury clown. I strained and huffed, certain I was being torn apart limb by limb. One Foot planted his legs anew, forcing my legs wider yet; a snarl was fixed upon his lips and glitter showed in his eyes and for an instant his sight locked with mine. "Push, bitch," I heard someone growl; One Foot's fingers probed inside me deep as a barge pole; he spat and yanked as I howled; I was aware of a great sucking, slurpish sound which seemed to arise from the entire car, and my guts ripping, then a swoosh, and then a great vacuum or hole suddenly opened inside my womb; this emptiness swept onwards and in the instant took hold upon my brain. My very bones seemed to have been scoured. Heaven help me, yes. My eyes opened and I saw the newborn gliding smoothly upwards, flowing like a skein of syrup between my bloodied legs into One Foot's nimble, fraught, embrace.

"Aye, duckie!" someone said. And henhouse cackles all around.

My husband held the child high in the one hand, smacking rump.

"Sir?"

One Foot's hand at last shot out and shook Big Mouth's lingering paw.

"Indeed, sir," One Foot said to him. "Indeed I have views."

I arose – "You will move the buttocks, sir," – and took back my seat.

But that our child was a beauty to behold and born in perfect health despite the setting I have described, I leave to more proper and learned annals in our history to chronicalize in detail.

We named her Oryxes II, in my tongue, and Foot of the Dogs, in our shared language, with more than a few exchanges between ourselves of the mirthful code.

Some little aftermath of tranquillity must have followed this birthing, for I do recall I was asleep when this Luther person disconnected himself from that throng of travellers occupying each dot and parcel of seat and aisle. My eyes blinked, I mean to say, and in the next moment I felt the crush of One Foot's body slung across mine and our child's, though not before I saw the flaming torch in arched flight upon our very selves. And every man and woman screaming and trampling away from the fire's orbit, without regard for neighbour or friend.

From this attack I suffered a few unremarkable burns, together with nose bleed from one or another wild elbow, plus tintinnabulation, plus gore everywhere, and nothing to do with that dress except fling it at the first bush. But later I gave this decision second thinking and coerced myself into reclaiming the garment with a good wash, plus tincture of lye, plus needle and thread. Oryxes was unharmed, and One Foot's diminishment only the little greater, though the nature of his disfigurations in body and spirit did have weight upon me wearisome unto my depths. His mind was in deep cogitation of these Jeffersonian principles thrust upon him, and this study tired him mightily. What had seemed obvious now seemed arguable, he told me, and the vice-versa. Each simple issue or statement of plain truth now arrived in his mind with interminable codicil, or long-winded preface, with gazette and appendices, or contrary council and allegation, and footnotes that went on into eternity. He feared his new scholar's mind was now in session with the full academic committee, and it tired him, it tired him, *it lays me low, my darling.*

Through the oily, coal-dusted windows could be seen vultures at glide with our traffic. They gobbled flesh as they sailed. When morsels fell from their beaks, crows swooped in from nowhere, with raucous chatter, to claim what was theirs.

At Yale, a woman wearing a scarlet bonnet had asked my husband which of these many eastern inventions he was witness to had most impressed him.

"The hammock," he said.

The president of that institution had taken us aside and said how sad he was that Meriwether could not be with us to celebrate my husband's ascension to the Chair. "Villains struck him down, you know. Years ago. On the Natchez Trace."

"Yes. My princess and I were much enriched by our association with him during the Expedition, as with our correspondence through the years."

"I understand you were most helpful to him during those difficult Louisiana years."

"Princess was."

The president bowed and kissed my hand. "We have much to learn," he said. "I understand your lineage can be traced as far back as the Middle Empire's Amenemhet." I bowed to him, fluttering an impervious hand.

"Mr. Clark, alas, is also in the grave," he said to my husband. My husband fidgeted. He regretted Mr. Clark's demise, but had never forgiven him his decisions in the nasty Black Hawk affair.

"What do you hear of Sacajawea?" he asked us.

Ah, I thought: dear old Sacajawea. Even Whig bankers loved Sacajawea.

"She is toothless now," I said. "Though still the charmer. Her grandchildren are strung throughout the Dakotas and Wyoming. They are all great warriors."

He sniffed. "I smell roses," he said.

At that minute a rock crashed through the window; agitators were assembling on the lawn.

The captain's man again appears by my side. A monkey clambers about on his shoulder. The monkey regards me with merry, attentive eyes, looking over my attire to determine if I possess anything that can be put to its own use.

"The captain regrets the food aboard-ship is all contaminated," the man says. "It is all at rot."

"Your captain has never heard of salt?" I ask. "Of smoke?"

"Unfortunately, the pineapple does not smoke. Regrettably, the orange does not salt."

He scratches the monkey's belly. The monkey gyrates on his shoulder, then produces an orange.

I snatch at this fruit and have my teeth sunk into it almost before it has left the monkey's hand.

"To your health, princess," the man says. He spins on his heels, the monkey chatters, and both are gone.

This man is not so bad after all.

Juice drips from my mouth. I have not eaten in a month.

Minutes later, the monkey returns. He hops about in noisy agitation at my feet, making horrendous noise. But he loses not a drop of what he has brought. A rum bottle bobs atop his head. He settles the rum glass in my hand, pours from the bottle, dances about once more, then rolls away like a wheel.

I hear gee-gaws of muffled laughter from the wheelhouse, and smile my own appreciation into the dark.

I mean not to dwell on my vicissitudes, being not the whiner type and finding such a parade of memories repellent to my nature, as earlier said. But there it is: history must be composed, if lessons are to be extracted and life ever improved and the winds again to sing.

All history, I mean to say, is not written in blood. To cite an example, I will mention the Night of the Trees. Soon after our train had crossed the border into Canada, it braked to sudden, lurching stop, and steam and dust engulfed us all. Urgent whistles rent the air and the very earth shook. The next moment passengers of every description were surging forth, the cars all but instantly emptying. Up and down the track people by the hundreds poured into the darkness, as though possessed by some claim of enthusiasm or madness beyond our normal call. Before one could make account for this, large beds of fire ba-roomed into being, these flaming campfires or outposts of light spreading far almost as the eye could encompass; in the shadows of these great flames an incalculable array of bodies swarmed this way and that, each man, woman, or child among them, it seemed, hastening to his or her objective as by some predetermined course and cause. Their heads and shoulders, sometimes the whole of their bodies, were soon obscured by their loads: massive trees, shrub plants, and flowering bush of every variety. These bodies in phantomish assembly, silhouettes at flow in graceful symmetry beneath the blackened sky. Others roved about in mysterious dialogue with pick and shovel, while numerous wagons pulled by horses barely larger than dogs arranged themselves in strange procession over the barren, ghostly plain, each of these instruments of transport piled high with mounds of black earth. In this rich cargo blinked pinpricks of mirrors all at steady flash, mica chips, my husband observed, and over these wagon loads rode a latticework of cages big and small. An extraordinary convergence of wild, plumed birds were at flutter within these cages; birds swayed upon the creaking carts with their heads under wing, or held forth as statuesque sentinels transcribing shrieks and clucks and throaty, rapturous song into the dark, implausible night. Still other conveyances arrived, some as though dropped from the starry sky. In these prowled a montage of beasts large and small, many of a species heretofore unseen in the new world, you would think; these beasts arranged either in quiet curiosity as to what mercies it was that awaited them, or in wild roar of outrage at what travesty already had ensnared them. Men and women of oriental cast were everywhere to be seen, come from nowhere to sound out their strange tongue to one another while applying tong and hammer to some spot immediately beneath where they stood. Transforming that spot in the instant and moving on decisively and with fierce muttering of excitement to the next chosen place; and the whole of this teeming terrain lit, as I say, by moonlight and torch – this flood of souls released to some higher plain of endeavour.

Oryxes nursed, cutting her eyes to right and left.

The night wore on. The mysterious work on the great plain beyond our windows continued without let up.

Six white butterflies hovered at my window. They disappeared the instant my eyes claimed them. Scant seconds later they were at soft circling wing in the air above my child's head. As one, they descended, settling on the baby's brow. I sped them away with a wave of hands, but the second my hands stilled they again dropped as one upon the child's brow.

"She will live sixty years," my husband said.

Or die, I thought, in six days.

One Foot grasped my wrists to hold them quiet.

"Six days or sixty years," he said. "Do not wage war against the stars."

I watched the butterflies traverse my newborn's face.

At this point in our journey we were days from even the smallest hamlet or outpost and indeed knew not where we were, or were bound; in the darkened coach, with all this before us, my husband's spirit had revived; he sucked at my one breast as Oryxes suckled the other.

"You will bring great scope to the assignment," I told him. "You will bring honour to us, and to Yale, and to the Jefferson Chair. In the spring I will take Oryxes home and walk with her among our pyramids."

So much was the sense of goodness upon us that we swore anew our vows, pledging a strengthened loyalty to all in nature that was tranquil and harmonious.

Through the night the army worked beyond our windows, and at daybreak when the great fires were nothing more than ashen piles a great virgin forest stood in seemingly endless stretch towards the horizon; the arid plain was no more. Birds were in bivouac in the trees, or in summit each to each, and beasts and fowl at roam among the foliage and dazzlement of blossoms.

Something unyielding in the heart had finally yielded, I thought, and created this amazing oasis.

In the distance one could hear mighty waterfalls, and witness their wet haze in the clouds.

Morning, now.

Those who had disembarked came on again as the sun rose. They wore their previous composure now, and showed no evidence of toil; they were eastern loudmouths in suit coats and boots, in quaint round-topped hats and string ties. They were demure ladies in unsoiled travellers' dress, in high-top shoes that still carried shine; they were strutting school-boys and young gentlemen in apprenticeship to a latitude of professions and trades. Boisterous soldiers, as drunk or ob-scene as they had been earlier, trooped in noisy combat or comradeship up and down the aisles, to fling themselves into whatever empty seat or lap their province of thought led them. Old men and women hobbled aboard, as bent by ache and disfigurement as when they had disembarked. Hardly the crew, you would think, to have wrought what they had wrought through this wondrous night.

The fat impresario of the railroad swung elbows, fitting himself again beside me into his old seat. His bloated, immaculate hand thrust itself One Foot's way.

"Now," he said. "You were saying. As a redman and savage, and one who has known the unblessed life, what might be your thoughts about that infernal Yale Chair? Every scalawag and dog to have his day? Is that your tune?"

"Them coolies," I heard one woman whisper to another, passing along the aisle. "I couldn't make out the single word! Must we have ignorant foreigners in pigtails building our railroads?"

Our boat chugs on through the night, aimless as a plank tossed into water. Our stomachs have soothed and we repose on the deck like bundles of hay dropped haphazardly over the rail. Wind rakes at old cuts in the flesh, and my bones acknowledge their age. The sky has blackened, we can see nothing. Our boat scrapes bottom, brushes invisible foliage, and one can feel the lean of a thousand trees; we lift uncertain hands to dislodge drooping vines. One hears an occasional splash in the water, nearby or in the distance, and the heart quivers: is it fish or one of our own, sliding away into the black mystery?

The captain's man again returns, on shoes as silent as the evening's character.

"A pillow, princess? The captain desires you should be comfortable."

Something else scrabbles across the deck, approaches me; already I have raised my knife. What does it want?

"It is only the monkey," the man tells me, "come with a blanket."

Indeed, it is the monkey. I can smell now the raw smell. I can hear the monkey scratching its fur.

"Cover the princess," the man says. The monkey chatters a polite reply. I see the waves of yet a blacker darkness, and cool air, and the blanket settling lightly over my legs. The hair on the monkey's hands brushes my face.

"No rum?" I ask.

The rum glass finds my fingers. I hear the slosh of liquid in the glass. I drink.

"Tell the monkey thank you," I say to the captain's man.

"No need to," he says. "You already have. You could talk that Egyptian tongue, he'd likely understand that too."

They start to go.

"Should be quite the show," the man says. "Quite the celebration. Whole country at fever pitch. You're coming home, princess."

It seems to me I can feel some timid increase in the boat's speed. Some added play in the waves. Some extra force in the breeze.

It occurs to me that I must have the captain's monkey. I must walk through the capitals of Europe, Asia, and the Far East. Through this continent and back again in the New

World. I in my princess dress and the monkey at my side, our hands intertwined.

Oryxes the First, I seem to recall, had monkeys and birds sealed with her in her golden tomb.

The railhead at Winnipeg, where we took on the cattle and into whose terminus we had been re-routed, was not an improvement, although it was here a man named Riel, said to be a rabble-rouser and menace to the earth's inner-tuning, furtively boarded and sat with us and recited his name. He spoke into his chest, although his eyes darted everywhere. He was an outlaw, on the run. Branded a traitor. His friends dead. So many of his people homeless, on their knees, or dead. Gutted end to end. The Great White Father was The Snake With One Belly and Two Heads. One head lived on the Potomac, the other up here. The snake's belly was fat with the dead. It liked the lard. The two heads saw little of each other. They did not need to. Such brains as the snake possessed were located in the belly. Or was up its arsehole, *forgive me, princess.*

Riel wore a bell on a rawhide cord looped around his neck. He drew back his coat to show us this. A handgun hung by the same cord. He had never fired this weapon, he said, without first ringing the bell. The ringing bell made him feel easier about the matter. It soothed his conscience and brought peace to the swans at swim in his head.

"What was decided with the Chair?" he asked.

Yes, he had been approached in the early days. The offer had chagrined him; he had believed himself unworthy. He was too angry. Although in those days he had trod about with six bells round his neck, and no handgun, or even a knife or stone in his pockets.

"Try One Foot, I told them. He's the bigger fool."

We shook with laughter at this.

"What news of Sacajawea?" he asked. "She always excited my blood, though her own ever ran clear. She was ever trimming my nails, inserting sticks into my hair or slapping tree bark onto my face. Correcting my French. I see her now, walking Paris streets under a gay umbrella, white poodles dogging her heels. Quite the savage, eh? Sacajawea could read one page of Latin in Clark's book, and thereafter speak the tongue with a sauciness and grandeur the match of Cicero."

Ah, we all thought. The old days.

"Where do you go now?" we asked.

He laughed, and waggled his head.

The baby wriggled on my lap, wanting to join in.

"A child shall lead them," Riel said. "Onwards into light." He tickled the infant's chin. "Never fall asleep on a tree's mossy side."

A man stalking the aisle paused at our chairs and leaned his face into Riel's. Riel tinkled his bell. The man straightened and hastened on.

"And what news," he asked me, "of the empire? Of the darker continent? How fares the princess, her heels raw from the Dakotas' lam. So far from home, and for so long?"

"Upriver, slave ship oars thump out the iambic beat. More and more vessels thicken the water. High tide is ever higher."

He withdrew a white handkerchief, and with it daubed his sugar under my eyes.

"Downriver, there's talk of a canal."

"Ah," he said. "The innocent life."

For a time within his environment our spirits lifted; we smoked and spat and dwelled on the eternities and toasted the baby.

He slipped away, and our train rattled on, again in ungainly lurch towards the Dakotas.

A night and a day passed. The vultures once more plied commerce with our route, gliding calmly by like gulls at a seaport.

Three days, four days, five.

Then there was this same Luther underfoot again and the train at crash against a boulder set up across the rails. By Plum River this was, and it engorged, and somehow in the stew of this my newborn's throat being had at, plus Luther's gang at pile between my legs.

You can see here my sketchiness, for I have little stomach for the chronicle. A body tires, it wants relief, and the mind, too, desires the pruning.

Then this mucous scampering away into grass.

But One Foot was wounded and his head a hollow bell and his eyes sightless in the aftermath.

"More rum, princess?"

"I thank you, yes."

"More?"

"Yes."

"To the top?"

"Yes."

We survived in these conditions and made on again, on foot now and following a path of stars, accompanied by the maddened cadenza of wolves at rove on the plain. Some two hundred of Luther's sordid fireboilers drove in hot pursuit, as we nightly reconnoitred the matter from our moonward levels. This, thanks to a scurrilous document nailed to tree stump and post by our enemies, affirming that the Chair brigade had under face of darkness routed that institution called Yale, murdering every woman and child while they slept and leaving in their wake naught but the stench of rotting flesh in which maggots of a special Egyptian-Injun variety were at swim, with the whole of civilization now at peril. And these blackguards now loose in unprejudiced liberty through the continent, with more of their infamy to follow. And all this at the will of a moneyed claimant to the French throne, in conspiracy with the English Influence along the Potomac – and many a decent kettle-tender, pig-swiller, blackie or redman the dupes of these knaves who dared make use of the Jeffersonian name. These despoilers of his hand-writ Constitution and defilers of the *of, by, and for,* who would usurp our land's very foundations.

"More rum, princess?"

"Dispatch the monkey for another keg."

"He's asleep, princess. Between yer legs."

We reside now in the wheelhouse, our features at dance under the globe of yellow lanterns. I sit on the captain's stuffed horsehair sofa, cold inside my bones, mindlessly rubbing the monkey's scalp. The monkey groans in his sleep; he has the sound of one grown weary and old from the drone of my voice.

The captain is steadily attentive to the wheel and only intermittently shows notice of me. He cares for his boat and would have nothing harm her on this journey. "Yer has the mission, yer takes it," he has told me. "Yer hopes to effect no damage to yer vessel what brings yer to or from it."

"Yer does?"

"Yer. Yer does."

I have been here the past hour, the pair of us saluting ourselves with each drink we pour down our gullets.

"Skaal!"

"Skaal!"

"Prosit!"

"Prosit!"

"To yer nanny!"

"To yer nanny!"

"Pura quanzu!"

"Pura quanzu!"

"A votre sante!"

"A votre sante!"

"Down the hatch!"

"Down the ruddy hatch!"

The captain is a piece of cloth new to my experience. I cannot make him out.

"I told yer," he says. "Yer takes on a mission, yer..."

Another lantern illuminates the boat's bow and some few feet of grey water. It illuminates the captain's weathered confederates. Ropes are entwined about their torsos as they dig in their heels, as they sway and pull. We are in shallow water; this tub is scraping bottom.

"We'll get yer through," the captain says. "No problem."

The monkey yawns, stretching his limbs. The right foot jiggles as he sleeps.

"I meant to ask," says the captain. "How's that Sacajawea? There were a woman could come at yer like oyster on the half-shell."

"You knew Sacajawea?"

"Why, my Lord yes. Like this us were."

He snaps his fingers behind his back, his torso at lean through a window. "Onward, boys," he shouts. "Another league onwards!"

It sounds silly. I help the monkey scratch at fleas, thinking that this monkey and I are walking down a Paris Street. We are creating the sensation, and why should we not? I shall not let the low-life deter me.

Go away, I will say. You with your small minds. Who else will flap warm blankets over me when I am cold? I will sit on a bench and debate with the monkey Jeffersonian ideals and the Napoleonic Code.

"That Riel fella were hanged, yer know. Captured at Batoche and strung up." The captain pauses to gnash the gears, to kick at some hum of engine irregular to his ears. "Oh, not so long ago. Quite a fella. Yer. My old sidekick, in my rough-and-ready days."

He turns and looks at me. It is the first time I have seen his face near a lantern, in good light. His face shows the cascades of a thousand years.

"Didn't know yer husband. Knew his father, though. Old Two Foot, yer know. Two Foot in the Water. Now there were a man could chew yer up and spit yer out. Yer give him cause. Not the man for that Chair, though. Not a Jefferson man. The way yer husband was."

Beneath the wheel, where the captain rests his leg, is my chained steamer trunk. I started with seven, and now am returning with one. I have gone up and gone down.

I root a finger into the monkey's ear; I ream the knobby flesh.

"Yer can go on with yer tale, yer know," the captain says. "Anytime yer like."

Yer. My infant daughter ripped from my chest and flung into the Plum, even as these same tormenters tore away my dress and dropped down astride me. Shouting insane currency in my ears. Another of Luther's gang standing by at the ready. *"We'll show you democracy!"* My child at squall in rapids and no shriek too many to proclaim the atrocity.

Jackals at gnaw upon our bones.

Later on, my child at float, head down and much bloated. I pushed the swollen child along in the tide. Go, I said. Why do you tarry?

I observed her spirit rove ashore some further distance along; it arose sprightly, and joy flooded my heart. But then her legs kimbered and the arms spun as in a cripple's dance and the head sailed loose of her frame and one arm spiralled eastward and the other westward and in the sky I saw lips nose eyes and ears all disassembled and whirling in wind and the next moment the form that remained in the water toppled backwards and sank into the fathomless bottom.

"Ujiji," the captain says. "Kigoma. Yer. By daylight. Then only three thousand more miles. Yer see slave ships in yer mind, princess?"

Yer. And the cry of the birds when their wings are axed and the sky is no longer theirs and the slave ships slip away with the bird wings stacked one upon the other and the night of all nights has come down.

"Yer. I thought yer was."

We are entering a lake mouth. A soft rain is falling; the leaves are dripping.

"More rum, princess?"

I think not.

A hush of people, come from nowhere, are lining the bank.

"Yer dress, princess? Yer think?"

Already he has unlocked and opened my trunk.

"Yer are their princess too, yer know. Yer are the Chair."

Yer. My bones, my beads, my princess dress. Sticks in the hair. My face painted.

Yer.

WHAT HAPPENS NEXT

I came out of my writing room only wanting what I was thinking of as a small break from the tedium of composing, endlessly composing, but actually just sort of sitting there, sitting in there, I mean, though *earnestly* sitting, *reverentially* sitting, you could almost say, though actually unable to get out of my mind that line in the Joyce Carol Oates memoir *A Widow's Story*, the line that goes *Why did you not fall in love with the many others with whom you did not fall in love?* which I have found is a darn intriguing line to be thinking about whether you are me or some other party. Why, yes, why? – is what I was in there thinking, that being the very same thing Joyce writes that she was thinking after the death of her husband of four decades – among other related questions she – and I, yes, after the death of my wife of four decades: what we were thinking. And also thinking What next? Is there a next, and if so, What? Then it dawned on me that maybe it was time for a well-deserved release from all that composing, or non-composing if such is how you prefer to see the matter, if, that is to say, you want to be absolutely literal about something that is none of your business in the first place. Except that it is your business, I guess, if you're reading this.

So that was the situation, up to a certain moment. Which certain moment arrived the very moment I quit that room. A woman I know, know very well, have known and loved through forty years, have been *unreservedly* intimate with a minimum three thousand times, that being her estimate – three thousand, just imagine! – and these physical encounters existing as the merest *prelude or introduction* – the *landscape!* – to the intimacy aggressively present in the entire *frontier of intimacy* as known and practiced by those of us so fortunate... *when... when this same woman* places herself directly in front of me, places herself between me and where it was I thought I was going, so close I dare not move, I dare not breathe, and what she says, says in this serious, no-nonsense way, is *Listen here, you, don't monkey with me, I know exactly why you've abandoned that room, I can see it in your face, you are quitting that room because YOU DO NOT KNOW WHAT HAPPENS NEXT, you cannot figure it out, you have not THE REMOTEST IDEA, and DO NOT think to blame it on me, do not so much as consider blaming it on JOYCE CAROL OATES, or on your father or mother or children or on our dog and cat.*

That is precisely what she said. And I, who at any other time might have claimed to *always* know what happens next, was now blind and dumb in that regard.

Her appearance was unanticipated, lovely – a thoroughly inconclusive – *next*. Now what?

Katherine Mansfield arrives in a yellow cab. She's wearing a nice hat. Look at her. A nice yellow hat with gold piping – a garden party hat! She's trying to pay the driver with a concrete poem found this morning in a broken tea cup. Among the tea

leaves! Who broke that cup? D.H. Lawrence broke that cup.
What did he call her? He called her loathsome! A reptile! A
loathsome reptile! Let's say no more about that. We may not,
because Katherine's taxi driver is speaking. "Not today, Lady!"
the driver is saying. "No poems today!" No one should talk
this way to Katherine Mansfield. They should not say, as this
driver does, "I will however accept as payment your pretty
hat." "Not my hat!" shouts Katherine. "I am going to a garden
party!"

This is outrageous. Someone must intervene. Jump up! I'll
pay the man! My wife is speaking. Heroic even in death – "All
right, Katherine, the nasty people have gone. Here, darling,
take this chair. Relax. Don't even think of seducing anyone
today."

"Too late, too late I did."